Praise for
House of Thorns

"A beautifully creepy tale of love, loss, and healing, *House of Thorns* will keep you just as trapped as Brier Hall until the last page is turned."
—Hannah Whitten, *New York Times* bestselling author of
For the Wolf

"Cleverly written, eerie, and atmospheric, *House of Thorns* is an intricate gothic tale that lingers like a haunting dream."
—Lyndall Clipstone, author of
Lakesedge and *Unholy Terrors*

"As gorgeous as it is spine-chilling, *House of Thorns* echoes with the question of grief, and what it does to those who have to the fill the missing space afterward."
—Chloe Gong, #1 *New York Times* bestselling author of
These Violent Delights

"Breathlessly tense and feverishly beautiful, *House of Thorns* will haunt you from the moment you step inside."
—Tara Goedjen, author of *No Beauties or Monsters*

"*House of Thorns* is an addictive read brimming with tension and intrigue. Strychacz's prose is what really sets the mood—it's emotional and evocative, soft and sharp in all the right places. This is a story of sisterhood, of first love, of being haunted in more ways than one. I found myself saying 'just one more chapter' over and over again."
—MK Lobb, author of the Seven Faceless Saints duology

"Isabel Strychacz's thriller about a girl who must return to the old manor by the sea, where her oldest sister disappeared, in order to save her only remaining sister is a beautiful and haunting tale about sisterly love, grief, and the lengths we will go to save our family. Lyrical prose, suspenseful pacing, and lots of heart make *House of Thorns* a stunning novel by an author to watch!"
—Joyce Chua, author of *No Room in Neverland*

HOUSE
OF
THORNS

Isabel Strychacz

SIMON & SCHUSTER BFYR

NEW YORK LONDON TORONTO SYDNEY NEW DELHI

SIMON & SCHUSTER BFYR

An imprint of Simon & Schuster Children's Publishing Division
1230 Avenue of the Americas, New York, New York 10020

SIMON & SCHUSTER BOOKS FOR YOUNG READERS
and related marks are trademarks of Simon & Schuster, LLC.
Simon & Schuster: Celebrating 100 Years of Publishing in 2024
For information about special discounts for bulk purchases, please contact
Simon & Schuster Special Sales at 1-866-506-1949 or business@simonandschuster.com.
The Simon & Schuster Speakers Bureau can bring authors to your live event.
For more information or to book an event, contact the Simon & Schuster Speakers
Bureau at 1-866-248-3049 or visit our website at www.simonspeakers.com.
Interior design by Hilary Zarycky
The text for this book was set in Adobe Garamond Pro.
Manufactured in the United States of America
First Edition
2 4 6 8 10 9 7 5 3 1
CIP data for this book is available from the Library of Congress.
ISBN 9781665942591
ISBN 9781665942614 (ebook)

For my daughter, Imogen Grace.
Once upon a time there was a precious little girl who lit up the world, and she was the very best thing out of all the good things that have ever happened, and I am so lucky that out of all the babies in every infinite branch of the wide and vast universe, this little one belongs to me.

HOUSE
OF
THORNS

DALEY

One need not be a Chamber - to be Haunted -
One need not be a House -
The Brain has Corridors - surpassing
Material Place -
—Emily Dickinson, "One Need Not be a Chamber -
to Be Haunted"

Brier Hall was always freezing cold, even inside. Even in summer. That's what happens when the spaces between the walls and the gaps in the floorboards are teeming with ghosts. Boiling over with memories. Sinking under the weight of those long forgotten.

That's what happens with a haunted house.

Even now I can remember every second of the two years I lived there, although sometimes I wish I didn't, and have often pretended as much to ward off the curious questions or the odd appearance of a rogue reporter who still finds us all these years later. Sometimes I'm able to convince them I'm not a Peartree girl—*Who? Sorry, you have the wrong person*—but for the ones who've done their research, pretending to have no memories is the best way out.

Oh, Brier Hall? No, I'm sorry—I was too young.

No, I don't remember.

I don't remember Brier at all.

It's all lies. The name is vinegar in my mouth. *Brier.* Seven hundred and twenty-one days of mounting dread. Brier. Over sixty-two million seconds of a slow decline into panic. By the end, all of us—me and Ali and Avery and our mom—were drowning in delirium. By the end, the real end, Avery was missing. Gone. They never found her body, which means all I have now are what-ifs and nightmares and maybes: Maybe she was under her bed and didn't hear us yelling her name. Maybe she was in the orchard. Maybe by the cliff. Maybe she was stuck in one of the ever-shifting rooms.

My life is now made up of maybes.

Maybe my big sister is dead. People say she is, that she *has* to be, because people don't just disappear into thin air for five years. And maybe they're right, maybe somewhere deep in the depths of Brier Hall, Avery lies dead in the ways you can see: stiff and unmoving and uncrying and unscreaming. And while the rest of us escaped, we are dead too, in the ways you cannot see.

And now, even now, five years later, we still get weird looks and whispers. We still get phone calls. We still get reporters.

It seems that everyone loves a ghost story.

It seems that haunted houses never go out of style.

ONE

The walk through the parking lot from the car to the school's front doors is long enough that any number of things might happen on the way, and I hate to leave anything up to chance. Once I open the car door and step onto the asphalt, it's ninety-seven steps. Anything can happen in ninety-seven steps. The earth itself might open and swallow me whole.

Stranger things have happened.

I know this firsthand.

I peer out the window, glancing back and forth like there's some tennis match going on, when really there's just a quickly emptying parking lot. All the kids are milling up the stone steps and through the doors; the first bell has already rung, and the tardy bell is ticking closer, and it's the last day of school so everyone just wants it over with already. I want it over with more than anybody, but I can't make my fingers grab the door handle.

Come on, Lia, I scream in my head. Screaming wakes me up. Screaming, even if no one else can hear it, is a way to stop the boiling water inside from spilling over. My breath catches. *It's just ninety-seven steps.*

My hands are jittery as I clench them in my lap, and I crack my knuckles, pops sounding throughout the car. I can hear my breath loud in my ears. I glance up into the rearview mirror—my face is pale and pinched, my blond hair loose around my face. It's my eighteenth birthday today, but I barely made an effort; I could hardly drag myself out of bed. I stare at my reflection, dark blue eyes the color of the deepest part of the sea looking back. Eyes the same color as my sisters'. Ali.

Avery.

I can't stop thinking about how I saw her today.

Her.

Avery looked seventeen years old, still, *always*. There I was, walking out of the coffee shop with an iced latte—the only way I was going to celebrate my birthday—in one hand and my phone in the other, and then there *she* was. I could feel her watching me, right in my peripherals. I'd frozen in place, cold trickling down my back despite the heat, and when I blinked she had moved. *Closer.* I could feel her breathing on me; a slight breeze wrapped around us and I swear a tendril of her blond hair floated around my shoulders. The knowledge that if I turned I would look her straight in the eyes was heavy on my mind.

And I couldn't.

So instead I ran to my car, fumbling for the keys, birthday coffee falling to the asphalt, splattering everywhere. Forgotten.

And now here I am, unable to get out of my goddamn car because there's a chance my missing—dead?—sister might be waiting for me.

Come on, Lia. My hands are shaking. I place one on the door handle and breathe out. I'm only ninety-seven steps away from the front doors.

Ninety-seven steps away from safety. Relative safety.

Because here's another thing I know: Buildings are not as safe as people like to think. I'm not talking structurally. The flat, sun-soaked town of Daley sits right on the San Andreas Fault, after all, so one would hope these houses are sound.

I'm talking about the bones.

The memories that lie awake in the floorboards, waiting for someone to step on them. Out they come with a creak. I'm talking about the things that live inside houses, all the screams and fights and happy birthday songs and secrets told. Those things don't leave.

Those things are dangerous.

It is ignorance, it is wishful thinking. It is the ostrich sticking its head in the sand, willfully oblivious to oncoming danger. It is the small child pulling all her limbs under the covers so the monsters can't get her. I *was* that child, and here is what I learned: Houses are not safe. Homes will not protect you. The buildings simply like to pretend, to lull their prey into a false sense of security.

Sudden movement flashes by the window, followed by a sharp *rap-rap* on the glass, and I jump in my seat, a strangled scream never leaving my throat. Stuck.

Avery?

Amid the remaining kids hurrying into school, Diya stands at the side of my car, peering in through the window at me. Her dark hair whips around her shoulders and she shakes it back.

"The tardy bell's about to ring!" she says through the closed window, the words muffled by glass. She then grins and shows off the bulging plastic bag dangling from her fingers. It has DALEY GAS MART emblazoned in blocky red letters on the stretched plastic. "Cupcakes!" Diya says. "Happy birthday!" Everything Diya says ends in an exclamation point, and she never asks me about my past:

two of the reasons I hang out with her and her friend group. I'm on the fringes, even after years. It's my own fault. I push them all away.

"Come on!" Diya says, and it sounds much nicer when she says it aloud than when I scream it in my mind. She cocks her head toward me, a flash of puzzlement finally crossing her face. Her eyes dart to my hand clenched on the steering wheel.

Get a grip, Lia! I scream in my head again, pinching the soft skin between my thumb and index finger until there're little half-moon crescents from where my nails have dug in. *Come on. Come ON!* There's someone waiting for me now. I have to get out of this car. My fingers are weak on the door handle. Legs: shaking. Mouth: dry. I tell myself that nothing can get me here in the parking lot of a bone-dry central California school. There's CCTV everywhere. There's Lori, the school security guard who holds court on her golf cart. There's a Taco Bell and a coffee shop and the Daley Gas Mart right across the street. Super normal. Sunny. All the shadows meet their matching objects and none of them reach out toward me with sticky dark fingers. Loitering kids who are tempting both fate and the tardy bell are filming each other doing shitty kickflips off the curb. They all have faces undistorted by my memories. They are all just kids.

Everything is fine.

I get out of the car.

One step. Two. I forget that I've done this before, that I've done this multiple times a week for months now. Each time feels like the first. Each time the anxiety roots me in place, dragging me down, down . . .

"Hey," says Diya, then trails off with a repeated, "Happy birthday . . ." Her voice dips low in uncertainty. "You okay?"

"Um. Yes," I reply, noncommittal, flustered. My chest is still tight; I can't talk when I can hardly breathe.

"Did someone say something?" she asks, still uncharacteristically serious.

I breathe out. Diya knows none of my inner issues, just the public ones. That's the problem: This entire town knows the Peartree family's public issues. A few years ago, the whole world knew, because a missing sister and fleeing from your house in the middle of the night get people's attention. The comments used to bother me, but now I try to just ignore them. I can tell when the questions are coming; I can tell if someone recognizes me because a light comes into their eyes and you can literally see the moment the pin drops that *that's a Peartree!* Now that I'm about to graduate, they tend to flip between "You're that ghost girl, right?" and "But was it *really* haunted?"

It was worse before when my sister Ali was also still at school. Because upperclassmen's questions tend to be blunt and hard-edged and not really questions at all: "Oh, Peartree. You're Ali's sister."

I hate all questions equally.

"No, no, I'm fine," I reply weakly, accepting the bag of gas station cupcakes from Diya with a small smile. She's still looking at me all concerned, so I offer up a slip of truth. "It's almost been five years since—since it all happened."

"Lia—"

"Honestly," I interrupt, "I'm fine, I promise." I shake the bag of treats. "Thank you for these, Diya. I think I just—I don't know. Maybe my senioritis is finally kicking in."

Diya gives me a hesitant grin and, as I follow her up the steps, we duck our heads at the glares from the front-office staff. "That's why your grades are still so good. My senioritis started sophomore year."

She's wrong; my grades are good because if I throw all my energy into homework, I don't have as much time to think about the reality of my life and the unreality of my past. They're good because one sister is gone, and the other is absent, and I'm the one who has to be perfect, who has to hold it together.

But I'm in pretending mode now, so I keep all this to myself and instead chatter aimlessly with Diya about birthdays and boys. Normal. *Be normal.*

We walk together into the O-Wing, the original building where all the English and arts classes are now held. The rest of the school looks like a prison, concrete and hulking, but not these classrooms.

Large windows and whitewashed walls cast early-morning light onto the original wooden floorboards. They're pitted planks that creak when you walk across them. I love this building but hate the floors.

Diya and I hurry through the door of our English class right as the tardy bell goes off. The class is in a last-day-of-school uproar, everyone talking over one another and signing yearbooks. The floorboards groan with every step as I walk to my desk. Just like Brier's had, years and years ago. Each creaking footstep brings back memories, hot and fresh, as though they've been waiting for a moment to make their appearance.

I try to push Brier from my mind as the wooden plank sinks slightly with an audible groan and *I know that sound I know that sound I*—I've barely been at school for two minutes and Brier is already forcing its way into my thoughts. *Not now. Not again.* I clench my fists, dig my nails into my palms once again. I kept them long for this very reason. To bring myself back to reality.

"Happy birthday!" sings a classmate.

I smile tightly, sliding into the desk, trying not to fidget. Trying to look *normal*. My fingernail polish is pink and peeling. A pink flake drifts casually to the floor.

Diya is still walking to her desk at the far side of the room, and floorboards are screaming under her. *No one is screaming, Lia.* My fingernails press hard, as for a single second I'm back there— *there*—and my head is filled with screaming. My mom's? Ali's? *Avery's?*

Don't think about that. Don't think about her.

Fingernails dig harder. I clasp my hands in front of me. Hard, harder. Painfully tight. I tried to focus on that pain, turn it into a spear of clarity. I will not have a panic attack in this classroom. I will not. *I already am—no, breathe.* I am okay. *There's no screaming. Nothing is wrong.*

I am not okay, and everything is wrong, but there is nothing I can do about it.

People are looking. Stop this. Stop this.

People *are* looking, and I let my hands drop to my sides, the back of one covered in red crescents, the half-moons of my fingernails.

"You okay?" murmurs Matteo, who's sitting next to me, and he sounds like he actually wants to know.

It's the second time I've been asked that in less than an hour, and it's not even nine in the morning. I can't read the look in his eyes—is it pity? Concern? Or maybe there is nothing there. It wouldn't be the first time I projected stuff like this onto others. I give a brisk nod: cool, calm, collected. I don't think he believes it.

Pull yourself together, Lia! Nails dig in harder and I breathe a long breath out, then sit up and square my shoulders. I can be fine for one class period. People pretend to be fine all the time.

The English teacher is a young woman just out of teacher training, and she obviously has her own case of senioritis. She sits behind the desk and surreptitiously texts someone as the classroom moves on around her. I feel so detached, as if I'm viewing the room from above my own body. I keep feeling the weight of eyes fall on me, and I know that just beyond the laughter and nonchalant chatting my classmates are watching me. Like I am some wild animal in a cage.

I need to get out of here.

I want to go home and bury myself under a mound of covers, but I steel myself. I don't walk out on things—I can just imagine my mom's face if I did. And I am a good daughter. I am the perfect daughter.

The floor creaks next to me, and although I know it's just Matteo shifting in his desk, I jump in sudden agitation as the sound crawls through my bones, scratching its way through. Avery's face flashes into my mind—Avery as I saw her this morning, as she crept just out of full view. The wisp of her hair curling up in the breeze, brushing my cheek. The blankness of her expression I could only see out of the corner of my eye. The shock of seeing her—no, of *remembering* seeing her, because *of course* I didn't see her—makes every part of my body go cold. It's the same feeling as when my sisters and I jumped off the rocks at the side of the cove into the water of Brier's private beach. That sudden full-body immersion of ice cold that shocks you into suspension. That locks your limbs as you're pulled under, as you sink down, down, deeper . . .

I gasp my way out of the water, out of the memory.

Is that salt in my mouth?

Get a grip get a grip get a GRIP—

Screw making it through class before leaving. Screw being the perfect daughter.

I'm standing before I even realize I'm standing. I was seated, I was underwater, and then suddenly I was propelled upward. I'm towering over everyone, swaying.

"Lia?" Matteo says.

"Lia?" Diya calls from across the room. I am back underwater. Her voice sounds like she's speaking from light-years away.

"Lia?" says our teacher, finally sitting up and shoving her phone under a pile of graded final papers. "Everything okay?"

"I'm s-sorry—I have to go," I say to her, to the room, to the air. "I feel sick." I would never make a scene like this usually—that's Ali's job—but I'm a senior and I never have to see any of these people ever again if I don't want to. I don't care what they mutter about me behind my back.

I avoid looking down at Matteo or over at Diya, where she sits with her other friends. Her normal friends. I can't bear to see their faces right now—I'm sure they have twin expressions of pity, of confusion, of *what-the-fuck-is-wrong-with-you.*

"I have to go," I repeat, my voice dull, as if I've been screaming. Maybe I have been.

I don't know much of anything anymore. Reality takes too much of my energy to be bothered with. Reality is where I'm a ghost to my own mom. Reality is where I hate my sister. Where Avery is dead. Where we're hundreds of miles from the house that still has us in its thrall.

I don't wait for a go-ahead. If I stay here another second, I'm worried I'll either burst into tears or have a full-blown panic attack. I can feel the edges of panic, inky black and fathoms deep, already creeping in and winding its way around my throat, my heart, my lungs.

But that can't happen. Not here. I turn and run out of the room, floorboards screaming as I rush over them, and let the door slam shut behind me.

BRIER HALL

You know something is wrong when your mom stiffens, her fingers trembling as she holds the letter.

You remember, don't you?

How your sisters don't notice. Nobody notices but you, because you notice everything.

You are the watcher, the watchful.

Her mouth forms a little O of surprise, and her expression is hard to read when she turns to you and your sisters, lying there on the floor spread out like bodies in a crime scene. The TV is blaring out some animated movie and everyone is engrossed but you.

"Girls," says your mom, and Avery flicks down the volume, ever dutiful. Her hair is pulled back in a ponytail, the same ponytail all three of you sport. It's an easy-breezy style, a three-kids style, a single-mom style. "Girls, I . . ." She sits down on the couch with a thump, like her legs have given out. Then she breathes out a word, a bad one, and you and your sisters stare at one another with wide eyes.

"What's wrong?" Avery asks, finally noticing what you have noticed since the start.

"It's your . . . your father," your mom says.

You all just wait, wide-eyed once more, but you don't feel much because *father* is a kind of nothing-word, a nothing-thing that doesn't seem to settle. Avery frowns, and Ali is squeezing her hands into little fists, eyes locked on her fingers as if they're the only real things that exist in this moment. Avery and Ali feel more when your father is mentioned; you know because you file away their reactions and their reactions are always so much more than yours.

"He's . . ." Your mom stops, the word on the tip of her tongue, and then she swallows it back and starts again. You can almost see her mind whirring, trying to figure out the correct thing to say. You know what she's thinking. You know what's happened. "He's gone. I'm sorry."

Avery is crying and hugging your mom, and Ali is softly punching her fist into a couch cushion, repeatedly, like her fist is a metronome. You sit and you watch and you know you should be sad but your entire world is here in this room, right now, and the fact that some man you haven't seen since you were a tiny baby is now gone can't quite seem to worm its way into your head. He was gone before, wasn't he? He was never here, and he isn't here, and he will never be here again.

You didn't even know him.

To you, he was already gone.

"Oh, Montgomery," your mom whispers with faraway eyes, and you remember *oh right*, that was your father's name, but it doesn't ring true within you. Montgomery Brier could be any-one. "Oh, what did you do?" You can barely hear her over Avery's muffled sobs. Is Avery crying because she's sad or because she's older and knows crying over a dead yet absent father is something that you should do?

Maybe you should be crying too.

After all, you always follow in your sisters' footsteps. You're a follower, a watcher, and you wait for their bright lights to lead the way.

"It says here he's left us his family's home," your mom says faintly over the din. "It's been in the Brier family for centuries, but he's left the home to us. To his girls." She glances up at you and Ali over the top of Avery's head. You meet her eyes. It's almost like she's talking just to you, only to you, when she says, "To you."

The words rattle into you. A home, a home, a home. A home that's been left to you. A home seems so much more than the tiny apartment you're in now, the single bedroom you share with your sisters. This is a house. A home is something else.

Something more.

You picture it. You can see it so clearly, like it's been waiting for you to imagine it just so it can pop into existence.

"Brier Hall. Home to the Brier family for generations."

Yes. Yes. The name rings like a bell within you, steady and loud and sure.

"It's in a town called Eastwind."

Yes, you knew that. *Eastwind*, you mouth to yourself, the syllables fitting themselves to your tongue. You knew it was Eastwind. You could feel it.

"On the coast."

Yes, of course: You can feel the salty breeze whipping your hair. The cries of hungry gulls circling overhead. The roar of the ocean.

"And he's left it to us in his will," your mom whispers again, her eyes glazed. "What the . . . what . . . ?"

Your mom is trying to make sense of the letter and Avery is still crying and Ali is still thumping the pillow, her eyes glazed.

You watch them all for a moment, this painting of agitation

and grief and anger, as if you are somewhere else. As if you are already inside the walls of your new home, watching this scene from far away.

Then you push yourself to your feet, walk carefully to the bedroom where your school backpack hangs lonely on the bedpost, and begin to pack.

The air is still and hot outside, which is exactly why Mom moved us all out here to Daley, California, a small city which should be called Middle of Nowhere. It is fully flat and its dark asphalt roads streak out in all directions, lined with squat houses and the neon lights of convenience stores. It has four identical coffee shops and even more hairdressers, and everything is golden-brown 99 percent of the time.

You can't smell the ocean from Daley.

I think that's why my mom likes it.

Because the smell of the ocean is briny and salty fresh and that's what Brier smelled like. Brier Hall, up on the hill. On that precipitous bluff dotted with gnarled crab apples and scrub brush, overlooking the Pacific, with its iron gates encrusted with sea salt. Gulls screeched overhead and everything smelled like cold breeze and wet sand and there was always an underlying scent of fish and seaweed and rot. Decay.

I lean against my car and breathe deep.

All I smell is Brier. Which is impossible.

"Hey."

I jerk my head up because—God. I'd know that voice anywhere, even in a whisper. Maybe *more* so in a whisper. I see a flash in my peripheral vision: blond hair, wide eyes, a fluttering hand. She's half-hidden by the corner of the science building, which juts right out toward the student parking lot. She peeks around the concrete wall and for a second all I can think of is *Avery, Avery, Avery,* but the voice isn't Avery's. It's Ali's.

My heart sinks. This is too much. I can barely deal with speaking to my sister on a good day, a day when I feel strong and bold and unforgiving. Not a day when I've run out of school, sidling out the front doors when the front office was quiet.

"Come here." It's hissed at me and that mere fact alone makes me want to turn around and walk away. But her hood is up and she looks small and young.

"What are you doing here?" My voice doesn't sound like mine. It sounds like someone's socked all the air out of me. It feels like that too.

"Just come here."

My feet walk of their own accord.

And then I'm standing in front of my sister. A quick peek shows sunken eyes and chapped lips and thin hair, and then I glance away. I can't look at her; I look over her shoulder at the trunk of some squat, ugly tree. I'm shaking like a leaf because just standing near Ali makes me want to scream. Scream loud. I tense up my entire body and listen to the wind, listen to the cars driving past, listen to anything but Ali's shallow breathing.

Sometimes I hate Ali so much, I think I might spontaneously combust just from standing near her.

"I need money," she says in a papery-dry voice, like she's ten thousand years old instead of twenty.

Fingers clenched. *Breathebreathebreathe.*

"Call Mom, she'll give some to you." Bitterness is all over my tongue. It flows off me like a waterfall, pooling at my feet. I see Ali's car in the adjoining parking lot, parked sloppily in two spaces. My mom bought it for her when Ali promised that she was clean and had a job and had to get around.

And my mom said, *I'm so proud of you for getting yourself together,* and got her a car. I saved up my earnings—mostly from babysitting until the moms found out I was Ali Peartree's sister and found other babysitters without notorious sisters—and bought a twenty-five-year-old Volvo for a thousand bucks.

Ali's bumper is smashed now.

Breathebreathebreathe.

I lapse back into stony silence because that's the only thing I can do around Ali. It wasn't always like this—not even close. And that's why everything *hurts.* If we were the type of sisters who'd never liked each other, then the past years wouldn't matter.

But the three of us had been close. The three of us had been *everything.* We were just the Peartree girls. Avery, the oldest. Ali next, and then me, the baby. It was always me and Ali. Ali and Lia. Me and Ali shared a room at Brier, and my mom would stroke our hair before bed and say that when she was pregnant with me, Ali, only a toddler at the time, kept pointing at her tummy and saying, "Me. It me."

And my mom assumed she meant *my sister.*

But what she meant was *me; herself.*

And then Ali and I would smirk at each other from our twin beds as the rain lashed at the windows and the ocean crashed far below, and our mom would finish her story by telling us that's why she named me Lia. It was just Ali, rearranged. Ali, but a little different.

It's why you're so close, she'd say. *You're the same.* And she'd cross her index and middle fingers together, hooking them around each other. Keeping them close. *Like this.*

Like this, we'd say, and cross our fingers back.

But Ali is before me now and we're not the same.

"Mom said she won't give me anything unless I go to rehab," Ali says, and rolls her eyes.

My jaw is clenched so hard, I think I feel my teeth crack. If I open my mouth they'll fall out one by one, shattering on the asphalt into a million pieces. I stare at the tree trunk behind her.

"Then. Go."

"Don't be stupid. I don't need to."

She should be crossing her fingers because that's what you do when you lie. *Like this.* That was a lie too. Ali ruined it. Ali ruined *us.* She can blame Brier all she wants, but instead of getting through it together, she pushed me away. Pushed *hard.*

Before, we were AliandLia, the same but rearranged, never apart. *Like this.*

But I guess what we didn't know then was that Avery was the one holding us together, and so without Avery all I got was screaming fights and words designed for death by a thousand cuts.

Now when I look at Ali, all I can see is her five years ago, her eyes glassy, face contorted as she screamed at me, *I hate you!*

When she screamed, *I wish I was never in this family!*

When she screamed, *I wish you had been the one who died instead of Avery!*

It was the only time Ali admitted our other sister might be dead instead of just missing. The only time, and it was to scream that she wished it was me instead.

My hands are shaking more now. I'm humming. I'm humming loud to drown her out and she's still talking and she's *begging* for money and I want to slap her. I clench my hands and it's not to stop the trembling, it's because I want to hit her. Hard. What kind of sister wants to do that to her sister? What kind of sister am I?

"Why do you need money?" I finally get out. I want her to say it. I want us each to stare at the other and I want her to realize what AliandLia has become, what she's done to us.

"I—" Ali bites her bottom lip, over and over, and her nervous habit is setting me on edge too. "I just—"

"I won't help you buy whatever it is you're on, Ali," I snap, turning to leave, to flee. "I won't help you ruin your life even more than you've already—"

Ali's hand snakes out, too quick, and grabs hold of me. For someone who looks so frail, she's surprisingly strong. She fixes me with a glassy-eyed stare. "That's not—I don't want—" She breaks off, swallows hard, then starts again. "Can't you feel it?" she whispers, her voice breaking. "Lia, can't you feel *her*?"

My breath catches. "What?"

"I can feel it," she says, her eyes darting nervously around the lot. I remind myself she's just paranoid, that the drugs make her paranoid, but somehow her words keep drawing me in. "It's calling to me. It wants me home, Lia."

"What?" I say again, because there's nothing else to say. A pit of dread is forming in my stomach.

Ali scratches at her arm. "Avery wants me to go to her. I've seen her. And I can *hear* it calling me, all the time," she cries. "I can't stop it, Lia. Don't you feel it too?"

"I—"

Ali lurches toward me, eyes wide and bloodshot, her hands scrabbling on my arm. My heart flies to my throat and I jump backward, jerking away from her, sudden terror overtaking me. Because this isn't Ali; this crazed person before me can't be my sister.

"Get the fuck away from me!" I say, the words coming out strangled.

Ali stops, breathing hard, and glares at me. There's anger there, and I think I see a flicker of hurt, and I immediately feel guilty. She opens her mouth to respond, but then:

"Lia!"

Someone hisses my name, and I whirl around, my hum dying in my throat. It's Diya, hurrying toward me, casting worried glances over her shoulder. She's holding the bag of cupcakes that I forgot on my flight from the classroom.

"Oh my god, are you okay? I was so worried about you, babe! Look, have a cupcake and—" She sees Ali then, and stops. "Oh. Sorry. I'll just—"

She has the Peartree look. She knows exactly who this is; of course she does. Everyone in Daley knows Ali one way or another, either because they've gossiped about her wild exploits or partied with her, or she's stolen something from them or they've warned their kids not to go near her. Like bad is something that can rub off on your skin.

Maybe it can. That would explain a lot about my family.

"No," I say because I want to get out of here. I turn away from Ali without saying anything and she doesn't even protest, she just melts away back to the car that my mom bought her for being bad. I walk toward Diya, trudging through my lake of bitter thoughts. A girl could drown in a lake this deep.

"That's your sister, yeah?" Her eyes are still on Ali. She's never met Ali in person, only seen her from afar when we were all at school together, or heard about her from others. Ali isn't the type of sister you want your friends to meet. Not anymore, at least. Once upon a time, Ali was my go-to, my everything, and my heart constricts again as I remember her as she was—as *we* were.

"Yup," I say shortly.

"Is she okay?"

"Ali's never okay," I reply. "I think that's how she likes it."

"I don't think anyone actually likes not being okay."

I sigh and scrub my hands through my hair, pressing hard on my temples. Talking with Ali—just those few tense words—has made my whole body tired as if I've just sprinted a marathon.

"Do you . . ." Diya takes a deep breath. "Do you want to talk about it?"

"About what?" I reply.

My voice must be ice-hard, because Diya takes a step back. I immediately feel bad; it's not her fault I can't bear to have real friends. It's not her fault she's tried to be kind to the girl who is in pieces.

"About . . . you know. Brier Hall." She says it in a hushed tone, as if a whisper will soften the shot of terror and longing that zips through me as she says the name. "That the five-year anniversary is coming up."

I hate that she calls it an anniversary, like our flight from the house is something to celebrate. "I don't want to talk about it at *all.*"

"Are you sure you don't?" she says, and the way she phrases it doesn't even sound like a question. And at this point, who even knows? Brier's in my waking thoughts and in my dreams. It follows me everywhere. And as much as I say I hate when people ask questions about it—and I *do*—it's like Brier is always on the tip of my tongue as a reason, an explanation, an excuse. As a *hey, remember when,* or a smile or a scream. There's a part of me that craves anything to do with that house.

Anything that shows me what happened there was real.

"And you'd listen?" I breathe.

She looks at me like I'm not making sense. "Of course I would," she says plainly. "The only reason I've never brought it up was because I didn't want to upset you. I don't know what happened there, babe—I mean, only what was on the news, but, like, you're my friend. We're friends, right? You can tell me anything."

The words cut right through me, and I open my mouth, ready to respond. Maybe to cry *thank you, thank you.* That's when it happens. That's when I see her.

Wispy blond hair. Long. Flowing around her body, caught in a current. Caught in a breeze from another place. Her mouth is open, moving, and her eyes are pleading.

Avery.

She's right behind Diya, close enough that I could push her to the side and reach out and touch my sister's cold skin, her hair. Her fingers list limply at her side.

Avery wants me to go to her. I've seen her.

Everything smells like fish.

I can't gag; I can't even breathe. My lungs are in a vise grip.

And then: "Lia?"

And I'm coughing and sputtering, and Diya's hand is around my upper arm, her fingers indenting on my skin as she holds me up. "Lia, talk to me! What's going on? You look like you've seen a—"

She stops abruptly, the words colliding in midair, dropping like stones. We stare at each other, long and drawn out.

"I'm fine. Just go back to class, Diya," I say, my voice scratchy and low. The skin in my throat is burning. "I have to go. Text me after school."

Diya is silent, and I can't read her face. Then she sets the bag of squashed cupcakes on the asphalt at my feet and hurries back inside.

The smell of rot and brine in the air is gone.

And *she's* gone too, as if she was never there at all.

THREE

The house is heat-soaked when I get home. It's one of the squat brown-stucco houses that line most of the streets of Daley, with a clanging metal screen door and no AC. The front hallway is tiled with dull reddish squares, and the rest of the house has beige carpet. It's a bland, basic house and my mom has rented it ever since we left Brier Hall. We rent so we can leave if we have to. We've had a house turn on us before, and we won't be eaten alive again.

There's nothing at all wrong with the house in Daley. It's a house no one can get lost in, where the rooms don't change or move and doors don't lock of their own accord. A house of tiny proportions, a house only ten years old. There has been no time for any ghosts to accumulate in its walls.

There are no ghosts inside at all, unless you count us.

But the weirdest thing? It doesn't feel like home. I've lived in it for five years and the walls still feel unfamiliar, the layout strange. Everything seems off, as if the house senses that there's something *wrong* with us and doesn't want us getting too comfortable. Maybe Brier has seeped into our skin, branded us as its own.

The weirdest thing? Sometimes I miss Brier Hall.

This is the thing I can never, ever say. Because you're not supposed to miss a thing that tore your family apart. You're not supposed to love a place that's haunted. But sometimes I remember Brier at the beginning. How excited we were to have rooms upon rooms upon rooms to explore. The musty smell when we first opened the front door, like the house had been holding its breath and was now sighing with relief that *we were here, we were here!* The garden with its waist-high grass, the orchard with its rows of gnarled crab apple trees, the crumbly path winding down the cliff to the tiny sliver of private beach. The tower that overlooked everything with its watchful eye. The crunch of the gravel on the long driveway, the creak of the wrought iron gates that kept us in and kept everyone else out.

Brier Hall, those gates said. *Brier Hall belonged to the Briers, and now it belongs to the Peartrees—and no one else.*

And I felt it. I was just an eleven-year-old kid when we arrived, but I *felt* that this place was mine. It watched us—watched *over* us—and it was ours.

The Daley house is not like that.

When I open the door and sidle in, I'm fatigued. Having a panic attack the first few moments of class and then talking to Ali . . . simply speaking with her in general exhausts me because I spend so much time just trying to focus on breathing. And then afterward . . . seeing *her* . . .

No, don't think about that. My hands curl in on themselves involuntarily, pressing in hard. *It wasn't real, none of it was real. You're home now. You're safe.*

How I got home is a blur. It happens sometimes, where I'll suddenly find myself driving home from the coffee shop and have barely any memory of what I did there. Or during school when I'd blink and class would be over.

When I'd pulled my Volvo into the driveway, I noticed my mom's used car was there too, looking a lot like mine: worse for wear. That seems to be our entire life post-Brier. *Things fall apart; the center cannot hold.* We studied that Yeats poem in English Lit last year and I know it's about the end of the world, but all I could think about was *Welcome to the Peartrees. Welcome to my life.*

"It's me," I call as I come in and shut—and lock—the door behind me. My mom, Ali, and I still introduce ourselves each time we open a door, because there was a time when doors opened and other things entered. There was a time when hearing the creak of a door from somewhere in the house didn't mean it was one of our hands on the doorknob.

"Hi," my mom calls back from the kitchen. She sounds more tired than even I am, which before this moment I thought was impossible. My whole body just feels like *slouching,* not walking. Walking upright is for people who don't see their missing, maybe dead sister.

Mom is sitting at the kitchen table. It's a cheap, flat-pack piece of furniture, and it's five years old. Everything in our house is only five years old—basically, everything is new. I think my mom decided this new, unhaunted house needed to be filled with new, unhaunted items. All our possessions stayed behind in Brier Hall the night we left. The night we *fled* is more accurate, I suppose, but that night is still blurry and hazy in my mind. I wonder what Brier Hall looks like now. Has the house righted itself? Has it unspilled Ali's milk and set all of Avery's books back on the bookshelf? Has it washed writing off the walls?

Or is it frozen in time, everything the same as it was the moment we stumbled out the front door?

I don't know. I guess I will never know.

"Mom?"

There's a short pause, and in the quiet I hear the slightest, tiniest exhale as my mom breathes out. Her hair hangs in a curtain over the side of her face I can see as she tilts her head forward; once blond, it has grown out at the roots until there is a choppy color change midway down. When she lifts her head, she's smiling with a smile that doesn't reach her eyes, not even nearly, and her eyes are red and rubbed raw, as if she's been crying.

"What's wrong?"

She doesn't answer me for a long time, then says, "Why are you home?"

"I felt sick," I say, a half-truth, but I know that I look terrible enough post-encounters with both my sisters to pull it off. "The school let me come home."

"Oh, I'm sorry, sweetie," my mom says. "And on the last day too." Her sigh could knock me off my feet. "I was about to leave for work." After we moved to Daley, my mom got a part-time job as a secretary at an insurance company. Boring. Quiet. *Safe.*

She doesn't mention my birthday, and I'm about to bring it up, to give a little reminder. But then she continues, "Have you heard from your sister?"

"I—no." The *no* is out before I can stop it. Because if I say yes, then our entire conversation the rest of the night will revolve around Ali. Ali, and what she said, and how she looked, and can I text her again, please, and can I call her, and *Ali Ali Ali* until her name doesn't even sound like a real word anymore.

"I haven't heard from her in almost a week. I'm worried—"

This is what I mean. How our world revolves around Ali now. I might as *well* be a ghost for all my mom talks to me. People only have so much brainpower to use during the day: Ali makes sure that she has all my mom's. Always.

"I don't want to talk about Ali," I say, my voice trembling. Mom's staring down into her mug of black coffee now and doesn't reply. It's like she doesn't even hear me. *Can you hear me, Mom?* I want to scream. I scream it in my head, pushing the words through the air. *Do you even remember it's my birthday? Do you even remember me at all?* She doesn't look up.

"I wish you would try harder with her," my mom says faintly. "She needs us. She needs *you.* "

"She doesn't need me." I get the words out through clenched teeth. She doesn't need me, but I need my mom. I want her to hear my voice, loud and uncompromising, and not interrupt to ask about Ali. And if she did, I could find the courage to tell her the truth: how I lost one sister to Brier Hall, and how Ali's been trying to follow in Avery's footsteps ever since. How I can't breathe when Ali looks at me. How I can't stand to be near her.

How Ali told me she wished I was dead.

She half-apologized a few days after she said that to me; a silly, shruggy apology like *Yeah, it sucked, but sorry.* Shrug shrug. Not *Sorry that your entire worldview shifted with just a few words. Sorry you'll hear me screaming that at you for the rest of your life.* She blamed the house and said she didn't mean it, and would I just forget it?

I wish you had been the one who died instead of Avery. Little girls don't forget stuff like that. Can anyone, really? Things like that sink inside and grip tightly and won't go.

She blamed Brier for everything. She said that's why she does what she does—to forget. She said Brier is an evil place. Not a place with evil, but an *evil place*. As if evil hung from the chandeliers and walked across the floorboards and smiled out the glass panes of the windows.

Can a *house* be evil?

Can an inanimate place be evil? According to Ali and my mom, the answer is 100 percent, without a doubt, unequivocally: *yes*.

But I'm not so sure.

I think Brier Hall loved us.

I think Brier Hall loved us so much. Too much, insidious and strong. It loved us enough that it just couldn't bear to let us go.

FOUR

text Ali because my mom makes me, and she peers over my shoulder until I've complied: **Mom says she hasn't seen you in a while. Text her.**

"You could be a little friendlier to your sister," she says, her tone disapproving, and I suck in air and squeeze my lips together before my words come out as flames.

No, I can't be.

"Okay," I murmur. I mean it as a throwaway word, an all-purpose sound. It's a question, a response. Most of the time, it's armor. I say it when there're other things I want to say but can't, or won't. *Your sister stole my wallet*—okay. *I read about you. You Peartrees are freaks*—okay. *No one believes you, you know, everyone knows you're lying about what happened there*—okay. It's a little ironic that the least-okay girl in the world throws up *okay* like a shield. But my mom doesn't have to know I don't mean it. "How's work going?" I ask, veering to hopefully safer ground, but by the sharp look I get in response I can tell that I've said the wrong thing.

"Terribly," she replies, flat as the sidewalk outside. She grabs her bag from the hook by the door and jangles her keys between her fingers.

I wince. When my absent father died, we were left a lot of money as well as Brier Hall. My mom got to leave her three jobs, got to freelance, got to craft pithy copy for magazines and blogs.

After we left Brier Hall we were flooded with interview requests and book deals, but my mom declined them all without even looking at them. Deleted every email. Screamed at the reporters, hoping for an exclusive scoop, who camped on the dead, dry patch of grass outside our temporary motel room as far from Brier Hall and the tiny town of Eastwind as my mom could get before we ran out of gas. She sat us down on the edge of the sunken motel bed and crouched in front of Ali. Morning was breaking slowly, creeping through the cracks of the dusty blinds, and the harrowing dark night when we'd left the house was turning into something worse. I remember the first thing out of my mouth was, "Where's Avery?"

I remember recoiling at the look they both gave me.

"Don't talk to anyone about what happened last night," she said. "Don't think about it."

I can't think about anything else.

"It wasn't real. Do you hear me?" She gripped my chin, made me look into her bloodshot eyes. There was a cut on the side of her forehead from where one of the very real doors had slammed shut on her all by itself. "None of it was real."

It was real. Avery being gone is real.

"Whatever they offer us, we won't take it. We have more than enough money."

And that's the thing. Because back then, Ali and I nodded solemnly, scared of what we remembered, confused by the fact our older sister wasn't sitting next to us. We believed my mom. And maybe back then it was the truth.

But it's not the truth now, even with my mom's secretary job.

It's a touchy subject. Of course I would bring it up now, at the worst possible time.

"I'll see you later, Lia," she says from the front door, eyes sliding to mine and then quickly away again, as if she can't bear to look at me for longer than a second. "You know, I feel sick too. Maybe what you have is catching."

Maybe it is. The door closes behind her, and I imagine strands of my soul, blackened with hate and grief, following her out the door. Catching her. Wrapping around her arms and legs. Then I get up from the table and whatever I have that's catching comes twining itself back around my ribs.

My room is dark and quiet when I shut myself inside, with the blackout blinds leaving only a thin sliver of sunshine. I don't flick on the light—there's the air of someone sleeping, lying undisturbed, and I don't want to wake them from their slumber. I edge myself onto the bed. *Come on, Lia, relax.* My own voice sounds false in my head, like it's not even me anymore. *Relax. You're okay.* But I'm not. None of us are. Maybe I could believe it if someone else other than myself was saying the words, but there *is* no one else.

I get out my phone and, in the darkness, I flick through my messages. There are many from Diya, some frantic and all caps—ARE U OK???—and some making an attempt at sympathy—I know it must be hard for you but I'm here if you wanna talk! and I want to understand.

I don't want to talk to Diya. I don't want to have to *explain;* I want someone who already understands.

There're only a few people who do though. My mom: a nonstarter. Ali: would make things worse. And Avery: too late.

You know who to call. All of a sudden, I can see him in my thoughts: not the way I know he is now, when I looked him up online and stared at his longer hair and half smile until my eyes blurred. I see the way that he was when I first met him, thirteen years old and the same height as me too. A mop of untidy dark hair and sparkling, considering green eyes. Running through the grounds of Brier Hall through waist-high grasses, screaming with laughter. Skinned knees and muddy jeans and skeletal trees just *made* for climbing. The good ol' days that morphed as seamlessly as a dream into the days I try to block out of my thoughts. The past that eats up my present.

And the whole time, he was there. He would understand, and he always knew exactly what to say to make me feel better.

I lift my phone back to my face, the bright screen making me squint. I don't have his contact info saved, but I know his number by heart. It's the number for a slow, old phone his parents gave him only for emergencies. He doesn't know my number, of course— that was part of leaving everything behind. We left Brier Hall, sure, but we also left the community of Eastwind, and the beach, and . . . him.

We also left behind ourselves.

After all this time, can I really call him? I know I shouldn't, that after so many years of radio silence I should just let things rest. But it's like I'm not in control of my limbs: Here I am, typing in each number carefully. Here I am, pressing talk.

The dial tone sounds in my ear, jolting me out of my trance, and I flatten my back against the headboard—something firm to center me, to hold me in place. My stomach writhes at the mere thought of hearing his—

"Hello?"

My bones crumble at the sound of Rafferty Pierce's voice. It's deep with a hint of rasp, of sleep. It's a man's voice, so different from when he was a young teen, and I'm immediately chiding myself because *of course it is,* but then he speaks again, "Hello?" and I can hear the same inflections, the same tone.

I can't say a word in reply. My throat is choked with five years' worth of tears.

There's silence, but the call is still going. We're both there, just breathing into the phone.

"Hello?" he says again.

I miss you, I think. *I'm so sorry I left without a word.*

More silence. But then I almost drop the phone when his voice suddenly sharpens, becomes suspicious, and he says: "Lia?"

I think I might gasp, just the tiniest bit. Nothing but an influx of breath, but I think he takes this as an affirmation, because he continues, "You don't need to say anything if this is you. Just don't hang up, okay? Don't hang up yet."

We breathe together, and just the sound of his breath makes me want to cry. My eyes burn, my fingers clenched around the phone.

"Lia," he whispers. My name sounds better in his mouth. I miss the Lia he's talking to. "Why did you—?"

He breaks off, but I know I can finish his sentence any number of ways. Why did you leave me? Why did you never call? Why did you forget about me, about us?

I'm about to answer, to find the courage somewhere deep down to say his name in reply and tell him I miss him and that he's the best thing in my memories, but I'm interrupted by a call waiting. Someone's trying to call me—*Ali*. Ali hasn't called me in years, and my stomach immediately plummets. Ali wouldn't call me unless she had to. Unless she really, really needed me.

I don't want to answer. But somewhere tucked away inside me lives the Ali I miss, the one who would shove me from a ledge just to pull me back with a shout: *Saved your life!* The one who still loves me.

I stare at the incoming call for a second before taking a deep breath, sending Raff an *I'm so sorry* he'll never hear, and accept her call instead. This is what he probably expects from me. Lia, the girl who disappears into nothingness.

"Hello?"

There's rustling on the other end, and then a whisper cuts through: "Lia? Lia? Are you there?"

"Yeah, it's me." I pause. "What do you want?" She sounds different from when I spoke to her only an hour ago outside Daley High; there's a note of underlying panic that trembles through her voice.

"Don't worry about me, okay? I'm fine."

I wasn't particularly worried before, but I am now. "What are you talking about?"

"You have to promise me something, okay?" She interrupts me, her words coming out too fast, rushed and tumbling over each other. I don't know what she's on right now, but I can't seem to put the phone down. "You have to promise me."

My jaw clenches tightly shut. "Promise what? What are you even talking about?"

"It wants us back with Avery. She's still there—I know it. It wants us too, and it's calling for me," she says simply. "It'll call for you next."

It. She can't be talking about . . . She's not . . . Get a grip, Lia. She's paranoid. None of this is real. I say it to myself: *None of it was real.*

"Are you trying to say that Avery is still at Brier Hall?"

There are rustles on the other end. Then: "Yes. She is."

"Ali."

"Lia."

"Avery's d—"

"She's not dead! I've seen her, Lia, and I can *feel* this . . . this pull. I think it wants us back there so it can have all three of us together. Which means Avery is still alive."

"Houses can't want things, Ali. Houses aren't alive." I say it with a lot of emphasis because I'm honestly not sure this is true, and if I sound convincing enough, maybe I'll convince myself too.

More rustling. I can hear wind blowing through the speakers, muffling Ali's next words. "You're wrong, Lia. And don't tell Mom about this call."

"Okay," I whisper.

"Lia?" She says my name like it's a life raft. I've only heard her say my name like that twice before, back at Brier Hall. Once when she screamed it down a shifting hallway. Once when she mouthed it to me as we lay under her bed, twisted together, hiding from the thing rattling the doorknob, trying to get in.

"Yeah?"

"Promise me one more thing."

I'm silent, waiting. She doesn't make me wait long.

"You have to promise you won't come looking for me," Ali says, "when I'm gone."

FIVE

Stepping through the automatic doors from the thick heat of Daley in the afternoon to the AC-cooled supermarket makes me feel like I can breathe for the first time all day.

It didn't used to be that way—for months after we fled Brier Hall and Avery disappeared, missing posters adorned the walls of every shop in every town and city on the West Coast. The police used a picture of Avery where she was smiling gently and looked like a perfect princess, and every time my eyes snagged on her face I'd end up paralyzed with grief, brushing away tears in some random aisle. There was a number at the bottom of each poster to call in the case of sightings or tips, a direct line to the Eastwind Police Station. They got a lot of calls, apparently, but five years later my sister's still gone.

And each day the phone rang less and less, and the missing posters blew away in the wind. And now I can go into a store and no one looks from me to the poster and back again; I'm almost invisible. Now I can shop without misery squeezing my lungs—it feels like stepping into another world here, a world where I can grab a cart and push aimlessly through the aisles. Which is, of course, exactly why I am here.

I want nothing more than to be somewhere else.

The wash of strip lighting above illuminates everything in its way, from the boxes of cereal to the butcher to the fresh produce. There are no shadows, no ghosts. No sisters.

I take the handle of the cart and push, keeping my head down. I don't even have anything to buy, not really, but my mom hasn't gone grocery shopping in a while so I can use that as an excuse to be here. Because otherwise the answer is that I just can't be at home, sitting still, my fingers aching to call *him* back, my mind turning over and over Ali's whispered words. *You have to promise me you won't come looking for me when I'm gone.*

She'd hung up before she heard if I promised or not. After a pronouncement like that, she just hung up and let my whispered promise be met with silence. A curl of anger reaches up inside me—as it always does when I so much as think of Ali—but it's extinguished almost right away. Because she's been gone many times before this, too many to count.

But this feels different.

This feels like my fault.

I remember everything I said to her in the parking lot at school, and everything I didn't say. How much blood was roaring through my veins and my head was pounding and my fingers trembling and the fire inside rose right to the surface. But that same fire burned away most of the anger and now there's just cold and ashes and a sick feeling whenever those words swim before my eyes. *Get the fuck away from me.* And now she's gone again.

There's a tiny voice in my head, small but insistent. Mocking. Unrelenting. *And you know exactly where she's gone to. Don't you.*

Yes. I know. And that's why I'm wandering around the rows of food, as if they can keep me in Daley, keep me from getting in my car and driving until I can smell the ocean again. I know what I'll do—of course I know—but the *wanting* is something separate. I both *ache* to go to Brier Hall and, at the same time, the mere thought makes my skin crawl. Two ends of a magnet.

Stop thinking of this. Think of something else.

Anything else.

The handle is sticky under my palms, even with the whir of Safeway's AC. My thoughts are shooting in all directions despite my attempts to corral them, but I stare at the vinyl flooring and try my hardest to rein them back in. Deep breath. Deeper. Focus on what's right in front of me: a pile of lettuce and radishes. Above them, a light flashes and then tiny overhead jets turn on, spraying the produce with mist. Despite their shower, the lettuce leaves look wilted and the radishes start growing mold. I stare. *What?* Nothing grows mold that fast, but I watch as a thick fuzz of white crawls over the pink skin of the radish. The skin bursts. The insides are black, black as tar. Rot.

The entire tray of radishes, decaying before my eyes.

No. I blink, squeezing my eyes shut against the blight before me. And when I open them once more, the radishes sit there innocently, skins gleaming red-pink and dripping with dew. They are normal. They are fine. Everything is fine.

"Hey!"

The voice comes from behind me, and although I pause, I don't turn. *Oh god, not a reporter. Not here, not now.* The reporters all but dropped away as the days ticked on without a single update in Avery's disappearance. I studiously avoided the podcasts and TV episodes. I could almost pretend it never happened. But as the five-year anniversary gets closer, I should've known someone might try to find me.

But then the voice says again, louder now: "Hey, *Peartree.*" And my stomach drops further, because the voice has said my last name not as a name or a question, but as a curse. Something disgusting that she spit out and is lying between us on the floor. It's not a reporter or a podcaster or a true crime aficionado. I spin around and take a step back. It's Kayla D'Agostino, a girl from Daley High I know of only through name and the fact that her social standing is way too high above mine to be standing this close to me. I have no idea how she knows my name, or why she's talking to me, but her arms are crossed, her fingers curled into fists.

"Um. Hi?" It sounds like a question because I can't keep my voice steady.

"Your sister is Ali, right?" Her actual question comes out as a statement, her voice flattening in the mirror image of mine, because she already knows the answer. Us Peartrees have the same face, the same freckles, the same golden hair. But it's never good if someone asks about Ali. Ali courts trouble with a smile: She wears it like a cape of feathers and the troubles flutter off and infect everyone they come into contact with.

"Hello?" Kayla says again, her voice full of barely concealed anger. She waves a hand in front of my face. "Are you listening? You're a Peartree, *right*? You're the girl from the haunted house?"

Oh god.

"Yes," I say cautiously, suddenly all too relieved that there's a cart between us. She looks ready to launch herself toward me. Her fingernails are manicured and long, filed into stilettos so thin they look more like lacquered talons. They're painted a dark, violent bloodred. I imagine her pushing the cart aside, wheels clattering. Imagine her talons transforming into claws. Imagine her hands around my throat.

She doesn't move, just tosses a sheet of dark hair over her shoulder. Then she points a finger at me, the tip of the stiletto nail aimed right where my heart is thumping away, far too loudly. "Your sister," she spits, "was in my *house*."

"What was she doing there?" I ask. "Were you hanging out?" The words sound so small, scared. I do not want to be scared. I don't want to be scared of Kayla, or the girls at school, or the people who pass by me on the street, or my sister, or my mom, or the house that ruined us. The house that still has its hands in our lives.

I don't want to be scared of anything.

I am scared of everything.

"Hanging out?" Kayla considers me, and I get the feeling she's checking to see if I'm mocking her. If I'm in on whatever my sister does. But she settles for a derisive laugh, and I can tell that at least she realizes that no, Ali and I are not the same. "No, we weren't *hanging out*. She broke into my house over the weekend while I was with Tyler in Tahoe and stole from us."

My mouth is so dry I can barely form words. I'm not good at thinking on my feet like this. I am not good at chess: I can't see two steps ahead. I can see what's in front of me, and even then it takes me a moment to process. I want to sit and think this through: Do I apologize? Do I cut ties with anything to do with Ali? Do I tell Kayla to leave me and my family alone?

"How . . . How do you know?"

"Are you saying I'm lying? We have footage of her on our home security cams! It's her, okay? She literally looks up at the camera as she takes money from my dad's wallet."

"I . . . I . . ." I am still the perfect Peartree. I have to be that girl. If I let in any of the fear that is battering at my bones, begging to enter, I will fall down and never get back up again. And me shattering would shatter my mom too. "I am so sorry, Kayla."

This white lie sticks to my tongue.

"I haven't seen Ali in weeks."

This lie flows easily.

"She's not in a good place."

Lies always seem more real when they're tied in with the truth. And this, at least, I can say with complete honesty.

Kayla crosses her arms and squints at me. "I swear to god, Peartree, I'm not going to let this slide."

"I understand," I manage. There is dust in my mouth, coating everything.

"My dad's a lawyer and he's already taking the footage to the police."

"Okay," I whisper.

Kayla stares at me for a second, her lip curling, and then she stalks away from me.

I stand stock-still, clutching at the cart handle for support, as if Kayla has taken a scythe and chopped my legs out from under me. I'm reeling—not surprised at what Ali's done, as I've had more than my fair share of angry confrontations from people in Daley that Ali has somehow wronged, deliberately or not. Stealing from the D'Agostinos? A typical day in the semicharmed life of Ali Peartree.

But she just took cash, nothing else. Enough cash to get herself where she needs to go. The encounter at school today, and then the phone call . . . she was letting me know she was going and letting me know where she's gone.

I realize I wasn't lying to Kayla, not really.

Ali is not in a good place. I don't know exactly what's convinced her that Avery is still alive and just biding her time in Brier Hall, but if Ali is going back there, I have to go too.

I loosen my hold on the empty shopping cart and leave it there in the aisle, turning and walking to the door. I can feel my breath come in short gasps with each footfall. Kayla's in line at checkout; she glares at me as she gathers her items, a set of shiny car keys wrapped around her fingers, jangling, but I ignore her and hurry out into the oppressive afternoon heat.

My dusty old Volvo will be hot and horrible, but I have to get to my mom. I have to somehow convince her to let me drive down the coast to Eastwind and to Brier Hall. Convince? I almost smile as I slide into the driver's seat, because nothing would ever convince my mom. I'll have to lie: something perfect Lia Peartree doesn't do, but I have to get home. *Home, home, home.* The words make their way through my mind. A chant. *Home, home, home.* I'm just not sure which home they mean.

Ali's not in a good place, and she's heading to a worse one.

And I need to get there soon, before another sister goes to Brier Hall and doesn't come back out.

SIX

A camping trip?" My mom takes a sniff and then a sip of her pink wine. I make sure to keep my Perfect Lia smile plastered on my face. I link my hands behind my back and give the skin at my wrist a sharp pinch to keep my thoughts from veering into panic.

"Yeah," I reply casually. "With Diya and some other girls. You know, to celebrate graduation."

"That sounds nice," my mom says, smiling at me with a tremulous smile. Another sip of wine; she considers the glass before her, then drinks again. "Where are you going?"

"Not sure," I reply, still casual. Pinch, pinch on my wrist. "I think Diya is still planning with the other girls. Probably Tahoe, though, I think," I add, remembering Kayla D'Agostino mentioning a Tahoe house. "One of the girls has a house there."

Another sip, and I can almost see her calculating how far Tahoe is from the edge of California, where Brier Hall sits on the bluff. Pinch, pinch, pinch. My wrist stings and I swallow hard, trying to anticipate what she will ask next. But then she gives a wan smile and says, "Sure, hon."

And why would she realize it? I've never lied to her before. I get up every day before my alarm, I go to school, I do my homework, I don't put a toe out of line. She doesn't have to worry about me . . . so she doesn't.

She sighs and flicks aimlessly through some channels on TV. "Are you feeling better?"

"Well . . . not really."

She turns to me and grimaces, even though she seems removed, like she could be looking at anyone. Like I'm not even really there. "It's hard, hon, isn't it?"

I drop the smile plastered on my face, all teeth, all fake, and my heart lifts. Maybe this is where we finally *talk*, where we talk about the past and the present and she asks me about my day and doesn't accept "It was fine" as an answer. Where she doesn't accept that my smiles are real.

"Yes," I breathe. "Yes, I—"

"Have you heard from Ali?"

Everything stills and my teeth clench together involuntarily, so tightly I can *feel* the ache blooming in my jawbone.

Of course we're not going to talk about me.

We always come back to the one who really haunts the Peartrees. I can't escape my sister even when she's gone. I'm sure Ali would love to know she's all we talk about, some ever-present force that settles over everything in our house.

Have you heard from Ali?

It's the one thing my mom and I always fall back on. I know my mom tries. I know this. This is why I also try so hard, why I keep all the strange, overflowing anger toward her and Ali and everyone tamped down deep inside. Because she's trying, but she doesn't *get* it, so instead of fixing anything we're just orbiting each other, crumbling to pieces, both of us trying and smiling and saying "Are you okay?" and "I'm fine" and "Have you heard from Ali?" and "No."

I only hesitate for a second before I shrug. "No, I haven't." Monotone. Short. *Stop talking about Ali! Stop mentioning her name! I don't care, I don't care, I don't care*—There's a ringing, some kind of buzzing in my ears. Except it can't be just in my head because it's *so loud,* and it's building in a crescendo, coming at me from all angles. Our entire house is filling up with sound, like standing too close to the fire alarm and having its wail cut right through you. I throw up my hands, pressing in against my ears, but it doesn't help in the slightest. And the *I don't care* that was in my head comes bursting out of my mouth, somehow, the words screeching out like a physical representation of the screeching in my head—no, in our house.

But why isn't my mom clapping her hands over her ears like I'm doing now?

"Lia!" she says, her voice loud enough to cut through the fire-alarm wail. The way she says my name, *Lia,* has edges. It's all barbed wire and sharp, and a second too late I realize that shutting out the noise that she obviously can't hear just looks like me not listening. Looks like I'm clapping my hands over my ears, *na-na-na, I can't hear you,* like a petulant child. Looks like I'm being rude—something perfect-child Lia doesn't do.

I drop my hands. The ringing in my ears is abruptly gone; there's just a tense silence now. My mom's lips are pressed tightly together, but her eyes flash at me in that mom way that tells me I've done something bad. Why do I feel like this silence is almost *mocking?* As if the ringing *knows* it was there and is hiding away just out of sight. It got me in trouble and now it's laughing as it watches the aftermath.

"I'm sorry," I say immediately. I edge away from the couch and toward the hallway, toward freedom from her flashing eyes.

"What's going on with you?" she asks, and she sounds so disappointed that even though I've been waiting for this question, my lungs freeze up and I just stare back at her. Shrug. Breathe in, out, walk backward, don't cry.

I mouth, *Nothing*.

She doesn't see my lips move because she's sighing and rubbing her forehead as if *I'm* the one causing this family to slowly implode. As if I, trying so fucking hard to make everything normal and okay, am the one making things worse.

"I try to let you do the things you want, this camping trip, hanging out with friends, but I just don't understand what's going on."

I mouth *nothing* again because my vocal cords don't seem to work anymore. I wonder who ripped them from my throat.

"I just don't understand what's going on with you and your sister," she continues.

My breath catches somewhere deep in my lungs. *Nothing*, mouthed again.

And then she sighs once more and looks up at me. She says, "I just wish you would try, Lia."

And all my held breath—stuck in my lungs, in my stomach—comes whooshing back up to my throat and there's sound again and the ringing in my ears hasn't simply crept back in, it has *detonated*. My lips move of their own accord, as if a puppet master stands somewhere above me, ruining everything with a smile on his face. The scream is so loud I don't even know it's my voice at first, the words tumbling over themselves.

"I wish *you* would try!" The screamed words echo back at me: I wish *YOU* would *TRY-TRY-TRY.*

The shock on my mom's face would be funny if it wasn't so very unfunny.

I have to get out. I stumble toward the open doorway, feeling as if my feet are ten miles away. Careening down the hallway toward the bathroom, I am a newborn, my legs wobbling beneath me. I have just learned how to walk and I should not be running yet.

I turn the lock on the bathroom door. The Daley house doesn't have thick, heavy locks that *thunk* into place, but I can feel the click as the door locks and that's enough.

"Lia Peartree!" my mom says from outside the door. She knocks, three little taps. She sounds stressed, strained, and a little voice reminds me, *You did that.* It doesn't matter how much I try, because just one thing goes south and then I bring everything crashing down. "What is going on with you?"

I don't answer. I just try to calm my ricocheting heart.

"Lia!"

I can hear her on the other side of the door. She's not knocking now, but I can see the shadows of her feet. She shifts from one foot to the other.

I stay quiet, so quiet she can't hear me breathe. Brier taught me to be this quiet, to keep my panic inside and my breaths silent so no one could hear. So *it* couldn't hear me as I lay there on the weathered floorboards under my bed, my eyes squeezed tightly shut, my heart squeezed in my rib cage, my fingers squeezed and interlocked with Ali's, lying next to me.

She wasn't as good at staying quiet.

Brier always heard her breathing.

The quiet is suddenly overwhelming, and I spin around and stalk to the bathtub. The Daley bathroom has no personality; it's a wash of white and beige. The only color in the room is from our toothbrushes standing on the sink—my mom's, mine, and the unused, untouched one that my mom keeps in case Ali decides to return—and the basket of cleaning supplies under the sink. The hot-pink and turquoise plastic bottles promise to keep every inch of grime away, to banish even the hint of scale. My mom wipes down every inch of our house every single night.

As if Brier is an infection that follows us wherever we go. For a second the image of the moldering, rotting produce at Safeway flickers in my mind, the radish skins splitting open to reveal the gelatinous ooze inside. Although the Daley bathroom is gleaming, the porcelain perfectly clean, I shiver.

The bathwater runs hot over my fingers, the copious amount of bubble-gum pink, floral-scented bubble bath I poured in frothing into a thick layer of white. This is what I need—a break. Just some relaxation time where I can shut off my mind.

This is what I tell myself as I undress and sink beneath the water, folding my arms tightly across my chest. My fingernails dig just above my elbows. I am holding myself together by a pinch of skin.

It takes a while for me to relax, but eventually the heat of the water seeps into my bones, loosening the muscles and letting my brain drift. I focus on the floral fragrance and close my eyes, edging my toes up out of the bath as I lower the back of my head into the hot water, sinking down. The bubbles rise around my neck and my hair spreads out, tendrils gliding and tickling gently against my chest. The water pressing against my ears dulls the sound of everything: the overhead fan, the distant radio from the kitchen. Everything is muffled except for my own breathing and the sound of my heart in my head.

This is what I needed.

Breath: steady. Heart: slow. I'm suspended in the water by nothing but my toes gripping the far edge of the bath, and I almost feel weightless myself, as if I'm drifting. This will make everything okay because nothing seems very real right now. With my eyes closed and the water cradling my body, I could be anyone, any-where. I could be a normal girl with no ghosts, no past, taking a normal bath. I could be back at the private beach at Brier, eyes closed as I float on my back in the salty ocean, my sisters floating with me, our fingers touching, brushing up against one another, reminding each other we're still there.

I could be not even real, and I'm just row-row-rowing myself down a gentle stream. *Life is but a dream* and all that.

Something brushes my foot: the tiniest shiver of feeling, as if someone has taken a tip of their finger and gently brushed it across the top of my big toe.

I push out of the water, my heart thundering once more into overdrive, but there's nothing there. *Jesus, Lia, get a grip.* I can't even take a bath without freaking out. My entire body is coiled, ready to spring, to jump out and run—where? Run from what?

The Daley house is fine.

Everything is fine.

I force myself back under the water, just to prove to myself that I can.

Because nothing is wrong. And everything is *fine*. As I sink down, the water rises up my neck, my chin, and over my lips, and I try to put myself back in the water at Brier with my sisters, cold salt water lapping in a gentle tide, the sun beating down on us, the air thick and hot. Those idyllic summer days before everything turned *bad*. But my mind won't go, not now. It keeps thinking to the touch on my skin. The soft brush of fingers.

Salt water, I tell myself. *Sun and sand and sisters.*

Ali, sinking beneath the water to swim silently under me while I drifted alone in the sea. Ali suddenly grabbing my foot and tugging sharply down, shrieking with laughter as I shrieked with fear, my mouth filling with brine. Sputtering, coughing. I still remember the way I'd choked, that petrifying moment when the water filled my ears and nose and mouth and for a single second I was drowning.

"It wasn't me, it was the monster!" she'd said, all defensive, when Avery had swum over to be the peacemaker, the referee, the oldest sister, as always. We had all tread water, hands scooping and legs whirling while sludgy kelp and the light touches of tiny fish brushed our toes.

I had sputtered and spat salt. "Monster?

"The monster who lives in the lake."

"This is the sea," Avery interrupted.

"The monster who lives in the sea," Ali said, her voice lowering, her legs eggbeating beneath the surface. Her eyes were very bright. "The sea monster. It has tentacles, you know. It waits for little girls to swim by."

"But there haven't been any little girls in this house before," I whispered back, because even though I knew it had been Ali who'd pulled me down, I was only little and I was too trusting and suddenly a sea monster who lived in the tiny private cove of Brier Hall seemed not just probable but absolutely undoubtable.

"It just waits," Ali continued. "It waits and waits." She smiled at me, and it was a wicked smile. An Ali smile. "It could wait forever to get you, probably."

And then Avery had snapped, "Ali," and had turned to me to assure me that Ali was lying and there were no sea monsters here or anywhere, while Ali screeched that we couldn't be sure though, could we? And then we'd raced one another from one end of the cove, arms windmilling with loud splashes through the water until dinner, and the sea monster was forgotten.

Except when it wasn't, like in my dreams of being pulled under the water. Water everywhere. Inhaling it. Feeling it fill my lungs, sloshing through my veins.

It could wait forever to get you, probably.

Is that what brushed my foot? Just one more monster from Brier Hall, reminding me that it's there, waiting, always waiting for me to come back so I can be pulled under? Eyes still closed, I can feel the panic rising. *Breathe, Lia.* Because of course there aren't sea monsters anywhere, not even at Brier Hall. And especially not in the bubble bath in flat, brown, lifeless Daley.

I open my mouth to take a deep breath, to smell the light powder-floral scent of the bubbles.

And I'm pushed under the water.

It's a single push from somewhere around my midsection, like someone stood above me and *shoved* down. Water fills my open mouth, sickly with soap and now tinged with a definite fishy taste.

A brackish smell. My eyes fly open as my face slides beneath the surface, and I breathe in more water in cold shock.

Because above me, through the rapidly dissolving suds, my sister stands and looks down at me. Avery. She looks like she did when I last saw this apparition, this vision: swirling hair, wide eyes. She looks exactly the same as she did the last time I saw her, on the last night in Brier. She stares at me with filmy eyes, looking perfect and beautiful, and then it gets worse, and it's just like the grocery store: She rots. It happens from the inside out, her skin withering, her hair loosing itself from her scalp and drifting like feathers down into the bath. Her nails blacken, and her mouth drops open in a wide and soundless scream. Then I'm screaming too, still under the water. Screaming and screaming and sputtering and bubbles stream from my mouth, the sound muffled by the liquid pressing down. And I'm closing my eyes against this dead-eyed Avery; this silent, pallid Avery who is disintegrating before me, who smells like the rotting seaweed flung onto the Brier beach by the tide.

I thrash up, ready to open my eyes and run, ready to scream for my mom, but when I do there's no one there. She's gone again, back to wherever ghosts go when they're not haunting their victims. The bathroom fan *whir-whir-whir*s above me, the constant sound a blanket of white noise. A sob comes to my throat, and I wrap my arms around my bare chest and hug myself tightly, skin slick with bubbles, then I spit out soap and grasp the edge of the bath, pulling myself out of the water. My nose and throat burn from where I've inhaled the bath—floral-scented once more; the putrid smell of rot having fled with the ghost of my sister.

I know it's not Avery.

Because there are no ghosts.

Because there aren't ghosts: not here, not anywhere. There are not ghosts or monsters or tentacle-laden things in the ocean waiting to snatch little girls from the surface.

But the words sound hollow, even to myself. I don't know if Avery is really dead—Ali certainly seems to think that she's not. Even the police couldn't call it death—after their investigations turned up nothing, they presumed she ran away. And if she *was* dead, would she haunt me? I don't want to believe she would. But if it's not her, then who?

I go to my room, shivering, the old towel wrapped around me scratchy and damp. My hair is stuck to my back in wet tangles. First: Lock the door. This lock falling into place doesn't make me feel better, not in the least. But it will stop my mom from barging in if nothing else.

I flick on all the lights and check the room. I shine my phone's flashlight under the bed, illuminating every dark corner. I open the closet, pushing in against the rows of hanging shirts and sweaters. I double- and then triple-check the locks on the window, and it's only when I've pulled the blinds across that I let myself sink onto the edge of my mattress. I can't stop shivering; I'm freezing cold. It's the kind of cold that sinks into your bone marrow, but I can't seem to force myself to stand and change from my towel into dry pajamas. I just sit there and shake, and shake, and shake. I listen to the thrum of the ceiling fan. The TV in the living room is on, some rerun playing, muffled by the Daley house's beige popcorn walls.

The studio audience laughs uproariously.

I sit and shake until all the noise blurs into a dull roar in my head, draining the fear from me and replacing it with a kind of nothingness. A numbness that spreads through my whole body, my plans and questions—*get to Brier, find Ali, bring her back, figure out what's happening*—coalescing into one single thought: *Go home.*

A duffel bag hangs on the end of my bed, so like the backpack I once packed for Brier all those years ago. I can still remember how excited I was with the single-minded surety that this new home belonged to me. Was *meant* for me.

And now I'm going back. And so I grab the duffel bag, throw it open, and pack for Brier Hall.

EASTWIND

The past is never dead. It's not even past.
—William Faulkner, *Requiem for a Nun*

SEVEN

Daley is a town made for leaving.

My mom is still asleep on the couch when I creep down the hallway, duffel bag slung over my shoulder, the half-drunk bottle of pink wine still open on the coffee table. She rouses herself just enough to give a reply to my "Bye, Mom."

"Lia?"

"Yeah. I'm going to Diya's."

"Camping trip?" The words are heavy with sleep.

"Yeah." I stare at her prone form, then murmur, "Love you, Mom."

"Love you too," she replies, but I'm already slipping out the front door. I can't let myself think of what I am about to do: not because I'm worried I won't go through with it, but because I know that I will. Regardless, I will. Brier Hall wants me to come, and I'm coming. I can't stop myself—I don't *want* to stop myself. I want to walk the creaky old floors of the home that belongs to me, that loves me, the home that desperately, dangerously needs me.

It feels nice to be so needed.

Even if my mom begged me to stay, I would get in my car and drive until I was at Brier Hall's front door.

I don't know what kind of daughter that makes me.

It's barely dawn as I drive through the dark streets of Daley, my packed bag on the passenger seat beside me. All the streetlights are on, bathing everything in a flickering glow. I'm the only car on the road, and it's easy to pretend I'm the only person in the world.

Before getting on the highway, I pull over, taking my phone from the cupholder. The first text is to Diya: I'm going away this weekend to meet my childhood crush again, ahhhh! But it's in my old town so I told my mom me and you are on a camping trip so please PLEASE cover for me! I promise all the juicy details when I'm back! Next I text my sister, just two words: I'm coming. I know she won't respond. If she's already at the house, I'm not sure if she'll even receive it. I'm unsure of anything to do with Brier Hall anymore, but not for long.

Soon, I will drive out of Daley. Soon, I will be driving through the gates of Brier Hall. Even covered with rust and creeping vines, the gates were majestic, rising in wrought iron curls from the ground as if they'd sprouted there like overgrown weeds. Did Ali sneak through them in the dark, the only living creature on a haunted estate? Will they still be vine-covered now?

I will know soon.

So soon.

As I turn onto the highway, I think of how I told Diya I'm going to meet my childhood crush, and for a moment all my thoughts on returning to Brier Hall are replaced by another homecoming, one that's only ever happened in my mind. It will be hard to be in the same town as Rafferty and not see him, but I know it would just make things more difficult. There're five years of questions and hurt and not enough time to wade through the tangle and make it out the other side. Maybe Rafferty is better held perfect in my mind, forever thirteen.

Maybe. But maybe not.

I compromise with myself. I won't see him—I *won't*—but I'll call him. Just one more time. This will be the last time, I tell myself. Maybe going back to Brier Hall will bring me closure with Rafferty too. I'll be able to put Brier and Eastwind and everything that happened to my family in the past.

I dial his number and put it on speaker. He'll probably still be sleeping anyways, and just hearing his voicemail would be enough.

I'm accelerating when the dial tone disappears and he answers, "Hello?" His voice is full of sand, drenched in sleep. There's a long pause, and I take a breath, and then Rafferty says, "I know this is you, Lia." Another pause, then, "I knew you would call me back."

I am shattering in the driver's seat. With every second I am shooting toward him at seventy miles an hour, the dark sky lifting around me, beckoning me on.

"Are you going to speak?"

If I can find the courage, I say in my head.

"Fine," he says after another pause. "How about I talk, then? Don't say anything if you want me to keep talking to you."

I can tell that he's smiling. I can picture his slow smile in my head, so perfectly, and a hot tear drips onto my cheek. It's as salty as the sea.

"Good," he says when I say nothing. "Lia—I've missed you." As suddenly as I had the urge to call him, the urge comes to hang up. I can't do this: this isn't fair to either of us. In five and a half hours I will be back in the town I left five years ago, where the boy I love won't just be a ghostly voice on a voicemail but a physical presence. But he won't know. I won't get to see him; I'll only see stone walls and my sister's angry eyes.

It's not fair. *Not fair.*

With shuddering hands I end the call and toss the phone into the back seat. I put my foot on the gas and roll down the window, letting in a convulsing shaft of wind that fills the car with an endless roar. The day is already warming, the last tendrils of the cooler night air being pushed out by the heady Northern California heat. Soon Daley's shimmering dry heat will be in the past. I am switching it for thick, drenching mist, for the ocean air that roils up over the cliff edge, for the walled orchard and the weeping willow, branches bent against the breeze, creating a cave inside that belongs to no one but the Peartrees. To nothing but the house.

I am switching the safety of Daley for the unknown.

A rush of anger at Ali claws up inside me. Ali, who *had* to return to the house. I suck my lip into my mouth, chewing furiously on it to distract me. But the thoughts come anyway. Surely she knows Avery isn't there, but she knew I would follow. She knew that no matter what, I would follow. I hate that she knows that. I hate that it's true.

I taste blood; I've bitten through the soft skin on the inside of my lip, and rust and salt fill my mouth. I lick it away, then stare as the road expands out behind and before me. The Volvo's greedy wheels eat up mile after mile of asphalt. My lip stings and my eyes water and my stomach churns as the mile markers pointing to Highway 1 get smaller each time, but I try to ignore it all. I've had lots of practice at pretending, but I'm alone in my car now, and the one person I can't fool is myself.

I'm terrified.

I'm terrified to return, to see the house, to have the last five years fold backward until the past envelops me again. I'm terrified that Ali will be there. I'm terrified that she won't be.

Brier Hall looms like a thicket in my head, and I was just fine without picking my way through its thorns.

I don't want to go back.

I need to go back. My hands are shaking on the wheel, but my foot is still on the gas. *Home, home, home.*

Don't come looking for me when I'm gone. I promised Ali, but I guess I lied, because I just can't seem to stop myself.

ARRIVAL

As soon as you step out of the car and onto the cracked asphalt sidewalk that is Eastwind, you know that somehow, you've been here before. This place feels familiar, like the hint of a smell from your childhood that brings back a fragmented wash of memories, disjointed and tangled with time.

You know where you are.

Your sisters stay in the car, Ali pretending to be asleep and Avery scribbling furiously in her diary in the front seat. Your mom leans against the side of the car, shielding her eyes from the rays of sun breaking through the cover of mist. The car is parked in the weedy, sandy lot at the very edge of Eastwind, and before you is a boat launch and a stretch of sand that serves as a runway for the crashing white-tipped waves.

You ask if you can run on the beach, just for a second, just to stretch your legs. Your mom agrees when your asking veers into begging, and you're off running, sand flying up from under the soles of your shoes before she can remind you to stay where she can see you.

The late afternoon sun edges out, and momentarily a wash of heat follows you as you run, skimming over your shoulders before diving back into the clouds. You stop by the boat launch, breathing deep the smell of brine and salt and seaweed that you remember so well.

"Hey," says a voice.

You turn; there's a boy there. A familiar boy. He's your age and he has dark hair and dark brows and green eyes the color of the far-out ocean, the place where the kelp gathers right under the surface.

"Hey," you say back. You're not supposed to talk to strangers, but he isn't a stranger. He's—

"I'm Rafferty," he says.

Oh, of course. Rafferty fits into your thoughts, Rafferty becomes the boy before you. As soon as he said his name, you couldn't help but think, *Oh, right*—some part of you, deep down, knew.

"Lia," you say, and Rafferty grins at you, like deep down some part of him knew too.

"You don't live in Eastwind," Rafferty says.

"Yeah, I do," you reply defiantly.

"No," the boy says in reply, crossing his freckly arms. "'Cos I've never seen you."

"I do too live here," you say. You can feel the truth of your words seeping into your skin. You can feel the truth in every grain of sand dusting your legs. "Just moved. I live in Brier Hall." You're proud. Brier Hall. The name sounds like a dream, like a promise.

Rafferty's eyes widen. "You're a Brier, then?"

"No," you say. "A Peartree."

"How come you're living there, then?"

"Because," you reply, "it's my house." A Peartree, yes, but still Brier-blooded.

He raises his eyebrows. "There're a lot of stories about that place though, you know."

"I know," you say, even though you don't.

Rafferty's eyes are very green. "It's supposed to be haunted."

"Yeah, I know," you repeat casually, even though you want to ask *By who?* All the ancestral Briers? Your father?

You don't consider yourself particularly brave: not like Avery, leading you through the world step-by-step, or like Ali, who faces everything head-on, with her hands on her hips.

If one of your sisters had whispered *It's haunted*, you would have been bright-eyed and terrified.

But when Rafferty says it, you don't feel scared.

Why should you be?

You're not scared; you don't need to be scared. Nothing can hurt you now.

You're home.

EIGHT

Lia," my sister whispers, "I'm scared."

We're beneath the bed, the wooden slats mere inches above our heads. We press ourselves together, tucking toes up, knees intertwining, fingers holding fast. *Like this*. Ali squeezes my fingers so tightly I think they might break, but every inch of my body is coiled, and if I try to speak, I will scream instead. Ali's body is still warm—we got out from under the covers and rolled under the bed frame as soon as we heard *it*—but the floor is so cold it feels wet, as if something is seeping up from the warped and pitted boards, soaking through our clothing, our skin. Maybe it is wet—did we leave a window open? I can hear the wind battering against the side of the house in a vicious snarl of salt and sea spray. During the day the water in the cove is our plaything; we swim and splash and bend the waves to do our bidding. But at night the sea turns into something else, something living, angry, dangerous.

There's a tiny sliver of moonlight that falls in a thin, wavering band on the floor a few feet away, and the light reflects in the whites of Ali's eyes. She is nothing but a wide-eyed shadow with squeezing fingers and a clenched jaw.

The wind keens outside, and the window rattles in its frame with the force of the gale, and then suddenly dies away as the stormy winds edge around the side of the house. For a moment, quiet.

And then the door to our bedroom creaks open, slowly, slowly. Ali's nails dig into my skin.

And—

And I know this isn't real. But Ali's nails *hurt* . . .

I force myself out of the memory. I am digging my fingernails into my own arm, and I let go with a gasp. Outside the car window, towering trees line the thin stretch of highway in tightly packed rows of dark green, suddenly opening to dry scrub grass and a view of the ocean below, before plunging back into a tunnel of greenery. I know this is a dream—a memory—and that's all. Something bubbling up from the depths of my subconscious as I get closer to Brier . . . but it feels so real, and even with seeing the scenery flash by outside the car, it takes me a moment to pull myself back out of the memory. In this moment, I remember everything, every second. The way the running footsteps woke us up; that initial moment of pure, undiluted panic where we stared at each other, too scared to get up, to move, to speak, to breathe. The first intake of Ali's breath, caught in her throat. Small hands on my smaller ones, tugging me out of bed and onto the floor. Slithering our way under the bed, snakelike and desperate. Footsteps: *Thud. Thud.* Pause, so long we almost let out our breath. Then: *Thud. Thud.* Closer. *Thud. Thud.*

Waiting. Hands over mouths. Quiet.

The creak of the door.

And—

I can feel the nausea rise within me. *It's not happening.* The trees are a blur of green, racing by too fast for me to focus.

I try to take deep breaths. A sign flashes by:

ARCATA 94 MILES
EUREKA 87 MILES
EASTWIND 22 MILES

I am rumpled and tired after the drive, but seeing that little word in the flesh sets a shot of anxiety and adrenaline roiling in my stomach. A huge car passes me, engine roaring, and all I can think is: *That's a car made for battle. That's the car I need for a trip to Brier Hall.*

A getaway car, ready and primed for when Ali and I inevitably flee the house.

Of course I don't know this will happen. Probably everything will be fine. I say this aloud to myself a few times, just to hear a human voice, but my words sound hollow even to my own ears. Still, speeding along with the windows down, radio playing bright and jangly pop songs, I am almost able to convince myself everything will be fine. That nothing will happen. Because haunted houses aren't real.

They're just stories.

So don't worry, Lia, there is nothing to be scared of; it's just a house. *Just a house.* Brier taught me many things: it taught me to be quiet, hiding under beds. To be wary of rustles from other rooms. To close your door at night so things can't slither in while you sleep. To close your eyes when you walk down the hallways so you won't see them stretching out before you to infinity, taunting you, reminding you that you aren't in *just a house* at all.

And it taught me to lie, too, to smile waveringly to the cameras and newscasters and reporters and podcasters and tell them not to worry. That there is nothing to fear.

It's just a house.

But I can't lie to myself, not for long.

"I'm fine," I say out loud. "Everything is fine." The turnoff is coming for Eastwind; it seems ridiculous, but I swear that among the gathering fog there's a change in the air. A pull.

It's calling for me. It'll call for you next.

My fingers clench on the wheel until my knuckles turn white, and I drive like that until all of a sudden my stomach gives a swoop as if I've rollercoastered down a hill, and *I know where I am.* I'm at the last few seconds of road before the turnoff and—yes, there—the sign looms suddenly out of the mist. EASTWIND, with an arrow pointing to the left.

I slow the car and signal left, blinker flashing. *Click-click-click-click.*

Maybe it's the fog that swirls around the car, but everything about this feels unreal. I can't be here. I'm not here, I'm in bed, and any second I'll wake up and journal about how my subconscious still holds the memory of the Eastwind turnoff and how in the dream it felt like I never left. I pinch the skin at my wrist but I'm still driving, and houses are peering out from between cypress trees.

This is real. Eastwind is surrounding me once again, and five years fold and collapse in on themselves. Eastwind then was a tiny collection of houses, salt-weathered and damp and lonely, and now it seems much the same.

I drive along the road, the cement crumbling and dipping into potholes. Lines of spreading Monterey cypresses bend toward each other overhead, forming a tunnel of trees. The huge trunks stretching up from the ground look like fingers bursting from the loam, and I keep my eyes on the uneven road before me. I don't look at the trees or the houses I know are between them, watching me, until the tree tunnel ends and is replaced by the main hub of the Eastwind community: the historic Eastwind Hotel, a stately layer cake of a building with weathered wraparound verandas on each of the two levels and huge mullioned windows with original warped glass. The American and Californian flags hang limply in the misty morning on either side of the double front doors, which are still painted a glaringly anachronistic teal blue. A vacancy sign is on the front doors, and I can see the shadows of movement from within the hotel as figures walk past the gauzy curtains.

Well, I know where I'm staying tonight.

I don't want to walk through those doors again because I know who they belong to. The Eastwind Hotel has been owned by the Pierce family for decades, and it's almost guaranteed there will be some of them wandering around. But I sure as hell am not staying at Brier Hall—not before I've found my sister, at least—and there's nowhere else in Eastwind to go. I can picture perfectly what I'd find if I kept driving: the tiny grocery store, the bakery, the library, the school, the arts-and-crafts boutique store almost exclusively patronized by the tourists that arrive every summer, the weathered houses of the locals, and the hut near the beach where bored, hung-over high school kids stand and market rented kayaks to passersby.

And beyond that? I can feel myself turning onto the long path that winds up the side of the coastal bluffs, even as I pull into the Eastwind Hotel parking lot. I can feel myself stopping at the ornate, salt-encrusted gates of my home—*home, home, home*—even as I throw the car in park and get out, wrapping my coat around me. The mist is low-hanging today, casting strange dulled shadows and settling a sheen of water over everything.

Please, please don't let anyone recognize me.

The last time I was here I was leaving, crying in the back of my mom's car. She was putting up missing flyers, and we'd had to visit the police station yet again to reanswer questions we didn't have answers to. *Did Avery run away? Did Avery tell you she wanted to run away? Did you do something? Do you know something? Are you keeping secrets? You know haunted houses aren't real, right?*

I put up my hood and push through the front doors of the hotel. There's a bell hanging above the door and it tinkles with a clarion chime before fading away, mingling with the footsteps of a couple as they cross the lobby, chattering about packing sandwiches for their trip to the beach. The young girl at the reception desk looks up, tucking her dark hair behind her ears, and I take an involuntary step back, because even though she'd older than when I knew her, I recognize her immediately. Frankie Pierce. She has green eyes and a smattering of freckles and her expression is serious, just like her brother's always was.

I can tell she doesn't remember me. She would always want to play with us on the grounds of Brier Hall, but she was a kid, whereas her brother and I were the queen and king of a sprawling estate. And she was only eight when we left Eastwind; to her my presence must have seemed a brief and fleeting dream.

I almost say her name, "Frankie," just to make sure she really is there before me, but at the last minute I swallow her name and soundlessly mouth it instead. She doesn't notice because she's loudly typing at the computer keyboard.

She glances up at me once more. "Hi," she says. "Welcome to the Eastwind Hotel."

I stare at the carpet. It's the same wine-red carpet that was here five years ago.

"Thank you," I mumble.

"Do you need a room?" she asks.

"Uh-huh."

She kind of narrows her eyes in my direction, but I keep my eyes trained to the ground and she must think I'm just a random odd tourist, because when she speaks it's in her friendly receptionist voice. She's thirteen and sounds like she's playing dress-up as an adult—she always wanted us to play dress-up with her before. She's good at it.

"Okay," she says, clacking again on the keyboard. "A single room?"

"Uh-huh."

"Okay." *Clack-clack-clack.* "Great. All guests get free breakfast here, so just come down between seven and nine. Will you need any information about your stay in Eastwind?"

I shake my head. The only thing I want to know is if anyone has seen Ali pass through, and that's the one thing I can't ask.

A family with excited, bouncing kids walks behind me, heading for the hotel's dining room, and I have to jump out of the youngest's way to avoid his excited journey toward food. My hood falls back, and the sudden resurgence of others makes me remember where I am. I need to get to my room; I need to get away from anyone else who might know me.

"No, I don't need anything," I say, turning back to the reception desk. "Just the room key, please."

"Sure," Frankie says politely, picking up a key attached to a motel-style plastic fob printed with EASTWIND HOTEL in gold lettering. She looks up to hand it to me, and stops. "Oh," she says. She squints. "Uh . . ." Chews on her bottom lip. "Do I . . . do I know you?"

"I—no," I say immediately, sure that the sudden panic bubbling up inside me shows clearly on my face.

"Are you sure?" Frankie says, her hand traveling to her hip in the slightly belligerent way that only thirteen-year-olds can truly master.

I'm saved having to respond by the bell at the front door jingling merrily, announcing another customer. *Thank god.* I snatch the key from her fingers and whirl around, ready to make a break for the stairs and the locked door behind which I will finally be safe and alone.

I turn right into someone else.

"Whoa," says the person, putting their hands on my shoulders and steadying me. "Are you . . . ?"

He meant to say *okay;* I know this because his mouth makes a little O although maybe he's just stunned.

Rafferty Pierce.

He looks like Frankie; there's still something in his face that is the same as it was when he was thirteen. It's the online photo I found of him made flesh. His hands are on my shoulders, fingers drifting into the soft spaces between bones. His dark curls are windswept and messy, and he smells like the sea. That's all I'm able to take stock of before he stumbles away from me like he's had an electric shock.

Then: "Lia?" He doesn't say my name like he did on the phone, lazy and slow; now the syllables are wrapped up in utter astonishment. "Lia Peartree?"

NINE

have dreamed of this moment infinite times.

The moment I return; the moment my blue eyes meet Rafferty Pierce's stormy green ones. For five years I've dreamed so vividly of this moment that I think surely somewhere, sometimes, it really happens, and there are infinite branches running alongside me where Rafferty and I are together and we are happy.

Sometimes in this moment he licks his lips, slowly, before saying: *You really came back. I missed you so much.* Sometimes we sit on the bed together, drenched in nostalgia and tears, remembering and laughing. Sometimes he is in the doorway, standing still, his hand fluttering toward me, stroking my cheek, taking in the realness of me. Sometimes his eyes widen dramatically like in the movies. *Lia!* He says it with so much love. He is tender. Sometimes he says nothing at all, but his eyes say everything for him. Sometimes he says nothing at all but hurries toward me, unable to wait, scooping me up in his arms and pressing his lips to mine. *Lia, I missed you.*

Lia, I love you.

Lia, I'm so glad you've come home.

I have created him in my mind: not the boy I used to know, my friend. In the past five years I have dreamed up a new boy, a boy who has aged with me, a boy who has always been there every time I close my eyes. A boy who is singular and perfect and lives inside my bloodstream. A boy who is a part of me.

I dream as I walk up the stairs to my room, the room key jangling unceremoniously from my fingers as I create other worlds for me and Rafferty to live inside of. Rafferty's footsteps are muffled by the thick carpet but I know he is there, and when I unlock the door with shaking hands he follows me inside.

The door clicks shut behind him and I raise my eyes to his.

There's always one similarity in every dream, no matter how the moment plays out: Rafferty is always happy to see me. Cautious, sometimes, but always happy. Because I am his and he is mine and we are the same.

But Rafferty Pierce, made of flesh and blood and bones and not of dreams, is before me now and he is stone. He is not the boy who lives within my mind. His frown is carved from marble, an angry god.

And we are not the same.

"You're back." His voice is flat.

Instead of answering, I just look at him. Every part of this very real boy before me I cast into my memory for when I eventually, inevitably, leave again. I was taller than him when we first met as kids, but not anymore, and he towers above me now, arms folded solidly across his chest. I trail my eyes over the way his dark hair curls around his ears, how a stray lock falls across his forehead, brushing the top of his furrowed brow. He's tanned and windblown, cheeks flushed: maybe from the salt spray, maybe from the red-hot anger ticking in his jaw as he looks at me. Rafferty: son of the sea, my best friend, my confidant. I was in love with him in the fierce way of a thirteen-year-old with her very first crush. If I believed in soul mates I might think that he's mine, except for the fact I haven't seen him in five years and I can't seem to do anything except ruin things.

Before, we would climb gnarled trees on the coastline until our fingers bled and swim in the freezing Pacific waters in the cove until we were numb and sandy and more salt than human. We'd play flashlight tag with my sisters in the grounds around Brier Hall: I was always on Rafferty's team, and we would hold hands so we wouldn't lose each other in the blackness. Together, we were wild, and I always thought that Raff would be the one to leave Eastwind someday. We had big plans, big adventures, lists for futures that included each other in them. We had linked pinkies and promised to always be best friends.

But looking at him now, he's settled into himself. He is salt-soaked and wind-stained like everyone here in Eastwind. It seems all the wildness has been drained from Rafferty Pierce, like dirty water swirling down the sink.

I am the dirty water.

Rafferty has washed me away.

For a second I think that nothing remains of the boy I used to know, and I work up the courage to whisper, "I should go." His eyes flash, and I suddenly know he's in there, my Raff.

Rafferty scoffs. "You should go? Yeah, that tracks."

"*Excuse* me?"

I know he's about to explode and I'm ready. I can't fight with my sister but I can fight with Rafferty Pierce. This was never a moment I dreamed of but now I want nothing more than to have Rafferty yell at me, to have him detonate. Raff's anger is still wild.

I want to scream at Raff. I want the fury to rocket around the room in a cleansing fire, and afterward in the new, bright, blank silence I want to kiss him. I have built him up in my mind and I want that dream boy to be the one before me now. I want to collapse into him.

"You heard what I said," Raff snaps.

"You weren't this mad on the phone," I say. "You wanted to talk to me then."

"It's different now."

"How?"

"Because you're *here*."

"There was nowhere else to go, Raff," I snap back. "You know that, this is the only place that—"

"God, Lia, I don't mean this hotel!" Raff says, his voice rising. "You're *here*, in Eastwind, and you just . . . you just . . . why are you acting like this is all normal?"

He's on the brink and I want to make him mad. It's a bad habit I have: I know now that things won't go how I want them to, so I start trying to make them worse. Making things go wrong is at least something I can control. "This is normal. This is just a town and we knew each other for two years when I was little and now everything is different."

We stare at each other, both of us defiant.

Then: "I know you know how I felt about you," he explodes. "You were my best friend, you were—you were . . ." He stops. His jaw is so tight that, as he swallows, I can see his Adam's apple bobbing above the collar of his white crewneck sweatshirt. "You left," he finishes. "You just left."

All my anger drains away and I sit down on the end of the bed, the soft mattress sinking beneath me. A bubble of anxiety rises in me, twining its fingers around my lungs and tightening. He doesn't seem mad now, he seems defeated, and I can't fight back against defeated. Now we've come to the point where we have to face the truth: I am the villain here. I am the bad guy. I stare down at my hands so I don't have to look at him. "You know why I had to."

"No," he says, and then very carefully comes and sits down on the bed as well, making sure not to let his leg brush up against mine. "No, I don't. No one does, Lia; you just left in the dead of night and the rumors—you wouldn't believe—"

"I bet I fucking would," I snap.

"Well," he concedes, looking slightly abashed. "Maybe you would."

It's so quiet I can hear him breathing. I count his breaths, listen to each reminder of his life.

"It's been shit," I say finally. All the air seems to have gone out of my lungs, but Raff is still breathing so evenly I pretend it's enough for both of us.

"Yeah?"

"Yeah."

"I'm sorry about Avery. About everything."

"Thank you," I whisper. Hearing Avery's name from someone who actually knew her feels worse than hearing it from the mouths of the reporters and police and the podcasters. At first, in the immediate aftermath of her disappearance, her name was like death by a thousand knives. So I began to sort of block it out. It wasn't *my* sister they were talking about. It couldn't be. *When did you last see Avery? When did you realize Avery wasn't there? Has Avery tried to contact you? Was Avery the type of girl to run away?* It's like when you say a word so many times that it no longer looks real. After a while, the Avery they spoke of was some made-up person totally removed from my sister. Someone whose disappearance I could cope with—more or less.

But when Rafferty says *Avery*, it's different. It feels like the first time I've heard my sister's name in years.

"I could've helped you through things." He sounds so earnest.

"No, you couldn't have," I say flatly.

"How's your mom?"

I swallow. *Pink wine and vacant stares and barely remembering I'm there.* "Bad."

"Ali?"

"Worse." I know my voice is angry, dismissive. *It's better this way, to keep Raff at arm's length.* I know it's true, but it doesn't feel true.

Raff sighs and scrubs a hand through his already tousled hair. "Lia—I'm sorry. I don't know what to say."

And because I also don't know what to say, and I'm upset and don't want to talk about this anymore, I end up mumbling a short and awkward, "Yeah."

"So you're here to what, do one last tour of your youth before college or something?"

I don't want to tell him why I'm really here, so I dissect his words and change tack. "I'm not going to college, actually. Not yet."

"Didn't you get in anywhere?" he asks bluntly, his tone cutting. I guess I'm not the only one who is trying to keep the other at arm's length.

"I didn't apply," I say, then add, "I started to. I don't want to stay in Daley but—"

"Daley?"

"That's where I live," I say. "Where I've been. It's five hours away, more or less."

"All this time you've been five hours away." He doesn't say it like a question, and he gives a short bark of laughter that doesn't sound humorous at all.

I nod and give a half-hearted shrug. "I started applying but then I had to write the essay, and I realized I haven't done anything at all. The only thing I could write about was, you know . . . *it.*"

My time at Brier Hall and Avery's life and disappearance have been reduced to *it*, the day *it* happened.

"And I found I couldn't do it." I shrug. "So no, I'm not going. I'll figure something out." Before Rafferty can ask me again why I'm here in Eastwind, I continue, "What about you?"

"Yeah, I got into a few places." He swallows, then says, "Dartmouth."

"Oh, you're smart now?" I say, and for the first time since I bumped into him in the lobby—for the first time in five years—Rafferty smiles at me. It's the exact same slow smile that shows all his teeth. It's the same grin he's had his whole life, and seeing it loosens something inside me.

"More or less."

"Less, I'd say."

"That's not what the college said."

"Oh?"

"They said I was on some genius-level shit."

"Yeah? Dartmouth said that to you?"

"Verbatim." He's still smiling.

"So what did you write about then? To fool some Ivy Leagues into accepting a small-town kid like you?" I mean it as a joke, but his smile subsides: first to a tiny uptick of his lips, and then a straight line, pressed together. "I'm—" I swallow. "I'm sorry—"

"You," he says abruptly. "I wrote about you."

The *sorry* trails off, dying in my mouth. *What?* The past few minutes of banter and smiles and pretending we're back to normal is gone.

"You . . . what?" I want him to laugh it off. To say it isn't so.

"I wrote about you. I wrote about how I grew up adjacent to the Peartrees, adjacent to the drama and the news and the infamy, but always separate. Never a part of anything, not really. I wrote about that, and how it changes someone. How it makes them see the world, and their community, and other people."

"You used me to get into college?" I croak.

"Yes," he says bluntly, staring right at me, his green eyes boring into mine. "I did and I don't regret it. It happened to you, but it happened to me too, and I'm allowed to write about my experiences."

A part of me understands exactly what he's saying. The events at Brier Hall *did* happen to this entire community. And then I left, never to be heard from again—until now. But still . . . I can't quite control the wild anger that rises up in my throat every time I think of him typing out an essay about me, my sisters. That house.

"Fuck you," I snap, crossing my legs and turning away from him on the bed.

"Fuck *you*," he snaps back immediately.

"You're not the same person you used to be," I say, whirling back to glare at him.

His eyes are clear and sharp. "No," he replies, "I'm not."

We stare at each other, and then I break eye contact. None of this is going at all how I imagined it would. Now I just want him to leave.

"Well, it was nice to see you again," I say. "I think we've said enough. Thanks for the catch-up, Rafferty."

He stands, bed springs creaking, the end of the mattress rising up in his wake. "You shouldn't have come back, Lia. Not after all this time."

"I didn't come back," I say. "Not really." I pause. "My sister is here, and I've come to make sure she's okay. That's it. That's all."

"You mean—you're going back to the house?" Shock colors his voice.

I make a tiny noise of assent, then stand and push past him. "Yes. And then I'll be gone again. That's my thing, isn't it?"

Raff is still standing beside the door, and as I reach forward to grab the door handle, I brush up against him. He inhales for a second, a sharp, angry sound, and then captures my hand in his calloused fingers. I hold my breath, my eyes flicking to his.

"That's really why you came back?"

"Yes," I whisper. He's not the same as he was, and we are not the same. Except maybe we still are, in a new and uncharted way. We are not the same kids, wild and free, but as I look into his eyes and watch as his jaw clenches tight, I gravitate toward him, just like I always did.

"Don't go back there."

"I have to," I say. "It's why I came." I nod with certainty, trying to convince myself. "It's the *only* reason I came back."

"Oh yeah?"

I nod mutely. Raff edges closer to me, closer, closer.

"Why'd you come back to Eastwind?" he asks again.

"My sister." I can barely get the words out.

"And?"

"That's it." I'm such a liar. But Rafferty doesn't have to know the war my own mind went through on the way here, convincing and unconvincing myself to see him again. He doesn't have to know how often I've thought of him over the past five years.

"And?" When I'm quiet he presses his tongue between his teeth, then gives a half smile. His voice is rough. "And?"

"What do you want me to say, Raff?" I say. "That I wanted to see you?"

"Did you?"

Yes.

He seems to read the answer in my face. "And what did you think would happen?" he says, his voice low. He takes a step forward and for a moment I'm sure he can read my mind, see every world I've thought up for us. I can see his lips crushed to mine, arms pushing me against the wall, and we're thinking the same thing, I'm sure we are, *we are the same—*

He puts a large hand on either side of my head, trapping me against the door. He smells like the salty air and the one type of bright-blue cologne that the all-purpose Eastwind grocery sells. I breathe him in and he dips his lips down to mine, hovering them above my own. My breath catches. *Oh my god oh my god oh my god*—I've never wanted something to happen more than this. Every bad part of being back in Eastwind fades away. I cannot hear Brier Hall's call. Everything is unreal; there is nothing in the entire world and all its infinite branches but us, right now, in this moment.

"Did you want *this* to happen?" he breathes.

I can't even speak. The world has paused itself.

I brace myself against the door as he leans closer, his lips brushing mine so that I can feel them move as he says, "We're not friends, Lia Peartree." And then he steps away from me, the sudden absence almost a physical pain. We stare at each other, coldly, and although everything is changed and ruined I know he knows my heart is breaking, even now. He says we've changed, but he still knows exactly what to say to make my breath catch. To make me smile. To make me cry. Raff swallows, then says, "We're not anything."

My teeth lock together so tightly, I think they might crack. *Don't panic.* It's rising within me, the scream, the tears. I nod quickly, ducking my head so he doesn't see when the tears begin to fall. I knew coming here that seeing Rafferty would only end badly. Why did I ever delude myself into thinking it might go well?

Hope is not the thing with feathers. Hope is wax wings and a long, hard fall.

We're both quiet.

I take a deep, wavering breath that comes out shaky. My fingers are clenched tightly into fists as the anxiety rears up. *So stupid, so stupid, so STUPID*—

"Are you ever going to forgive me?" I manage to say, the words coming dull and fast. He has knocked me out and he knows it.

Raff has stepped back, away from the hurt he's caused. "Do you want me to?"

I raise my eyes to his, looking at him through a blurry veil of tears. I can't read his expression: part pain, part blue anger, part guilt. The tip of his tongue is pushed out into the corner of his mouth and I can see this teeth moving as he chews on it, something he used to do all the time when we were kids.

When I was nervous, I'd create fists so tight my nails would leave half-moons on the flesh. When Raff was nervous, his tongue would come out and his teeth would start moving. Sometimes I used to see him spit blood.

My fingers are fisted now, and as I look at the tip of Raff's tongue, I realize some things never change.

Do you want me to?

I know that I could end this now, it could all be over with one little word. *No.*

Do I want you to forgive me? No. I'm leaving.

No.

This has already gone so badly, and I could put a stop to it before things get worse. But instead, I do the wrong thing.

I want to tell him I want to be friends again, that I wouldn't have minded if he'd kissed me against the door, that he was the best part of living at Brier, that I've missed him every day. But instead I just say, "Yes," and somehow that feels much like the same thing.

Rafferty clears his throat and says, "I'll consider it."

"Maybe you could stop by again after you finish work," I say.

"Maybe," he replies, opening the door and stepping out. He pauses on the threshold. "Lia? Don't go back there."

I can't meet his gaze. "I have to."

"Lia." His voice is quiet now. "Don't."

And I think I finally realize what Ali was talking about when she said that Brier Hall was calling to her. Because I can feel a pull in my bones drawing me toward the gates. I don't think I could turn back now whether I wanted to or not.

"I'm sorry, Rafferty," I say. "I have to do this. I have to know what's going on, and I have to find my sister." I don't mention which sister I mean.

He sighs, then shakes his head and moves toward the door. "You're making a mistake. That place is bad news." Then with one more shake of his curls he backs out into the hallway. The door clicks shut behind him, but not before he lets in a guest of heavy silence that comes bearing the gift of memories ready to drag me under.

HOW TO FORGET

I watch as you play.

Dashing up from the cove and into the briar patch: thorns scratching at your arms, Rafferty with a hand over his mouth to stifle his breathing, fingers linked, huddling together. Do you remember? The whites of his eyes shine brightly in the moonlight and you stare at each other and then peer out of the thick foliage, waiting, waiting . . .

Movement in the dark. Panting, and then a flash of shadow. You're filled with adrenaline and Rafferty winks at you, the signal, before you both click on your flashlights and jump out of the underbrush, thorny vines tearing at your skin.

You shine the wavering beam of light at Ali and Avery, two shadowy forms making a break for home base. You scream out, "One, two, three, four, five!" and your voice is tossed by the wind. I hear you anyways.

Your sisters slow to a walk and you gather in the dark in a tiny huddle.

"You're out!" Rafferty yells, running over as well and joining your group, backs against the wind. He smiles at you, gummy and wide. He is always smiling at you. I watch him want you, but I want you more. "We win!"

"It's not fair," Ali grumbles, crossing her arms. "Ave, tell them they can't hide in the briar patch. It's not fair that *we* can't win because we don't wanna get all scratched and hurt and—"

Avery grabs at your arm, pulling up the thin material of your long-sleeved shirt. Tiny scratches make their way up and down the skin there and you and Rafferty smile proudly at each other, coconspirators and reigning champions of flashlight tag. You hide where I can hide you.

You were always the smart one.

"You're bleeding," Avery says.

You pull your sleeve back down. "Not really." They are just tiny scratches, nothing more. I make sure of that. The briar hides you well—it is the perfect place to run to for cover. The thorns often prick you as you shimmy to safety, but it is a small price to pay. Do you sometimes imagine tiny droplets of your blood falling like rain onto the thirsty ground, the thick, overgrown gardens of Brier Hall growing wild and untamed because of you? You are here forever now. You and Rafferty both.

The wind roars by you, tumbling up from the sea, and you think it sounds like words. Like it's Brier, screaming at you, although you don't say this out loud because whenever you do your sisters give you a *look* like you've said something ridiculous.

But they just don't understand, do they?

"Are you hurt too, Raff?" Avery asks.

Rafferty shakes his head. He has a tiny twig in his hair and you pluck it out. "Look, you're turning into a tree."

Raff laughs, but no one else joins in. Ali kicks at the gravel path with the toe of her shoe, arms still crossed and a stormy look on her face. Avery looks worried, still holding on to the sleeve of your shirt.

"I checked the briar before, for you," she says. "I didn't see you."

"Well, we were there," you say.

You know I hide you well.

"Briar patch is out of bounds from now on," she says.

Your protestations are cut off when the porch light flicks on, the buzzing of the light breaking through your arguments. The front door slowly creaks open, and then your mom's head pokes out. "Dinner's almost ready, kids," she shouts. "It's too dark, come on in now, okay? Rafferty, d'you want to stay for food?"

"Yes, please!" Rafferty yells back.

"You all stayed away from the cliff, right?" your mom calls out as she goes back inside.

"Yes," you all call back as one, giving each other guilty looks as the lie resounds into the house. You quickly move to safer ground in case your mom comes back out to check, and you romp through gravel and overgrown grass toward the front door, still slightly ajar, welcoming you home.

"Hey," Avery whispered to you as you took off your muddy shoes on the porch. "I know you and Raff have a hideout somewhere in the briar, don't you? Where is it? Because I *did* look there and I couldn't find you . . ."

"No, we don't," you reply staunchly. You aren't going to give up the location of your secret fort, even to your sister. You watch as Ali stills as she slowly unties her laces, listening to us. "We were there."

"You're a liar," Ali pipes up. "Liar, liar."

"No," Rafferty says, suddenly appearing behind Avery. "No, she's not. We *were* there the whole time. Maybe this place just doesn't want you to find us. Maybe it just likes us more."

Ali narrows her eyes at us. "You're all liars," she snaps, then stomps into the hallway in her socks.

Avery looks at both you and Raff, who crosses over to stand next to you, like a guardian. You don't need him as protector—you have me.

Avery looks at you seriously and whispers, "Don't go back down there at night."

"Ave," Rafferty begins.

"Just say you *did* have somewhere in the briar that you liked to go," she cuts off Rafferty. "A place where maybe we can't seem to find you when you're in it. If you *did* have a place like that, you can't go back in there." She swallows hard. "I have a bad feeling about it."

"What?" you ask curiously. "Why?"

Avery starts to speak, and then shakes her head and shrugs instead. "Promise me you guys won't go back in there."

You and Raff exchange a glance.

"I promise," you say.

"Me too," Raff agrees.

Avery nods, lips pressed firmly together, and then heads inside. It's only after you hear the door to the kitchen open and close that you and Raff bring out your tightly crossed fingers from behind your backs, and the white lie slides away with the wind.

Like this.

TEN

brace myself as fragments of memories flash by: scratches from the briar patch. Raff's smile. Little white lies.

We never listened to Avery, even when we should have. The memory of her voice is so real in my mind that I look around the hotel room just to make sure she isn't standing behind me, but—*of course, Lia, of course*—there's no one there.

I collapse into the chair by the window. I've been wandering in circles around this tiny room ever since Rafferty left it, stuck in a whirlpool of memories and half-remembered dreams. My stomach feels sick whenever I think of how our conversation went. In all my imaginings over the years, I never let myself imagine a meeting where everything went so horribly wrong. I can try to fix things, but that's only if Raff returns. Raff's *maybe* and *I'll consider* didn't exactly give me much hope, and I guess I can't blame him if he decides to just leave the past in the past.

The fog outside has lifted the tiniest bit and I can see the tower of Brier Hall rising above the tops of the trees. It's just a dark behemoth in the growing gloom outside, but then as I stare, my eyes drawn to the walls like moths to a flame, a light flicks on in the window.

My fingers curl automatically on the window ledge.

No.

Ali?

Yes, it's Ali. Of course it's Ali, because Ali is at the house and no one else is. I raise my hand to my chest and press in hard on my rocketing heart. *Deep breaths.* I've thought about leaving, about running away, almost nonstop since Rafferty left, but every time I start throwing my toothbrush and coat back into my overnight bag it's like something physically stops me in my tracks. *Don't go. Don't leave. Stay.*

The light coming through the mist from Brier Hall suddenly flicks out, plunging the bluff into darkness. You could almost imagine that there's no house at all. That it's all in my mind. That I've come to a place I've never been with people I've never met, and that I've invented this entire history of loss and pain.

I wish.

There's a knock on the door, a sharp *thud-thud,* and I spring up, almost afraid to answer. We don't knock in the Daley house. For months after fleeing Brier Hall I would have nightmares of knocking doors and the slow creak of them inevitably opening after. I'd wake up screaming with Ali next to me, trying to shake me awake.

"Hello?" I waver. *Is the door locked? Yes.* Not that that would help much in Brier. *But you're not in Brier. Not yet.*

Deep breaths.

"Hey," comes Rafferty's deep voice. "It's me. Ah—Rafferty." As if I don't know.

I open the door. Rafferty stands in the hallway, wearing an East-wind Hotel shirt. It's untucked, hanging long over his jeans, and his hair is messy as if he's run his hands through it one too many times. In one hand he carries a to-go box, and he holds it out to me.

"I brought you this."

I wordlessly take the box and peek inside. A grilled cheese sandwich huddles next to a large helping of fries.

"Dinner," he says. "I bet you didn't eat."

"N-no," I whisper.

"You don't have to hide out," he says, folding his arms over his chest.

"I didn't think the rest of the town would want to see me."

An eyebrow arches up. "You're assuming the rest of the town even remembers you."

"Considering my family brought dozens of reporters and haunted house enthusiasts to this town, I'm sure they'd find it hard to forget. We single-handedly turned this town into a circus."

"I mean . . ." He pauses, sounding almost amused. "That's true."

"So I think I'll lie low for a while."

"Suit yourself."

"You remembered me, though," I say, keeping the words quiet so he can pretend he didn't hear them if he wants to.

"Yeah," he says slowly. "I did. As you said—I found you hard to forget."

I can feel him staring at me, so I stare down at the grilled cheese instead. "Thank you," I mumble to the fries.

"It's okay," he says, and even though he sounds slightly amused, I don't want to look up and meet his gaze. Then: "So are you going to let me in or do we have to do this outside in the hallway?"

"I don't know," I say. "Are we going to continue yelling at each other?"

"Maybe," comes the reply, and I chance a look up. He's still in the doorway, framed against the light, and he's definitely smiling now. It's not quite his signature smile, but it seems genuine enough. *I'll take it.*

"Okay," I say, retreating into the room. I leave the door wide open and he follows me in, kicking the door shut with his foot. I sit down on the bed, pushing myself up to lean against the headboard, and start picking at the fries. Do you get the person who you hate food? A tiny flicker of hope warms my stomach. "Thank you for the food. And thank you for—for coming back." I stumble over the words.

"I said I would."

"You said you *might.*"

"Yeah, well, I don't know why you thought I wouldn't. Leaving's your thing, isn't it?" He doesn't say it with any malice; I don't think he's trying to hurt me, but something inside suddenly snaps. One too many digs. One too many tiny, hurtful comments that have been building and building, and when I next speak, I scream.

"Rafferty Pierce, I was thirteen years old!" I slam the to-go box down onto the bedside table, fries flying into the air. The words rip themselves from my throat. "*Thirteen!* I didn't have a choice!"

"You could've called! I tried and tried to call you, to process, to help each other—"

"I was *grieving!*" I scream. I hear the faint sound of a shower being turned off in the room next to me; I'm sure I'll get complaints, but I can't bring myself to care. My missing maybe-dead sister is stomping through my head, and how does Rafferty think he can turn this into *his* thing? "I'd just lost Avery—"

"We all lost Avery!"

"But she was *my* sister! Mine, not yours! She was mine, and you'll never know what it was like to lose her and to live in that place. And if you really are going to keep acting like it was a *thirteen-year-old's* fault that I didn't call then you're not anything like the boy I thought I knew and you can get out of my room *now*." I stop, breathing hard, and there's a ringing silence as we stare at each other, wild-eyed.

Then suddenly Rafferty moves toward me, and before I can even comprehend what's happening he pulls me into a crushing hug, his arms locked around me. My cheek is resting against his collarbone, pressed into the crook of his neck. When he speaks, I can feel him murmuring against my hair.

"You're right," he whispers. "Lia, I'm so sorry. I don't have an excuse. I just—I'm just sorry. I missed you and I . . . when I saw you again, I just didn't know what to do."

I breathe in a shaking breath against his neck. It's our first hug in five years and I let myself melt in his arms, closing my eyes against the sudden flush of tears that threaten to spill.

"R-Rafferty," I whisper in return, "I missed you too. And I am sorry—"

"No, stop," he mumbles. "There's nothing to apologize for. I was so stupid. Selfish. Can we just . . ." He raises his head slightly, trying to meet my eyes. He takes a fingertip and wipes away a lone tear making its way down my face. "Can we try to start over, Lia?"

"I would like that." I would like nothing more than that, and hope begins filling my chest as Raff breaks away from me and gives an uncertain smile.

"Can I sit?" he asks hesitantly, his eyes drifting from me to the spot on the bed next to me. All our words are coming out as questions now, trying to keep this tenuous new peace.

"Sure," I say, hoping it sounds nonchalant even as my heart begins to ricochet. Rafferty crosses to the other side of the bed and sits down, his back pressed against the headboard and his long legs stretched out next to mine. I can feel him there next to me; I am aware of his every movement, his every breath. We sit quietly for a while, the sound of the waves crashing in a distant melody. The room grows gloomier around us.

"I can see the house from my window," I say.

Rafferty's hand finds mine on the bed, his fingers interlacing, squeezing. I hold my breath as my skin lights up at this touch. I don't want to break him out of this quiet reverie, where he might realize what he's doing and stop.

"Are you sure you want to go back there?"

No. Yes. "I have to," I say finally. "Raff, can I ask you something?"

"Well, I certainly can't stop you," he replies, and even though he's still holding my hand his words are wry, a little biting. I know there's still anger and hurt there, and what I'm about to say probably won't make it any better. But I have to ask.

I take a deep breath. "What . . . what do you remember?"

"About Brier Hall?"

The name falling so easily from his lips gives me a full-body shake, almost a sob, and Rafferty's grip on my hand tightens. "Yes," I whisper. "I want to know what you remember—because I want to know I'm not alone. That I didn't make it up. That I'm not just imagining something that never was."

Rafferty is silent for a moment, and when I chance a quick glance at him, he's staring at the wall, his eyes glassy, glazed over. Remembering. "I don't know," he says finally. "I've tried so hard to forget, you know? Looking back, some of it feels like a bad dream."

A huge wave of terror crests inside me, and I'm about to have a full-blown panic attack in front of Rafferty because *I've made it up, I've made it up, I've made it up—*

"But I remember," Rafferty continues, the words dragging, "that you were scared."

"I was scared," I whisper. *I was scared, yes.* It extinguishes the frenzied fire inside, just a little, and I focus on Raff's hand in mine. Something real, tangible. The feel of his fingers wrapped around my own, his thumb stroking my palm.

"All of you were scared," he adds. "All of *us*."

"It was all real."

"Hey," he says softly. "Lia, look at me for a sec." I tilt my head against the headboard, meeting his eyes. "Are you listening?"

I make a sound low in my throat. "Mmm."

"Lia, the house is not haunted."

I want to look away, but Rafferty's clear eyes have a hold on me. There's no hint of deception in his gaze, only honesty, but my entire body rejects his words.

"You're the one who told me it was," I whisper. "When I first met you."

"When you first met me I was eleven!" he says incredulously. "I was repeating rumors. I probably wanted to scare the new girl. But it's not true. Okay? Brier Hall is just a normal house."

"Mmm." I make the sound again, nothing more than an acknowledgment.

"There's no such thing as ghosts."

"Okay."

"Or hauntings."

"Okay."

We're still looking at each other. "You don't believe me, do you?" he says finally.

"I know what I saw," I reply. *Most days.* I remember seeing Avery back in Daley, the smell of fish and rot. That happened. I experienced it. Does that make a thing real? To distract myself from the sour feeling inside, I add pointedly, "You were there too. You saw things too, you know you did."

This time it's Rafferty who makes a noise of acknowledgment.

"You said you were scared too," I forge ahead. "What scared you, Rafferty?"

He swallows. "I don't know."

"Yes, you do."

"I don't remember."

"Yes," I say, "you *do.*"

There's a sigh, long and hard. Then: "Avery," he whispers. "I remember that Avery . . . wasn't always Avery."

My entire body goes cold. I know exactly the times he's thinking of; I can see them replay in my mind almost as if Avery is in this hotel room, acting out the past.

Rafferty and I had been exploring the house, wandering the still, ornate hallways. We'd started in our hideout in the briar patch, then hacked with sticks at overgrown plants outside, and now we had breached the impenetrable walls of the Brier. Our sneakers, damp and muddy, lay discarded by the front door.

"I've found a new hideout," I whispered to Rafferty as we crept up the stairs and down the hallway. "It's just for us. No one else can get in. And Avery doesn't know about it—she can't tell us not to go in." I dropped my stick by the banister, ready to show him the place I'd discovered.

It was one of those days when the mist had descended over the bluffs and drenched all of Eastwind in thick fog, and although we could hear the sound of the waves breaking against the cliffs outside, the windows just showed a blanket of swirling gray. The house inside was quiet; the number of rooms meant that it was easy to lose things: wooden sticks, damp sneakers, older sisters.

"How do we get there?"

"This way," I told him. "But we have to be quiet." I put a finger to my lips and shushed him, the *shhhhhh* hissing out and echoing around us. We tiptoed down the hallway toward the door at the very end, set deep into the stone wall.

The door had fascinated me—fascinated all of us, really—since the very moment we'd moved in. All the doors in Brier Hall were old, with wooden paneling and thick, heavy locks, but this particular door seemed even older than the rest, as if it was the only thing on this windswept bluff before Brier Hall was built up around it. It was pockmarked and gouged, and sunk deep into the wall, the huge blocks of stone keeping it safe and enclosed.

Ali believed it was always locked, but I knew it wasn't. Not really. Because on one particularly boring day I had watched her struggle with the handle, jerking it back and forth, until I had pushed her hand out of the way and gently turned it to the left. The door had opened right away, creaking inward to show a set of stone stairs leading upward.

Ali had glared at me murderously before mumbling something under her breath as she stomped away, furious.

But I led Rafferty toward the door—because where else would a hideout be hidden but inside a door with steps leading up, up, up?

"It's locked," Rafferty whispered, turning the handle again and again. The key wouldn't turn, and I could hear the lock rattling.

"No, it's not," I replied, stepping up behind him and jostling him out of the way. I knew it would open for me. Everything in this house had always opened for me since the moment we moved in. I knew that seeing others struggle with the doors and getting lost in the maze of hallways shouldn't make me glad, but I couldn't help it. I always felt a flicker of pride.

A turn of the key, sliding easily in the lock. A twist of the handle. The door groaned as it opened.

"How'd you do that?" Rafferty said, impressed, no longer whispering.

"Magic," I replied smugly, the pride rearing up.

It wasn't magic, of course. It was just the house, our house— *my house.* The house that liked me better. The house that loved me more.

"What's up there?" Rafferty asked, staring up the winding steps. A cold draft wafted out, curling around us both.

"The hideout," I replied.

"But what's at the top?"

I didn't know—I'd never reached the top, but I wasn't about to let Rafferty know that. "Oh," I answered airily, "first we have to get up the steps. They go up forever, probably."

"Then how will we get to the hideout?"

"We'll figure it out," I said. Rafferty nodded but then just stared through the open doorway. Neither of us wanted to make the first move up the steps.

Lia . . .

I heard my name; I know that I did. My name, called out from somewhere deep within the house. My body answered before my mind was made up, because I was braver back then. I stepped forward and turned to face the beating heart of Brier Hall.

"Lia! What are you doing?"

I spun around, Rafferty quickly moving behind me. Avery stood there, looking down at the ground, one hand on the banister and one on her hip. Her long blond hair was in a braid down her back, a tiny pink ribbon tied in a bow on the end of it. Even in jeans and a hoodie she was perfect and golden.

I was about to answer my sister, to make up some excuse about exploring and games. Because I couldn't let her know about our new soon-to-be hideout. Not after she made us promise not to use the briar patch anymore.

But then Rafferty shifted next to me; I could tell right away he was uncomfortable. His fingers brushed my own, lightly, and I was sure it was a warning but I wasn't sure why.

"What are you doing?" she asked again, her voice harder this time. "Why are you going up there?"

"We're just—" I began, but was cut off by Rafferty.

"Avery?" His voice was equally hard, but there was something else wavering there too: fear. "A-Avery?" With a soft sidestep, he edged in front of me.

I peered out from behind his shoulder.

"Get away from there," Avery snapped. She started walking her fingers crablike along the wooden railing, watching them in apparent fascination, as if she didn't realize she was moving them herself. It was so wholly unlike Avery that I didn't move; I just watched her watch her hands crabwalking their way forward, trying to piece together why my older sister was acting so strange.

The heavy tower door creaked shut behind me, its hinges moaning long and hard.

"Avery?" Raff said again, his voice shaking now.

And then Avery's eyes drifted from her fingers up to us, and then we were screaming, because there was nothing of Avery there at all. I knew it must be Avery, but the person before me didn't look like my sister anymore. Someone older, stranger, was standing in her place as if she'd been plucked up and replaced without anyone noticing. Her eyes stared at us as if not really seeing, as if she wasn't really there at all. Something else was looking at us from Avery's face, and I closed my eyes, grabbing frantically for the security of Rafferty, tripping as I tried to run backward.

I reached out blindly and a hand caught mine, steadying me.

"What is *wrong* with you guys?" It was Avery's voice, Avery's *own* voice, and when I opened my eyes I looked into my sister's sweet face, only seventeen, her eyes worried but her own. Rafferty was ahead of me, halfway down the staircase. He paused and looked back at me, at Avery.

"What are you up to?" Avery asked again, staring between the pair of us in apparent confusion.

I wrenched my hand from her grip and hurried after Rafferty, reaching for his outstretched hand instead. Our wild eyes matched each other's as we took the stairs three at a time, Avery's voice, bewildered and hurt, echoing after us as we ran for the front door: "What's wrong? Where are you going? What did I *do*?"

I can see us so clearly racing down the stairs, shoving our feet into wet shoes and taking off into Brier's grounds. When I peek at Rafferty again, I can tell he's remembering the exact same scene.

"And you think that was normal?" I ask him, my voice moving us out of our reverie. "She was older, she was *obviously* not the same person."

"I didn't say I think it's normal, I said I think it has nothing to do with ghosts."

"Then what?"

"I don't know, Lia." Raff sighs. He's still holding my hand, as if he's forgotten. His thumb circles my palm briefly and I focus on that, on the feel of his skin. "But I'm still worried about you going up there alone."

"I'll text you when I'm there," I say. "I can text you every day to let you know I'm safe." I pause. "I mean, if you want me to."

"Call me," he says abruptly.

"What?"

"Call me," Rafferty says again. "I need you to call me, not text." He pauses too, like he's trying to figure out a brand-new sentence structure that makes more sense with the impossible words we're speaking. "I want to hear your voice," he says finally.

"Because anyone can be anyone over a text. How will I know it's actually you?"

We're looking at each other, but I can see Avery reflected in both our eyes; the older Avery that wasn't actually the Avery we knew but someone else, peering out.

"A call," I agree.

"Please be careful."

"If there's nothing wrong with the house, then there's nothing to worry about," I say, biting the inside of my cheek because I know he's so wrong, and Brier knows he's wrong. "Anyways, I'm always careful."

"You didn't used to be."

"Things have changed."

"I know. Everything's changed. Between us"—he raises an eyebrow at me, and I look down at my lap instead—"and it sounds like between you and your sisters too." He pauses, then amends, "You and your *sister*."

Ali. Yes, everything has changed. It's hard to even know where to begin; how can you catch someone up on five years of falling apart? "Yup," I say, my voice tight, and say the only words I can find. "I hate her."

"*Hate* is a strong word." Rafferty sounds all quiet and sage, but he doesn't get it. What I hate is people telling me how I feel.

"When I think of Ali, there are no pretty words, Raff," I say. I don't really know how to explain myself, but for him I try. "My stomach clenches like this"—I raise the hand he isn't holding and make a fist so tight my knuckles turn white—"whenever I think of her and I can't breathe and my heart races like I might be sick.

Sometimes I can't speak or move or think and I become nothing more than a statue who stands there and just *shakes* because she's ruined everything. So yeah. There's just hate. That's all."

Rafferty's shoulder is pressed against my own, and I'm sure he can hear my heart pounding through my chest.

"That doesn't sound like hate to me. It sounds like . . . sadness."

"I don't want to talk about this," I say. "I don't want to talk about *her*."

"And yet," he says, "you're here."

"I know," I say, and then stop, because there's nothing more to say. I know I am here. What I don't know is why, not really. *I wish you were the one who died instead of Avery.* I don't know why I'm still following my sister to the ends of the earth. Why I will always follow Ali to the end of anywhere. A part of me knows that deep down, Raff is right. My anger is a mask for something sadder, something deeper.

But there's a part of me that doesn't want to forgive Ali. Hating Ali has forged me in fire. I am who I am because of where I've been and what happened there. I am who I am because Ali made me that way. Without that, who am I?

"Lia?"

"Hm?" I just want to sleep. My body feels heavy, like lead. And Rafferty's hand in mine is so warm.

"I'll come with you if you want me to."

I tilt my head up; he tilts his down. There're mere inches between our faces. If we whispered to each other now, the words would float between our lips like a kiss.

"Really?"

"Yes."

"I thought we weren't friends anymore, not really."

Raff squeezes my hand. "I thought we were trying to start over."

I study him, trying to see the boy he was before. My friend. I know he's still hurt, maybe even angry, but like he said about Ali— maybe that anger is just hiding the sadness that bubbles beneath. Maybe he just missed me like I missed him, and neither of us quite knows what to do with all those feelings now that we're sitting next to each other.

"But you think the house is normal. Just a house, nothing more."

"I don't know what I think. But I *do* know that things like this are easier if you're not alone. That place . . . normal house or not, there're memories there. I don't want you to drown in them."

I smile a little, and when he says he'll meet me early tomorrow I smile and nod, and I don't let him know that the memories and feelings and grief and confusion have already closed over my head and pulled me down. I'm no longer drowning in them—I've already long drowned.

ELEVEN

We load up my car, neither of us speaking. The fog from the night before hasn't lifted, and although all of Eastwind is draped in a heavy shroud of white my eyes keep drifting past the roof of the Eastwind Hotel in the direction of Brier Hall. I can't see it yet, but I know it's there.

I can feel it.

Is this what Ali felt all the way back in Daley? I can feel the house digging into me, pulling me toward it. My mouth is dry; I keep taking tiny sips from the coffee Rafferty bought me, but nothing seems to help.

Raff keeps glancing at me.

"I'm okay," I tell him the fifth time his eyes slide over. "Really."

"I would understand if you're not." He's backlit against the fog; he stands in a sea of white soup. I imagine the fog growing, the swirling gray canvas stretching up, covering me, choking me.

"I am." I can hear Ali in my mind: *Liar, liar.*

"Are you ready to go?"

I can't speak anymore, so I just nod before sliding into the driver's seat. Rafferty gets into the passenger side and tosses his backpack into the back seat. *It's time.* My fingers tighten on the steering wheel and I know Rafferty clocks the movement but he doesn't say anything.

Eastwind whirls around us: kids on scooters, shirtless boys

carrying surfboards in the direction of the beach despite the cold, cars appearing out of the mist with kayaks strapped to their roof racks. As I drive by them not one of them notices us—why would they? They don't know who I am or where I'm going. They don't care. My breath hitches. *Deep breaths.*

"I know this is hard," Raff says. "Knowing you'll soon be back there." He says the words haltingly, but as I glance over, I see his eyes are bright. They spear me in place with their intensity. He is still the slow-smile boy I knew him as, but there is something more there. Something hidden beneath.

"A little bit," I say, because it's what he wants me to say. My body is abuzz with terror and anticipation and I can't parse out which is which. Soon I will be back there—home, home, home.

"What do you think it'll be like?"

I shrug. I don't know—and that's what I'm scared of. What will we find? My sister, I'm sure. The house, vacuum-held and untouched by everything except the dust of five years. Or will there be signs of life, like a line through the dust-covered floorboards where something has crept along? I know there must be things that live at Brier Hall, things that—unlike us—never left. I shrug again to give myself something to do.

I am fragile in his eyes. I am a jumpy, nervous deer in headlights who breathes too fast, who speaks too much about nothing and too little about the things that people want to know. I am a Peartree girl, damaged and broken and afraid.

"Lia, I'm here," he says. I breathe in, out. I focus on his words. *I'm not alone. Not this time.*

The turnoff comes soon, too soon. We're almost at the beach

and boat launch at the end of the road when a narrow road branches off to the right. There's no sign, but I watch as a couple quickly hurries across the stretch of road.

The road to Brier Hall doesn't need a sign.

I don't realize I'm shaking until Rafferty says, "I'm here, Lia," again. "It's okay." A car behind me beeps; I'm stopped in the middle of the road with my blinker on. *Click-click-click.* I swing the car up the road. There's bile in my throat.

The road is packed dirt, littered with pebbles, and it bends through the cypress trees, climbing upward for twenty seconds before the road turns to gravel and the gates of Brier Hall suddenly emerge out of the fog and stop us in our tracks.

A hush fills the car as I throw it into park. I lean forward, unbuckling my seat belt and almost pitch myself over the dashboard trying to get a better look. The gates rise before us, huge and imposing, rusted over. They're shut, and a thick chain and padlock is looped around the center curls of framework, but the padlock hangs open.

Someone beat us here. Someone is already inside.

I just hope it's someone I know. I hope it's someone alive.

"I'll get the gate," I say. My voice sounds strange, like it's not my voice at all. Rafferty doesn't move to stop me as I open the door and slide out of the car. The chill hits me first, and the air wraps itself around me, thick and cut with the smell of the sea. This feels like a dream: Even walking toward the gate, the gravel crunching under my feet, seems like it's happening somewhere far away. Like someone else has slid into my shoes and has forced me into a corner of my body to wait while they take over. Which of these sharp stones sliced my hand open five years ago? My middle finger bends down into a fist and caresses the raised scar tissue on my palm. The cut was deep—I still remember how the sudden searing pain cut through my terror on my frantic run away from the house—and the scar runs from one edge of my palm to the other. Slicing right along my life line, as precise as if a surgeon picked up a scalpel.

I force myself to raise my eyes and look up. *Look,* I scream inside my head. *Look where you are.*

Home. It rises before me, behind the gates and up the winding path, looking almost exactly as it did the day we left. Brier Hall is made of dark stone. Impenetrable. There are large windows filled with glass, discolored and warped by time, and ivy creeps up the front of the house, hanging like curtains by the front door. When we first moved in, I was the one to open the gate, pushing it open with all the strength of an overexcited kid, bubbling over with enthusiasm for this new life. It looked like a castle then. With its stone walls and turrets it looked just like something out of a storybook, and it was all for us. For me.

I unhook the open padlock and chain and push open the gates. I can't tear my eyes from the house, afraid if I blink it will disappear. I grasp the rusty chain tightly until there's a sudden prick of pain in my hand. I drop the chain to the ground with a cry. Blood wells on the pad of my finger and I stare at it, something like relief flooding through me. Because this is real. This isn't a dream, this isn't a memory. I am here, I am home.

Rafferty rolls down the window and peers out at me. "Lia, are you coming?"

"I'll walk," I say automatically. The house is only a minute or so up the drive anyways, and I don't want to be stuck inside a car. He nods, getting out and switching to the driver's seat. The car rumbles past me and I watch it go.

A magnetic pull drags me forward. That's what it feels like— like I'm not in control of my movements. One step. Two. Sitting warm and safe in my Eastwind Hotel room was just hours ago, but I feel like it happened in another lifetime. Like maybe the past five years were just a dream, and any moment I'll wake up, bleary-eyed and bed-headed in my iron-frame bed, Ali's warm body curled against me like a cat, her fingers laced with mine. A nightmare, that's all.

Like maybe I'm not coming home—maybe I never left.

I crunch up the path, toward where Rafferty is unloading our overnight bags onto the gravel. I walk past him until I stand pressed against the cool leaves of the ivy that climb the stone arch curving over the entrance. I can hear the waves crashing into the rocks down below behind the house, and I let my eyes close for a moment, so the sound rushes over me. Again, the strangest feeling of déjà vu creeps up the back of my neck. I half expect to hear Ali and Avery shrieking up the overgrown path down to the cove, for the front door to swing open—*Come in, come in!*—and my mother's voice to come singing out, reminding us to stay away from the cliff's edge and then calling us in for dinner.

But no voices come, and when I open my eyes the huge door rises before me. It's pockmarked and pitted, carved with curlicues that form roots, stretching down like long fingers. In some places deep gouges slash through the intricate carvings—from years of use or more dangerous things, I never knew. My entire life centers on

Brier—all my thoughts and feelings and my very being are tied to this place, this door, these walls. But Brier was here before us. And Brier will be here after.

I put my hand on the doorknob, turn, and push.

I know it will be open—it would be whether Ali came here or not. Just like the open gate, I don't know if Brier has been opened by soft shaking hands or something more . . . strange. But Brier always opened for me before, and so I'm not surprised when the door swings inward with a deep, long groan. Beyond is darkness: the stone porch and the curtain of ivy cut through the heavy fog. Just inside the door I see the outline of a table, but nothing else.

Go inside! I tell myself sternly, repeating the words over and over in my head until they begin to sound like they might not even be words at all. But I don't go inside; I stand on the threshold. I am a vampire, hungry and wanting and desperate, teetering on the doorstep, waiting to be invited in.

"Oh, you're in." Rafferty's voice is loud behind me, and I can't help but cringe at this sudden influx of noise. A disturbance that *I* have brought here. There's a tiny breeze that floats through the front door, like an outward sigh, and my stomach tightens. There was a *feeling* in that house-sigh; I don't think Brier is happy I've brought a guest.

Brier doesn't have feelings, Lia, I remind myself, still hovering, wraithlike and uncertain, on the doorstep.

But I can't help the feeling that roils through me, crystal-clear: *A Peartree should know better.*

"You had a key, Lia?" Rafferty says, stepping up beside me, holding both our overnight bags in one hand.

"No," I reply, and Raff has the understanding to at least look disconcerted for a moment before a smile creeps onto his face, like he thinks I'm teasing him. I know there's a part of him somewhere inside that believes in the truth of Brier Hall, but he finds it easier to bury in the sunlight hours than I do.

He throws out a hand, pushing the door open fully, and walks inside. I follow in his wake, mouse-scared and jumpy, and then I'm looking around, taking in the house I've been fearing and hating and missing for five years.

We're in the entrance hall; it's a large corridor with wood-paneled walls hung with framed paintings and, in the middle of the right-side wall, a huge elk head is mounted above us. Its shining black-beetle eyes stare at us blankly. Closed doors line the entrance hall, and at the far end a curling double staircase lined with a thick, violent red carpet rises on each side of the room, meeting in the middle. Right in the center of the hall there's a small round table covered in a thin layer of dust. A mason jar of dead flowers sits in the middle, their petals a coronet around the jar's base.

Something isn't the same as when we left, but I can't quite put my finger on *what*. The house looks the same as it did when we lived here, albeit a lot dustier. I stare at the elk head, at the wall beneath it. *Something should be there. Something was there the night we left the house.* My mind feels hazy, wrong. Just what that *something* is rests on the tip of my tongue, but I can't quite remember.

Rafferty puts down our bags in a clattering pile at the foot of the table, and I hush him without meaning to, the *shhhhh* leaving my mouth before I even really realize what I'm doing.

Raff raises his eyebrow at me, a tiny smirk playing in the corner of his lips. "Lia." He catches my hand in his own and squeezes it bracingly. "Lia, it's okay. Who am I gonna disturb?"

There's a long scream from somewhere in the house—not loud, not nearby, but like the echo of a scream. It comes from far away, and at first I think I imagine it until I see Rafferty jump in shock.

There's the sound of a door shutting—not here, no, from another floor, somewhere far above us.

"Hell*ooooo*?" calls out Rafferty, drawing out the word.

If it were a movie the sound would come back to him, echo, doubling over and flinging itself back toward us. His *hello* would ring against the glass of the mason jar and skim over the paintings. The dust-covered crystal chandelier above us would tinkle with the sound—for the drama, you know. For the fright, for the tension. But there is nothing; it is as if Rafferty never even spoke. The house has swallowed the sound. My fingers curl into themselves involuntarily, my fingertips brushing the thick scar.

Brier Hall knows I am here.

It knows I am home.

GONE HOME

"I can't believe this," your mom says as she stares up at the house, muttering so softly you're unsure if you're really supposed to be hearing her at all. "This is—this is ridiculous, this is—"

The walls of Brier Hall—home, home, home—rise up, stretching toward the darkening sky. Your little car, loaded to the brim with suitcases and sisters, is tiny and ant-like in the face of the swath of dark, wind-battered stone before you.

All you can think is this is like a fairy tale. This is a castle and you are its queen, arriving home, finally, after many long years away.

It's been waiting for you.

You can tell by the way the door creaks open, welcoming you inside.

Welcome home, welcome home, welcome home.

"God, did they not even lock the door?" your mom snaps. "Have they just left it open for anyone to come in?"

You know "they" refers to the estate agents and the lawyers and everyone who's been descending on your family like vultures the past few weeks, just as you knew "that man" always referred to the nothing-noun of your father.

"No one else could go in," you whisper, and through the open window of the car, Ali's eyes snap to you sharply. "It's open just for us."

Your mom just laughs tiredly.

You don't care if she doesn't believe you. You know you're right.

Carrying boxes into Brier Hall feels a bit like déjà vu; every time you turn your head there's something new to recognize, something new to pluck at your heart with a *Remember me?* Remember this? Once all the bags and boxes are piled like a turret in the entrance hall, you and your sisters sprint for the stairs. The hallways twist away from you, the house a maze of rooms and doors and windows, but you know your way.

The room's windows look out over the Pacific, and when you push up one of the windows you can hear the waves far below. There are two iron-framed twin beds side by side, and as soon as you throw your backpack down on one Ali skids into the open doorway, eyes wide.

"Is this your room?" she asks.

"Yes," you say certainly. You can feel it in your bones. This is your house, and this is your room. Meant just for you.

"Can I—can I be here too?" Ali asks, the words tumbling out. You stare at her for a moment, wondering why your brave and bold older sister, who finally has a chance at her very own room, wants to still sleep side by side with you.

You shrug. "Okay."

Ali tosses her backpack on the floor next to the other bed and sits down, the mattress squeaking under her. "What do you think of this place?" she asks you finally.

"I love it," you reply automatically, as if the words were sitting in your mouth just waiting to break free.

Ali is silent, and she looks away from you and doesn't meet your eyes again the whole evening. She stares into her bowl of bright-green pea soup from a can at dinner, not even reacting when your mom waxes poetic about fresh starts. She silently drags her suitcase up the staircase to your room and gets under the covers and stares at the ceiling even when Avery comes in and curls up at the foot of Ali's bed.

You and your sisters are not used to sleeping apart, and Avery lingers until finally your mom comes in to shoo you all to bed.

"A story?" Avery begs. You see how her fingers curl around one of the bed's metal spindles. She doesn't want to leave; she doesn't want to cross the hall to go to sleep alone. When she sees your mom wavering, she pleads, "I bet you'll be able to write some really good books here, Mom. Please tell us one of your stories. Pleeeease."

"Okay, okay," your mom finally acquiesces with a smile. It doesn't take much to convince her; she's a writer and she's told you all stories since the minute you were born. Stories of magical lands and queens and kings and little girls who took on the world.

In your mom's stories, all little girls are strong and fierce and unwavering.

In your mom's stories, all little girls end up victorious.

"Do you know what I'm going to write my next book about?" your mom begins, her eyes shining. She pauses dramatically. You hold your breath.

"A woman whose ex leaves her a big house." She smiles.

"A house on a cliff?" Avery pipes up.

"Oh yes."

"With the sea crashing right outside the windows!" Ali crows, then makes loud sound effects for good measure.

"Somewhere that smells of salt," your mom says, nodding. "Got it."

You clear your throat. "And can she have three little girls?"

"Absolutely," says your mom. "She has the best three girls in the whole wide world."

You and Ali meet each other's eyes for the first time all night, and when you smile, she tentatively smiles back.

"What will happen to the three little girls?" Ali whispers. The waves crash against the cliff outside fiercely, and you imagine them slowly eating away at the mud and earth until the whole house tumbles from its lofty place and plunges into the sea.

But you know Brier Hall wouldn't let that happen.

Brier Hall protects its own.

Your mom stares out the window into the night, and when she turns back to the three of you on the bed she has a tremulous look on her face, like she wants to cry.

"Mom?" says Avery after the quiet goes on too long.

"What will happen to the girls?" Ali says again. Her hands are tightly fisted around sections of her blankets. You watch as your mom's upper lip trembles. As she takes a deep breath and talks in that fakey-happy way.

"What happens to them? That's tomorrow night's story." She gets up off the end of the bed quickly, beckoning for Avery to come with her.

When she reaches the doorway, Ali calls out, "Mom?"

Your mom turns. "Yeah, baby?"

"It has a happy ending, though, doesn't it? The story of the three little girls in the house on the cliff?"

The silence warps around the room.

"Of course it does," your mom says finally, and then flicks off the light.

124

BRIER HALL

Fear and guilt are sisters.
—Shirley Jackson, *The Haunting of Hill House*

TWELVE

I am a moth, flinging myself at a candle flame.

This is what I think as I slowly mount the stairs leading up to Brier Hall's second floor. As I ascend, the thick red carpet runner sinking beneath the soles of my shoes, I hear the sounds of Rafferty moving around in the library, one of the rooms right off the entrance hall. I'd left him there as he paced around the perimeter of the wall, trailing a finger along the spines of the old books, occasionally looking back at the track that cut through the dust. As if he was making sure there *was* a track, as if he was checking that this was actually real.

I couldn't read the expression on his face, and when I left, I murmured something about going to look for Ali, and he didn't try to stop me.

The sounds of Rafferty get quieter as I move up the grand staircase, trying to take in everything all at once. A layer of dust coats the walls and furniture and the frames of the huge paintings that overlook the hall, but still—it's so *beautiful*. The word reverberates through my head. Beautiful. And it is. Beautiful and watchful and terrifying.

And *perfect*. Everything is in its place, just as we left it. For a moment I'm sure I remember running and screaming, the house in disarray as we fled, but . . . I must be misremembering. Because everything is perfect.

The eyes of the Briers in the paintings track me as I move. The entrance hall and walls above the staircase are filled with them—my mom always hated the paintings; she'd mutter about the Briers still lording over her even when they were gone, when it was *our* house. But she never took them down either, and so we spent those two years under the watchful gaze of Briers past.

When I reach the landing, the muffled sounds floating up from the open door of the library fall silent, cut off as if the soothing sound of Rafferty—the sound that reminds me there's a living, breathing person in this house besides me, and that I'm not alone—is nothing more than a recording. I hover on the landing, torn between heading further into the house and running back to check on him. To make sure it wasn't just a dream, to make sure he's still here.

And you won't leave?

No.

My fingers brush the dark stained wood of the sweeping banister, and suddenly there comes the sound of a door shutting from down the hallway. Somewhere in the depths of the house, out of sight.

I hesitate only a second before moving forward.

Ali?

I want to scream her name, scream it until she appears before me, a kid again. Skinny-armed and freckle-faced, tanned from every day spent down in the cove, a wicked gleam in her eyes, a story of heroes and princesses and gods and monsters on her lips. But I can't bring myself to break the thick silence that's fallen over the house. I can't even hear my steps as I walk onward, taking in the wide hallways and tall doors, the long side table set against one wall, a vase of fresh wildflowers, colors vivid and brilliant in white daisies with golden centers and tall sprigs of bluebells.

I walk a few steps forward, then stop.

No.

I turn slowly, eyeing the wildflowers. There is no dust here; there is water in the vase, clear and unmuddied.

But . . . but that can't be right.

I'm staring right at the vase, but my eyes refuse to believe it. *How . . . ?* I shut my eyes, squeezing them so tightly closed that fireworks of light explode behind my eyelids in starbursts of red and yellow. *Breathe, Lia. When you open your eyes, they'll be how they should be—dead.*

I open my eyes. Fresh wildflowers innocently sit there before me.

I shut my eyes again. *They'll be DEAD; they'll be withered five-year-old flowers in a dusty vase.*

I open just one eye, peeking out through a slit barely wide enough to see though. But—there's dust. Muted colors. Faded. Old. My body unwinds, my breath loosening. *There,* I tell myself, and with a tiny gasp of pain I look down to see my fingers uncurling, deep indents from my fingernails in the flesh. I hadn't noticed.

I leave the appropriately withered flowers behind and continue along. At the end of the hallway there's a stained glass window, panes of glittering green and blue sending shifting curls of light down onto the carpet. *So beautiful,* I think, and then the next thought worms its way into my head so quickly, I don't even realize I'm thinking it: *There's nothing to be afraid of here. Not in a place this beautiful.*

I don't think the thought is my own.

The sound of another door closing reverberates around me. *Breathebreathebreathe—*

"Hello?" I call out in a whisper. "Ali?"

The hall splits beneath the stained glass window, continuing to branch out in meandering halls left and right. I peer down each corridor, counting the long lines of closed doors and hoping they won't suddenly shift and change. "Ali?"

From the right corridor, there comes the long, slow creak. I watch as the door opens, swinging so slowly that the swish of it on the carpet sounds like a sigh. There's only a crack showing beyond the door, but I think I see a sliver of light. An invitation.

Please, please let it be Ali.

I take a step toward the open door, just as a shadow passes in front of the flickering light beyond. Someone is in there, I knew it. *No,* I correct myself. *Ali is in there.* I have to believe this to make my feet keep moving.

I'm halfway to the door at the end of the hallway when there comes another creak from behind me, the telltale sound of another door opening. I spin around, my heart ricocheting into overdrive, just in time to see the door at the opposite end of the hallway open too. Both doors cracked open, identical. Waiting. *Like this.* They are the same, they are both reaching out for me . . .

I take another step toward the doorway with the light dancing behind its partly open door.

And then: The door on the left opens wider, and a thin face peers out at me. "Lia!" It's Ali's voice, and in that moment I don't care if it's real; I don't care if the house is trapping me like a fly in its spiderweb. Because what is *I hate you* anyways but an easier way to say the other words I cannot? The house knew what *I hate you* really means, and now Ali—or something that wears her face—is before me and it's all I can do to not run to her. I made it so easy for Brier Hall, I think. I really thought I was stronger than this.

And then Ali says my name again: "Lia!" She says it like it's something sharp, adorned with knives. And even in a whisper her tone is so angry that it cuts through the haze that's pulling me toward the other open door. "Get in here!"

"Ali?" I repeat.

"Get in here, *now!*"

I let her voice pull me along, away from the light-filled room and toward her folded arms and set mouth. She is a wave carrying me deep into the dark.

She slams the door behind me when I finally get into the room, and I shake my head. Everything feels slightly foggy, but a few fleeting, sticky thoughts cling to the last cobwebs in my mind: *If Ali is in here, who did I see in the other room? Who opened the door? Who turned on the light?*

"You're here," I breathe.

"Yeah, I am. And what the fuck are *you* doing here?" Ali snaps. She's angry, but when she looks at me I think I see a flash of fear in her eyes. "I told you—I *told* you not to come after me!"

"You can't say something like that and not expect me to come!"

"You weren't supposed to come," she repeats.

"Well, that's me, the disappointment," I snap in reply.

Ali sucks in a sharp breath, then turns her narrowed eyes on me. "I heard someone else. Who's here with you? Why have you brought others?"

"He's not . . ."

"He?"

"It's—" I stumble over the words. "It's Rafferty Pierce."

She lets out a harsh laugh. "Oh, great. You've come here and are just right back to it, huh?"

"It's fine," I say, unsure why I'm trying to convince her. *You don't care what she thinks about you. You don't care.* "It's fine, because Raff doesn't believe in, you know . . ." *Haunted houses* is on the tip of my tongue, but I'm not sure if that's a label that even fits this place. I have no idea what Brier is. I only know what I think I saw, what I think I experienced. "He doesn't believe in places like this."

Ali looks like she knows exactly what I was about to say. Her face hardens. "This place doesn't give a fuck who believes in it."

Now that the last of the fog in my head has dispersed, I cross my arms against her and curl my fingers. Typical, that I've come all the way here to help her and yet she still only has nothing but bladed words.

"We're allowed to be here," I say, and I hate that my voice shakes. "It's my house too." *Get to Ali* has been my mantra for the past few days, and now that she's before me, I would rather be any- where else. Her skin looks fragile as paper and purpled under her eyes from lack of sleep and too much shit in her veins. With one deep breath I think I could blow her over if I could stand to look at her. One deep breath and I could huff and puff and blow her house down. I don't want to meet her bloodshot eyes, so instead I turn my gaze to the room we're in. Everything is familiar all at once:

It's Avery's room, dark blue bedspread neatly tucked, a backpack hung on the back of the chair, wispy white curtains moving in an invisible breeze. The walls are painted white, the dark wainscoting wrapping around the lower half of the room. There's a small pile of loose-leaf papers and an amethyst-colored notebook on the desk in the corner, and Avery's stuffed bear sits alone on the bed. There doesn't seem to be dust in this room; it doesn't feel like a room of a ghost, uninhabited for five long years. It feels like Avery has just stepped out, like any moment the door will open and she'll come bounding in, golden hair streaming behind her.

I cross to the bed and reach out a trembling finger to brush the fur of the teddy bear. Its black-thread eyes are trying to tell me something. *Did you see where Avery went? Do you know where she is now?*

"I don't want you here."

"I don't care."

"I'm here for Avery," Ali says, her voice deadly quiet in the room. I can feel her watching me, but I can't tell what's she thinking. She switches moods whiplash-quick, whereas a few moments ago she stood small and unsure, one of the thin, weathered trees in the orchard, now her stare is red-hot and iron. With her crossed arms and lank hair, she seems both like a petulant teenager and a wizened old lady. Ali is everything all at once, except for one thing: She is no longer mine in any way.

"Ali," I say, trying to keep my voice in check. "Avery is *dead*."

The word is a live thing. It writhes on the floor between us. *Dead, dead, dead.*

Ali licks her lips. "Is she?"

"Yes," I whisper. "It's been five years, Ali. No word. No sightings. She's gone. She has to be." I swallow.

"Then why are *you* here?" Ali sneers.

"You!" I cry. "You! I followed you because I didn't want to lose another sister!"

It's the most honest thing I've said to her in years, and in return, Ali chuckles low in her throat. "You liar. You're here to reunite with your little crush and—"

"Shut up!" I say, and I can't keep my voice from shaking. "You don't know—anything." I struggle to even get the words out. I tried so hard to get here, and now . . . what was even the point? I curl my fingers in against themselves, trying to find that calm place, trying to not let my anger come boiling out. Trying to stop myself from running out the door.

"You don't know anything," mimics Ali in a cold, lilting voice that sounds nothing like me. "I'm sad little Lia, so hard done by, boo-hoo, everyone pay attention to me . . ."

Breathe.

I can't breathe.

"Pay attention to *me*?" I gasp. "To *me*? You think anyone notices me at all?"

"Cry me a fucking river," Ali says dismissively, and finally I look at her, ready to rage, to scream, to lash out and let myself do everything that I want to do to make her hurt like I hurt, to make her hurt like she hurt me. But when I meet her eyes, I stop. There's a glint there, something lurking behind her pupils. It's like a younger Ali is looking out at me, a younger Ali who is full of sly smiles and mischief. It's Ali and not Ali, and it's brushing back hair with Ali's fingers, narrowing its eyes at me with Ali's eyes. "What are you looking at?" Ali says, and it smiles at me with Ali's lips.

And in some ways I guess I haven't changed at all, because just like all those years ago when Avery was both Avery and not Avery, I turn and run. Back down the hall—the door at the other end of the hallway is shut now, and the floor before it is thick with dust. There's no hint that it had ever been opened in the past five years, much less five minutes ago. There's the vase of wildflowers, bright and verdant with life: As I sprint by, they wither before my eyes, and then continue decaying until the cloying scent of rotting flora is thick in the air. I run down the stairs, taking them three at a time. The door to the library is closed, and Rafferty doesn't come to the door to see what the commotion is.

The front door sticks when I try to open it, groaning in its frame, and for one heart-stopping second I realize what I've done, and that it's over now, and Brier won't let me leave again. And then the door comes free, creaking on its rusty hinges, and I'm out. The chilly fog envelops me, wraps itself around me.

The thought comes again: *There's nothing to be frightened of! Stop running.* Again, I don't think it's from me. *Stop running, Lia. Turn around. Come back inside. Come home.*

I force myself to move. Hurrying along around the side of the house, wading through untamed gardens thick with overgrown weeds that reach for me, scratching and tearing at my leggings.

Wouldn't it be nice to look for your old hiding spot? It's in there somewhere now, deep in the briar patch. I would hide you like I used to hide you. No one would find you. You would be safe.

I pass the orchard with its uneven rows of gnarled apple trees, bent under the weight of shiny red-gold apples. They look like jewels.

Stop and try one, the thought comes. *They look delicious.* The voice in my head seems beseeching now. *Wouldn't it be nice to sit down in the grass and lie back with an apple, like you used to do? Rest a little. Stay a while.*

"No!" I scream, the word tearing from my lips painfully. "No!"

The path to the cove is more winding than I remember, switchbacks curling down the side of the cliff, an approximation of steps cut into unwilling soil. The voice has fled; there's nothing now but my own breath heavy in my ears, and a buzzing, loud and insistent. It's the same buzzing that rocketed through my head when I yelled at my mom, and the knowledge lies certain somewhere inside me that if I can just get down to the cove and throw myself into the waves, it will stop. I don't know how I know this, but I do.

I skid along the path: Above me, the bluff rises, adorned with tufts of grass and clods of dirt upended by my flight down. Atop it all sits Brier Hall; from this angle it looks menacing, looming. I turn my face away and hurry onward, breathing a sigh of desperate relief as I make the last switchback and jump down the final steps. My shoes meet sand. The waves crash onto the shore, expanding out before me in one huge swash of roiling blue. The current can be strong in this cove, hemmed in on the sides by sharp rocks.

For a moment I think I see a dark shape moving beneath the water, just past the line of the drop-off, where the sand under our feet suddenly would fall away downward.

"Into nothingness," Ali would say in a serious whisper as we treaded water a few feet away.

"Probably just like twelve feet down," Avery replied. "Maybe twenty if we go even farther out."

"No, forever," Ali said staunchly. "Into nothingness, down and down. It's not called the Never-ending Zone for nothing, you know."

"It's *not* called the Never-ending Zone, though."

"That's where the monster lives," Ali added. She smiled at me, eyes glinty, and shook her salt-crusted hair so that water droplets sprayed around like drops of blood. "It lives in a big house just like we do and it keeps a light lit so it can find its way home."

"An underwater light?" I said doubtfully.

"Yes," Ali replied, as if it was obvious. She lowered her voice. "It's probably listening to us right now. Waiting."

"No, it's not," Avery said with a sigh. She turned to me. "Lia, don't worry, it's *not*. There's nothing in the water but fish and seaweed." With an eye roll and another hard-done-by sigh, she kicked her legs up and floated on her back, staring up at the sparkling sky above us. It was a perfect day. I remember that.

Ali splashed over to me. "Fish and seaweed and the monster that waits in the Never-ending Zone. Avery doesn't know. She's never been down there."

"And you have?" I whispered, because I trusted too much.

"Duh," said Ali. "How do you think I know?"

"Mom says you're just telling stories."

"Well Mom's not here, is she? Everyone's always saying I'm wrong, but they don't *know*, do they? Mom's up in her office writing." Ali waved a wet hand toward Brier Hall, its massive walls and windows watching over the three of us splashing around in its cove. "She doesn't know. Anyways, who are you going to trust? Me or Ave?" And then she smiled at me because she already knew the answer.

"Are you still talking to her about the monster?" Avery's voice snapped from where she'd floated a few feet away.

"No," Ali said immediately.

And a moment later, I followed up with a soft *no* too.

I'm confused when I find myself up to my waist in the water, shivering as my bare toes—*when did I take my shoes off?*—sink into the sand. Everything smells fresh and salty, and the dark shape I swear I saw moving beneath the water is gone. There're just fronds of seaweed coiling around my wrists like manacles, and hundreds of tiny silverfish that dart around my body in a sinuous school. They glitter in the sunlight, and I want to dive down into the water and swim with them, mermaid-like and free, my legs lengthening, my arms becoming fins, my skins crusting over with brilliant silver scales.

They would know about the monster who lives just beyond the drop-off. They would be able to tell me if Ali's tales are true, if it is waiting for me, if it is glad I have returned.

I close my eyes, face turned to the sun, my heart rate slowing. Meeting Ali in the house seems like a dream. Maybe it was. Maybe I got out of the car and came right to the beach. I'll ask Rafferty later. Right now, I can breathe easy. Some people are scared of the ocean, scared of its vastness. But not me. Not the Peartrees. When Brier finally squeezed its arms around us too tightly, the three of us would stay in the water for hours, shivering when the sun began to set, too scared to return to the wooden walls of our supposedly safe bedrooms.

I take a deep breath of sticky air. *Breathe.* Then another. *Breathe.* Then—

I cough as a horrible smell wraps its way into my throat, my nose. My eyes fly open, and I look down and see fish.

The silverfish, belly up and floating aimlessly on their backs. Some sliced open as if by an invisible knife, the pinkish white of their insides spilling out into the water, their gelatinous eyeballs frosted over and staring up at the summer sky, but not seeing it— and this is real, because I can feel it, I can feel the waves and the cold water sluicing through my fingers. I am still, carved from bone. The waves suck around me as I stand at the center of an eddying pool of suddenly dead and decaying fish.

THIRTEEN

The rotting smell of the silverfish clings to my skin, even as I trudge back up the path and through the matted grass, holding my shoes by their backs. No voice inside calls to me: I pass by the orchard and the briar patch in a haze, the pull toward them gone for now. There's movement on the porch and I stop dead for a second before Rafferty moves into view.

"It's so weird being back up here," he says. "So . . . dusty." When I don't reply, he pauses and looks me over, noticing for the first time my soaking clothes and the puddle around my bare feet. "Are you okay? What's happened?"

"Yeah, fine," I mumble. "I just . . . went for a swim."

Rafferty raises his eyebrows at me, and then a line forms between them as he suddenly frowns. "A swim? What? It's freezing."

I knew it wouldn't work on him. I shrug helplessly. "I was down at the cove."

"When did you leave the house? I didn't hear you go."

I think of screaming in Avery's upstairs bedroom, of my rush down the hallway, of the flowers decaying as I ran by. Grappling loudly with the door, frantically trying to get it open. I don't know how to say all this to Rafferty—that I'm pretty sure he didn't hear me because the house didn't want him to. I don't even know if he would believe me. Thinking about how to phrase it makes me want to sink down on the steps and fall asleep.

"I'm not sure," I say simply, willing him to understand that there's something wrong here in this house. "I was being pretty loud." I pause, then add, "Ali's here. Just like I knew she'd be."

"You've seen her already? I haven't heard her in the house," Rafferty says, looking momentarily disconcerted by the fact that someone else has been moving around the rooms without his knowledge. I think of all the things that move around Brier's walls in the dark, in the night. What the hell have I gotten us into?

"Well, she's here," I say, then shake my head and stare up at Brier Hall's front facade. "It's just hard being back here."

Rafferty nods, then makes a strange, lurching movement like he wants to take my hand and then thinks better of it. "Do you want to talk about it?"

"I . . ." I try to think of what I would say. *Yes and no. I don't know how to tell you I don't know what I want. That just being here makes my brain feel foggy. I don't know which thoughts are my own anymore and I've only been in the house a few hours. I was standing in the sand and then I was standing in the ocean, and I was staring at the sky and then I was looking at a pool of dead fish all around me, and I don't know remember any of the in-betweens. I don't know what's going on, and I wish I wasn't here, but I know if I tell you any of this, you'll make me leave, and somehow leaving here would be worse than staying.* "No, not really. Should we just go inside? It's been a long day."

"We've only been here, like, an hour," Rafferty says with a grim smile.

I sigh. "I know." Then I shiver in my wet clothes as a strong breeze curls around me. I turn to look at the waves crashing down beyond the edge of the bluff. There, at the horizon, the sun drops low in the sky. It takes me a moment to process what I'm seeing, then I whirl back to Raff. "We've only been here an hour." It's not a question. It's the truth.

And yet the sky is growing dark.

"Rafferty." I can hear the panic in my voice. "Rafferty?"

Rafferty pulls out his phone and squints at the screen, then meets my eyes. "It's eight o'clock."

"The sun is setting. How can the sun be setting?"

"Just relax," Rafferty says, although his voice is shot through with fear now too, and he is not relaxed. "Just—that's not possible, so let's just relax and think things through. When did we arrive?"

"I don't know," I mutter. "Like nine in the morning?"

We stare at each other. Somehow we've been here more than eleven hours. Somehow we've lost a whole day.

I'm shivering hard now, shaking where I stand, as if one big gust of salty air might blow me away like a leaf. Raff moves forward, pulling off his hoodie and offering it out to me.

"I'm fine," I say, teeth chattering.

He steps up to me and pulls the hoodie over my head, tugging it down over my arms. He smooths down my mussed hair, then holds his hands on each side of my head.

"We're not going to be scared," he says forcefully.

"I'm not scared," I mumble.

"None of this is real," he says. "This is all just—a trick, or something."

I don't reply to that. I don't think he even believes himself. He keeps his hands on my cheeks for another second and then steps back. I feel unmoored, as if a part of me is still floating in the waters of the cove, being submerged by rogue waves. Some part of me has been unleashed, set free. When I turn my face from Rafferty's to the cold stones of the front of Brier Hall, I'm battered by memories.

What do you remember? I'd asked Rafferty at the Eastwind Hotel.

I remember we were scared, he'd replied.

And we were. But now I remember why.

I catch at the memories as they drift past my unanchored body.

"There were others in the house with us," I breathe. "Don't you remember?"

"There were no others," Rafferty replies. His voice is firm, but then it breaks and he shakes his head and continues, "God, Lia, what am I supposed to say? It *can't* have happened how we remember it."

"'Total Eclipse of the Heart,'" I whisper, my throat dry, and I watch as Rafferty grips the porch railing so hard his fingers turn white. I can see the memories flickering in his eyes; the way we'd be deep in the lonely halls of the house, the light fading, a board game spread between us, and then we'd hear it: the sound of someone humming. We weren't scared, not at first, because your brain looks for pathways that make sense. And our brains told us that someone humming from a lost room in the house was Avery, it was Ali, it was my mom.

Until it became clear it wasn't any of them. Until we were all gathered in the kitchen and the forlorn notes of "Total Eclipse of the Heart" started drifting in from the other room. My mom started singing along while the four of us kids sat at the table, frozen, staring at one another in sudden, piercing fear. Our wide eyes asked silent questions: *So it wasn't you? All this time, it wasn't you?*

I watched as Ali's eyes flicked to the kitchen door behind where Rafferty and I sat at the table. She met our gaze and mouthed, *The door's open.*

Was I imagining it, or were there sudden footsteps on the other side of the door? Avery's hands were shaking on the table. No, this was real.

My mom continued to sing as she stirred the chili on the stove, oblivious to our silence. Ali's hands clenched into fists. I couldn't breathe; I couldn't turn around.

The music suddenly stopped, plunging the room into thick silence. My mom turned around, her "Why'd you stop the song?" trailing off as she looked at us quaking. "Kids?"

I kept my mouth shut; who knew who might be listening?

"It wasn't us," Avery said finally, when it became clear none of us were going to respond.

"Who was it?"

We all shrugged.

My mom put down the spoon on the counter and crossed to the open kitchen door, poking her head out. For the briefest moment I swear I saw *something* outside the door, and snapped my eyes shut, the scream making its way into my lungs. Before I could let it out, my mom returned. "The front door's locked, you guys. This house is old, and so are the appliances. Must be faulty wiring."

She sounded so sure.

But I knew I'd seen something.

And from then on we'd continue to hear that song, drifting through the hallways. Reaching out for us.

"That wasn't real," Rafferty intones now, not looking at me. "Something bumped the music player or something."

"For over a year?" I snap back. The memories have been seeping through the locked gate in my mind, but now the floodgates have cracked open. I'm drowning in the confines of myself. "And we would hear people yelling—screaming—crying. What about that?"

He crosses his arms like he's guarding the entrance to the house. "It must've been one of you."

"You're blaming it on *us*?"

"No, but I think sometimes kids can get swept up in something like this!"

"Oh, yeah?" I scoff. "Where'd you hear that?"

"Therapy, Lia! Years and years of it!"

I take a deep breath. "Can we not fight about this?"

"I'm not trying to fight. I just don't want you getting swept up in—" He waves a hand, then rubs his forehead. "Fear's a powerful thing. If you don't watch out, it'll take over."

"Did you learn that in therapy too?"

He narrows his eyes at me. "Yes."

"So that's why you're here? To keep an eye on me and make sure I'm okay?"

"Yeah," Rafferty says. "Something like that. To make sure you're okay. To maybe show you that this house wasn't what we thought it was as kids. That it's not something we have to be scared of."

"Sounds like a big ask."

He holds out his hand and I trip forward to take it. The front porch squeaks underneath my feet, and I'm still shivering, but his hands are warm. "I can handle it." He gives me a hesitant smile, then cocks his head toward the front door. "Come on. Let's make— well, dinner, now, I guess."

"Okay," I mumble, following him inside. Rafferty locks the door, staring at me pointedly as the lock turns and clicks.

"Locked in tight. We're safe and sound."

I raise an eyebrow at him. "If you say so."

A voice from above interrupts us. "Well, well," it drawls. "Rafferty Pierce returns to Brier Hall." My sister is up on the second floor by the stairs, leaning over the railing and staring down at us. Her hair hangs lank, her eyes are sunken. I try to see her from Rafferty's view: five years on, seeing another of his childhood playmates once again.

Rafferty's faces betrays no emotion. "Hello, Ali," he says softly. "How are you doing?"

"You're in my house," she snaps.

"Your sister invited me," he replies evenly.

"You think we're imagining things," she says. She leans farther over the railing like a broken doll. I want to yell out to her to *be careful* but Ali has never been careful a day in her life. And she wouldn't listen to me anyways.

"I don't know," he says. "Look, I'm trying to be honest here. I think some of the things you experienced—"

"*We* experienced," she cuts in, and Rafferty shrugs in acquiescence.

"Okay, some of the things *we* experienced have been built up over time. They've become monsters in your own mind."

"My sister is gone because of this house!" Ali shrieks. Her hands tighten on the rail and I get a sudden fear she'll launch herself up and over the railing, but instead of falling she'll fly down toward us, hands turning to claws.

"Your sister," Raff says gently, "disappeared *in* this house. But look—just . . . just look." He takes out his phone and scrolls through until suddenly the beginning mournful notes of "Total Eclipse of the Heart" begin pouring from the speakers.

I tense immediately, bile rising in my throat as pure memory hits me over the head. Ali lets go of the banister and comes raging down the stairs toward us.

"Shut that off!" she screams.

"Look—" Rafferty holds out a hand to ward her away as she snatches for his phone. "It's not scary! It's an eighties song! We don't have to be scared of it!"

Every part of my body is tightening in panic.

Bonnie Tyler sings about falling apart, and then *I* am falling apart as the music swells around our little trio huddled in the entrance hall. I lay a trembling hand on Rafferty's arm and shake my head.

"I get what you're trying to do," I say. "But please turn it off."

Rafferty stares at me for a moment, then abruptly shuts off the song. "Okay. I'm sorry. Too soon. I was just—"

"I know," I whisper. "Let's just forget about it, okay?" I head toward the ajar kitchen door, trying to breathe normally, evenly. Ali follows right behind me, almost tripping me with every step as she

147

hisses angrily about Rafferty in my ear. I elbow her in her side as I push on the door with my foot. It creaks open and I look up, and Ali looks up, and I know by the way her breath catches that we're somehow seeing the same impossible thing.

Us.

Us, sitting at the kitchen table, little and white-faced and bright-eyed and terrified.

'm halfway to the front door, jumping over the duffel bags that are piled in the entrance hall, by the time Rafferty catches up to me and grabs my arm.

"Lia—Lia, what's going on?"

I just shake my head, unable to speak. My heart is a rabbit's heart, tiny and racing and fragile. I don't know how to tell him what I've seen. I don't *want* to tell him because that would mean I really saw it—saw something. It can't be real.

It wasn't real.

Raff's fingers grip each of my upper arms as I suddenly sag in his arms.

"This place . . ."

"It's not good for you to be here," Rafferty replies. "Let's go, Lia. You found your sister and she's fine, so—so you did what you came to do."

I shake my head silently. *You found your sister.* One of them, yes. Is that the only reason I came? I know that Ali is looking for Avery, and there's a part of me that needs to look for her too. Even though it's fruitless. We searched. The police searched. The town searched. Avery was never seen again after the night of the storm.

I know she's gone. There's no other explanation.

My own face, little and wide-eyed, staring back at me through the kitchen doors. Or maybe there are just so many explanations that don't make sense, that my mind just can't figure out.

"This place is getting to me," I whisper.

"Then let's go," Raff says again, more urgently, and I wonder what I must look like to have him look so worried. I want so much to just nod and agree and let him lead me out the front doors and away from Brier Hall and all its memories. I don't realize I'm crying until Rafferty gently wipes under my eyes, his fingers coming away wet. "Lia. *Lia.*"

"I can't," I whisper. "I have to stay." I straighten up, clenching my jaw hard in an attempt to stop the errant tears. I make sure to grab one of the duffel bags—to give myself something to do with my hands—and then walk stiffly back toward the heart of the entrance hall where Ali waits, her thin, bruised arms tightly crossed.

Like this.

Her eyes track me. As I brush by her, the edge of the duffel a barrier swinging between us like the pillow walls we used to make when we sometimes shared a bed, she whispers, "You saw us too."

It's not a question, but I can tell by the way she watches me go that she wants an answer. A confirmation. I'm halfway up the grand staircase when she suddenly shouts, the loudness of it jarring in the too-quiet hall: "You saw them too, didn't you? You *know* there's something weird going on here!"

There's nothing going on. Ali is paranoid. Ali is troubled.

You know this. You know this.

I take the rest of the steps two at a time, the duffel bumping unceremoniously against my hip as I run down the upstairs hallway.

I enter a room and slam the door behind me, then lean against it.

It takes me a moment before I look up, and when I do, my breath leaves me.

I'm in my own room. My old room. My feet have taken me right back, and the pure familiarity, the rightness, makes me feel so hollow it's like a piece of myself has been carved out.

The two twin iron-frame beds sit pushed with their headboards against the wall, framed by windows that look out over the cove far below. Everything is untouched and covered in a thin sheen of dust, and I bite back a sob, because apart from the dust, it looks exactly as it did the night we left Brier. Our beds are unmade, striped covers thrown back. Ali's duvet is half on the floor. Two dusty, empty cups sit on each of our bedside tables, and the tops of our two dressers are covered in half-filled-in homeschooling papers, piles of Baby-Sitters Club books, drugstore makeup and sparkly nail polish bottles. Ali's pile of interestingly shaped rocks and shells taken from Brier's beach is lined up across the back of the dresser like a museum. This whole *place* is a museum: All these things are me and I am them; they're the fuchsia lipstick and pink and green tubes of cheap mascara and the math homework I got bored with and the loose and littered colored pencils and the still-smiling teddy bear that made me who I am now. Everything is in disarray—but now that I'm inside, the stale, disused air has fled.

Ali and I might've just left the room.

The doorknob rattles behind me, just for a moment, but in that brief split second my heart rises to my throat, choking me, as my mind filters through all the other times the doorknob has turned and someone I didn't know was behind it.

"Lia?"

Rafferty—just Rafferty. I open the door and there he is, wild-haired and stormy-eyed, a fraying backpack slung onto his shoulder. He takes in the sight of me, rigid, fingers clenched into fists, and then gives me a smile that is both familiar and sad. The smile of someone who used to know your every thought. I'm immediately reminded that no matter how close we used to be, and how easy it is to fall back into each other, we're still unknown to each other now. These new versions of each other are strangers.

"You okay?" he asks lightly.

"Does it look like I'm okay?" I mumble, crossing over and hesitantly sitting down on the edge of one of the beds—*my* bed. The frame creaks loudly beneath me, unused to the pressure. It's unsteady, just like me.

"Not really, no," Raff says. "But that's just going off of the running away and the shouting and the—" He freezes up like a statue and clenches his fists.

"Yeah." I manage a smile. "All that."

He kicks the door shut behind him and drops his bag to the floor, where the contents clink mysteriously. "I wanted to check on you."

"You just didn't want to hang out with Ali while I was up here."

"That too," he replies. In the silence, he looks around, and I see the moment it hits him. He blinks slowly and licks his lips, then nods. "Your room. Ah."

More silence. I could drown in it.

Is a room still yours if you haven't been in it for five years? It *feels* like my room. Everything about this place is sad and lonely and *mine*.

I nod at the bag on the floor, anything to break the quiet. "What's in there?"

"Well, I'm glad you asked." He goes down on one knee and opens the bag with a flourish, where the top of a glass bottle pokes out. "Liquid courage. I took it this morning from the hotel—I figured you might need it. Hell, *I* need it." He runs his hand through his hair, then meets my gaze. "You want some?"

"I could use it," I said. "Will you get in trouble?"

"For this? When your family owns the only hotel in town, there's not much you can get in trouble for." He crosses to the other bed—Ali's bed—with the bottle in one hand and two East-wind Hotel shot glasses in the other. Setting them carefully on the bedside table, he pours us each a shot.

The sharp smell of vodka cuts through the salty air, and for a moment I wonder if Ali will come bursting through the doors like a hunting dog latched onto a scent.

"Don't tell my sister," I whisper. "Make sure she doesn't know—doesn't find this."

Raf turns the bottle in his hands. "She can't handle it?"

"She'll say she can," I reply. The words come out bitter even though I try to keep things light. Like thinking about Ali drunk and screaming and fire-eyed is something that's easy, something that isn't death by a thousand cuts.

"Then do we trust her?"

"She's proven again and again and again that we can't," I return.

"I can't take more of Ali lying to my face that things are different now. They're never different." I twist my fingers together and keep my eyes down. Everything is blurrier now, and I realize my eyes are filling with tears.

"She's had the same hard time as you, though," Raff murmurs. "Maybe we should cut her some slack and just see—"

"Cut her slack?" I interrupt, voice rising. "Raff, I cut her slack for years. How many chances do you give someone? Infinite chances? Just one after the next, doling them out like gold stars? I don't have infinite chances, okay? I can't keep saying, 'Sure, keep breaking my heart, have fun!' I can't do that forever! I can't do that! I don't care!"

My voice raises into a screech, but Raff's expression doesn't change. He is a rock in a storm. He just eyes me, then whispers, "You do care, Lia. You've cared about her so much for so long that it's ripping you apart."

"I—don't—*care*!" I shriek, my eyes welling up with tears, unable to think about how maybe he's right about me and Ali. Maybe my hatred isn't hatred at all, but love, love so angry that it feels like something else. He is right about something, though: I am ripping apart. I can feel it as I cry. My body is breaking apart, my bones turning to dust.

Rafferty reaches out and grips my fingers in his own. "I'm sorry, Lia," he says quietly. "I'm sorry for all of it. For her, for you, for your mom . . . I'm sorry we never found Avery."

Her name cuts like a knife.

Avery, the reason we're all back here.

"Me too," I say, wishing the tears on my cheeks would evaporate. "I . . ." My voice breaks, and I cut off, mortified. I hate that I'm here, I hate that I'm falling apart. I hate that Rafferty is seeing me fall apart.

"Does Ali really believe she's still here somewhere?"

I nod.

"And . . . what do you think?"

"I . . ." I stare at Rafferty sitting on Ali's bed and the words leave me, because I suddenly realize that the covers beneath him are no longer covered in dust. They're clean.

Instead of pausing to consider what that could possibly *mean*, I instead grab the two full shot glasses and pass one to Raff.

"Cheers," I say, then toss it back without waiting for him to do the same. The sharpness of the vodka burns down my throat. It feels good; it chases away the feeling of wrongness that I couldn't seem to shake.

"I don't know what I think," I whisper. "But Raff . . . I think there's something wrong in this house. I saw something."

"In the kitchen."

"Yes."

"What did you see?"

"You won't believe me."

"Try me."

I gulp. My mouth is dry. "Okay. I saw myself. You. All of us. Little. Scared." He's looking at me incomprehensibly, like the words I'm speaking don't make sense. Maybe they don't. None of this makes sense. "You didn't see anything?"

He shakes his head and begins pouring a second shot for both of us. I wonder if this is how it started for Ali. If she was just numbing the gaping wound where Avery once was, where the memories were kept, and then suddenly she was too numb to remember how to stop. Numb enough that love for her little sister, her remaining sister, turned to hatred.

But not numb enough to know she'd rather have Avery than me.

I force the sudden flood of grief to turn to anger instead. My hatred is red. It burns away the tears that threaten to fall once again. I won't cry over Ali, not again, not here. I won't think of what Rafferty says. I can't fall apart now.

"I didn't see anything, but I believe you," Rafferty says. He shrugs and stares out the window to the darkness beyond. "I believe you, Lia. Look." He holds out his hand toward me, extending his wrist. There's a battered gold watch there. "Look," he says again.

I take his wrist gingerly.

"My watch says it's midnight," he says plainly, his voice nearly a whisper.

"No." I shake my head, even though I can see the little black numbers as clear as anything.

"Midnight," he repeats. "Yeah."

"It was eight when we came inside."

"I know."

I laugh hollowly, and the sound seems to echo around the still room, bouncing off the big, old glass windows. I wonder how loud a scream it would take to shatter them. Instead I clear my throat and say, "We've lost another four hours in the time it took to talk to Ali and come up here . . . ?" My mind eddies. Yet another thing that isn't possible. *Add it to the list.*

Rafferty stares at me, grim. "Yeah." Then he reaches forward and clicks his shot glass against mine. His hand trembles. Vodka sloshes over the edge and trickles down my fingers. "Cheers to figuring out what the fuck's going on in this house."

"Cheers," I murmur.

Instead of falling apart we give each other strained, forced smiles and down the shots.

"Raff, are you scared?" I ask in the ensuing silence.

There's a pause. He's staring down at his hands, fingers clasped tightly around the glass. From somewhere outside in the hallway, there comes the creaking of floorboards, and he looks up and meets my gaze. "Yes."

I thought that hearing it would make me feel worse, but it doesn't. I feel stronger, calmer. His yes is forcing me to stay sane.

"We're going to stick together. It's like you said back at the hotel—there's no such thing as haunted houses."

He snorts. Pours another shot.

"No such thing as ghosts."

"Yeah, well, I'm reconsidering."

"Or hauntings."

"We've lost an entire day, Lia!" His voice is hoarse. "What else would you call it?" He passes me a full shot glass, then continues seriously, "We're sticking together, as you said. I don't know what's happening here but if time is doing its own thing and you're seeing . . . things . . . we need to keep each other in check. Keep each other safe."

I nod. There's something building in me, a mix of anxiety and fear and whirlpooling emotion. *Safe.* I hope we will be. I don't have the best track record of keeping people safe in Brier Hall.

"So. To do: Stay safe. I can do that." *Probably.*

"Stay safe and figure out what's going on."

I nod. "Raff," I begin hesitantly. In the light from the bedside table lamp, his face is bathed in a soft golden glow. Maybe it's the alcohol warming my words, making them come easier. Maybe I'm just desperate to not be by myself in this tomb of a bedroom without Ali, without anyone. "Will you stay with me tonight?"

Rafferty hesitates. "Lia . . ." His voice is almost pained, and I peek up at him.

"Not—not like that," I say quickly, even though a part of me means it exactly like that.

"Oh yeah?" The Raff from the hotel is back, the one who is all grown up, the one with the slow smile.

I can feel the vodka now, and for a moment I wonder what Raff would do if I just leaned forward across the empty space and kissed him. I want to imagine he'd kiss me back, that his hands would come up and tangle in my hair, that he'd say he'd forgiven me and wanted me.

"A little bit like that," I admit.

Raff sighs, and before I have a chance to be mortified he says, "It's different now, Lia. We don't even really know each other anymore."

"Of course we know each other," I shoot back. "Don't say that, Raff." What I don't say: *We were best friends. You meant everything to me. I loved you then, as a young teenager, and I love the you I made up in my head. I bet I could love the you sitting in front of me too.*

Raff holds up his hands in a placating sort of way. "You're

right. But things have still changed. We're different people. And as much I might like to stay . . ."

"Raff . . . I just don't want to be alone." I feel silly the moment it comes out of my mouth, silly and pitiful, but it doesn't change the fact that it's true. "Please. That's it, the only reason, I promise. Please, will you stay?"

Rafferty sucks in his bottom lip, his eyes never leaving mine. "Yes," he says.

"And you won't leave?"

"No. Will you?"

"No. Like I said—we're sticking together." I lower my voice so it's just a murmur, as if saying the words softly will make them have less of an impact.

"Right. And we'll figure out if—somehow—Ali's right, and Avery is still here. Still alive." Raff holds up his shot glass. "So cheers to us—to who we were, and who we are now," he says for a second time, then pauses. "And to Avery, wherever you may be."

I clink my glass against his and try to ignore the way my heart clenches. "To Avery," I echo, and I can't keep my voice from shaking.

We both tip the glasses and toss our shots back in sync, swallowing.

And then we're spitting out liquid and spluttering and coughing and gagging, both of us suddenly choking on salt water.

FIFTEEN

My eyes open suddenly, abruptly. I'm awake as if I was never even asleep in the first place.

The realization that something is *off* hits quickly, like drinking something too cold too fast. For a moment I can't pick what's wrong: here I am in bed, tucked in tight. Then there's a thudding noise, and I sit up to see the light from the open door illuminating the open window, banging on its hinges in the wind, rain flying in.

See? Nothing's wrong. It must've blown open when one of Eastwind's many storms swept toward the bluff.

I swing my legs out of bed and have crossed the room and closed the window tightly when all at once two things hit me.

First: Rafferty is no longer in the bed next to mine. It took us a while to fall asleep after the salt water shot incident, but—just like everything that happens in this place—there was nothing we could do about it other than whisper placations in the hope that one of us would eventually believe it. He fell asleep in Ali's bed.

We're sticking together.

We're keeping each other safe.

He's not there now. The bed is empty.

Second: The bedroom door is open. The hallway light is on. It was locked when we went to bed—I made sure of it.

I stand at the window. *Deep breaths, Lia. Come on. Deep breaths.*

Deeper. The scream is building inside me and I clench my fists so hard I imagine them turning to stone. I imagine the stone growing, spiderwebbing over my skin. Rooting me to the spot. I imagine—

Snap out of it, Lia!

The voice is loud in my thoughts, and I fasten my eyes back to the door. It's funny how at Brier five years ago, the door would be closed and locked, and the door handle would shake and rattle as someone tried to get in. Now, an open door is worse.

But there're a million explanations. Of course there are. Rafferty went to the bathroom to get some water. Ali, wandering the halls, searching for our sister.

I move toward the open door, hesitating in the doorframe. The hallway outside it flooded with light and completely empty.

"Ali?" I whisper. "Rafferty?"

The hallway swallows the sound. The gilt-framed paintings on the walls watch as I take a step forward, my bare toes sinking into the thick wine-colored rug. I'm hesitant at first, but then I push myself out into the hallway, taking a deep breath. This is my house. I won't be afraid. *I won't be. I won't be.*

"Ali?" I call loudly—*I won't be afraid*—and this time my voice echoes down the hallway, rebounding in on itself. *Ali? Ali? Ali?*

For a second I imagine the hallway twists and curves, warping, the doors at the other end shifting nearer to me. I blink and the hallway rights itself.

I blink and the door at the far end of the hallway—the door to Avery's old room—clicks open.

I blink and a girl is stepping out—she's turned away from me, and my first thought is *Ali,* and I swell up with relief. I'm about to call out

161

to her when she turns to face me, and the "Ali" on my lips unspools.

Avery watches me, still as a hare in the gaze of a fox. She looks different from my memories—older, somehow, her features more refined, her eyes sharper. Still, I'd know her anywhere. Avery, my sister. She *feels* the same, even standing at the other end of the hallway.

I blink, and the Avery standing there is no longer the strange, aged version but the Avery I remember—freckly and blond and barefoot, her face serious and scared.

"Avery!" I gasp, reaching out, my fingers desperate, as if they can touch her from twenty feet away. A tiny part of my brain reminds me that Brier can't be trusted—that not everything I see is real. Can't be real. But the rest of me hasn't caught on, and adrenaline is coursing through me. My feet are already moving. "Avery! It's me!"

Avery, my sister.

She turns and runs back inside the room she came from, slamming the door shut behind her.

"Avery!" I think I'm screaming. I reach the door, slamming into it, but no matter how much I rattle the handle, it stays shut. Locked. Doors in Brier Hall would never stay locked for me when I was a kid, not ever. But now I'm crying and screaming and throwing myself against the door, and the door won't budge. "Avery! Avery!"

My thoughts narrow in on just her name: Nothing else is real. Screaming something in the dead of night will do that.

I rattle the doorknob, turning it this way and that.

For a second I think I hear crying, screaming, but I can't tell if it's coming from inside the room or from me.

And then the door opens.

I burst into the room, tear-stained, panting, and I look around. The room is dark and shadowed, even though the room I saw Avery disappear into was brightly lit. Something moves in the shadows, and then a form appears.

"Avery?" I whisper.

The form moves into the light of the window. Ali's gaunt face stares back at me. She's shaking, and my anger explodes at the thought of her laughing at me in here while I was desperate and panicked to get in, to get to Avery.

"Why didn't you open the door?" I scream at her.

"I didn't know it was you!" she yells back at me, sinking onto Avery's bed, trembling.

"What do you *mean*? Who else would it be?"

"I didn't know it was you," she repeats, in a whisper this time.

I'm still warmed by my anger, but Ali is cold and blue to my red-hot, and I begin to calm down. "I was yelling for Avery. How did you not hear?"

Her fingers are still shaking, but she raises her head to look at me. She's still, as if she's holding her breath. "No, you weren't."

"What?"

"I said *No, you weren't.*"

"I was—Ali, I was yelling, crying. I saw Avery in the hallway. I—"

"No one was yelling. All there was was banging. The door was rattling, shaking. I thought . . ." Ali swallows. Her knuckles are white, fists tensed. "I thought it was happening again. But this time I was alone."

There're footsteps in the hallway, and we both whirl around as Rafferty appears in the doorway, eyes heavy with sleep.

"What's going on?" he mumbles.

"Where were *you*?" I ask, trying to keep the panic and accusation from seeping back into my voice. Everything puts me on edge. Merely *being* here makes me snap.

Raff stares at me blankly. "What? I was sleeping. I just woke and heard you guys arguing."

I'm cold all over, my anger doused, no embers. "You weren't there, Raff. I woke up in the night, and the door was open. I went looking for you."

"I locked the door before bed."

Ali interrupts, standing abruptly and glaring at us both. "Obviously this place is playing by different rules."

We're playing a game where we don't make or know the rules. A game whose rules are changed by an unseen hand. I'm a half second from telling Ali and Rafferty that I'm leaving and not coming back, but then I remember the Avery I saw in the hallway. The *two* Averys. One young, the girl I remember, and one older. Different.

Who was *she*?

I let myself be hustled in a daze back down the hallway by Rafferty, who doesn't seem to understand the way the last half hour has sapped my energy. But how could he? As far as he knows, he woke up, walked down the hallway, and found me and Ali in Avery's room.

That's it. That's all.

My knuckle throbs—it's raw and red, the skin ripped from where I clawed at the locked door. *Real.* No matter what Rafferty says, no matter what Ali says, this proves it was real. Doesn't it?

Ali files in after us and shuts the door, locking it behind her.

"What, you're staying with us?"

"Is that a problem?"

"I thought you were mad that Raff and I are even here."

"There're bigger things to worry about, okay?" she snaps, turning away from us and facing the door. "You can sleep," she says. "I'll watch the door."

"Ali, just—"

"It's fine," she says, and I can't read her face when she adds, "I'm not scared."

I think of Rafferty, gone from his bed when I awoke, and not gone half an hour later.

I think of a door shaking on its hinges, screams unheard.

"I'm not scared," she repeats.

I think of two different Averys in the hallway, and I realize that I'm scared for her. She's my sister, after all.

"I think," I say, "you probably should be."

HAPPY FOR A WHILE

You worship your oldest sister. It's obvious as you sit there, watching her, both of you leaning against the banister, legs sprawled down the stairs. Avery is carefully writing on some homeschool worksheet. Math questions. *If three little girls go into a house and one never comes out, how many remain?*

Her hair is in two neat braids and you brush your own hair down, wishing it was just like hers. Your fingers snag on a tangle; you pull out a bramble covered in tiny, spiky briar thorns. For a moment you're worried you're turning into a briar girl, and you take a minute to let your imagination run wild, picturing yourself turning into a bramble, thorns erupting from your skin like scales. Everyone in town would run from you, scared, but you'd be safe here.

You toss the bramble aside before Avery sees it.

"Don't you have some homework to do?" your sister asks, not looking up from her work.

You sigh, hard. It's raining outside, droplets hammering against the windowpanes, and Rafferty's mom wouldn't let him come up to the house in such bad weather. You couldn't find Ali in the maze of rooms no matter how much time you spent calling her name, so sitting with Avery is the next best thing.

"I don't want to do homework," you say, making a face.

Avery tugs gently on a lock of your hair, and gives a wry smile.

"You have to. One day you want to move out and go to college somewhere, don't you? Get a job?"

"No," you say. "Not really."

Your sister looks amused. "No?"

You lean your head against her shoulder. "I don't want to grow up."

"Of course you do."

"No," you insist.

"But think of the opposite of not growing up," Avery says, her tone big sisterly. "Just stuck. Everything the same, nothing changing."

"I don't want anything to change," you reply stoutly, because now you've chosen your course with this argument and you won't be swayed by logic of any kind. "I want to stay here with you forever." Every sunny day out in the orchard, in the cove. Brambles in your hair forming crowns: queens of Brier Hall. Stormy days spent roaming the house, running up and down the hallways. Scratching your initials onto baseboards, banisters, bedposts: anything and everything to leave your mark, to show that this place is *yours.*

"But what about Rafferty?" Avery asks in a singsong voice, and you feel your cheeks warm.

"You know?" No one is supposed to know how Rafferty makes you feel. How you write his name on the back of history worksheets that you never give to your mom. How you roam the wilds of Brier's estate, hoping his hand might brush yours. Accidentally, of course.

"It's a big sister's job to know."

"Don't say anything," you warn, because you can already hear

Ali's incessant teasing. Avery mimes locking her lips and throwing away the key.

"Not a word, I promise. But you can't get married in a huge fancy wedding one day if you're stuck in this house with your boring big sister." She makes a face, crosses her eyes.

"You're not boring," you reply. You always did know what to say, didn't you?

"Well," she says with a roll of her eyes, but she smiles.

"I want to live with you forever."

You want to live here *forever.*

Don't you.

Don't you?

"Okay," Avery says, already turning back to her homework, the ghost of her smile still on her face. "Sure."

"Really." You're insistent. The rain pounds above you, drowning out everything inside you except this one truest thought: *You want to stay here forever. Unchanging. Infinite.*

"Okay, okay, I promise," Avery says. "Me and you, we'll never be apart."

And you make her pinkie promise then, just to be sure.

SIXTEEN

The light wakes me again, but this time it's the weak daylight pushing through the overcast sky outside and not mysterious lights from the hallway. Instead, waking up in my little iron-frame bed feels familiar. It's something I've done hundreds of times before, and it feels like I never left.

No one's in the room and the door is wide open, but it's not frightening. Last night's panic seems like a dream. Maybe it's just the dark that riled me up. Maybe the echoes and memories were too much to bear on the first night back in Brier.

Maybe Rafferty was right.

As I get dressed, I scroll aimlessly through my phone. Everyone's celebrating summer, and I'm here.

There're texts from Diya:

OF COURSE I'll cover for you. My lips are sealed.
Even though I'm the least likely person EVER to want to camp.
Helloooo? How did the meetup go?
You okay?

I'm about to reply with a text when I see I already have. *What?* I stare at it. There's an excited, affirmative text with too many exclamations and too little truth. I have no memory of typing it, of sending it. I carefully find my mom's messages and—yes. There's another text there, apparently from me: a text about Tahoe and s'mores and bad signal. I haven't sent these, but there they are before me, real as anything.

I set the phone on the bed like it's red-hot. I know I should keep my phone with me, but I don't want it touching me with the phantom texts that I've somehow sent. *I didn't send anything.* I leave the phone in the room and hurry out the door. *Don't think about it.* I try to push the confusion, the fear, from my mind. If I think about it too long I'll panic, and I can't panic. Not now.

Brier is quiet and still as I walk through its hallways. Last night is just another memory to file away in its walls. For a moment I sit down on the top step of the grand staircase, resting my cheek in the palm of my hand.

One breath, two.

Light is filtering through the windows of the entrance hall and despite everything I can't help but survey the hall before me, with its shining parquet floors and gilt-framed paintings and giant chandelier, and think of how *beautiful* it is.

How wonderful this place could be.

If Brier had a body, it would be made up of my family members. Brier would be the Peartrees: drowning, angry, and in a well of reliving memories—but not without good moments too. The mornings we got up early and went out exploring the misty headland. Flashlight tag in the dark. Pancakes on Sunday mornings. The smell of the sea and the heather. Swimming in the cove until dinnertime.

I'd almost forgotten.

It wasn't all bad. We were happy for a while.

And as I sit, I can remember myself sitting in this exact spot five years ago, Avery next to me. Telling me that we'd never be apart. We'd pinkie promised and everything. But now here I am, without her.

My tears cut trails of salt down my cheeks, and I wait until they're dry before standing and taking the rest of the steps two at a time. I don't want to dwell on the past of my own accord when this place finds a way to throw me headfirst into it anyways.

I find Rafferty in the library, sitting on the floor with a half-eaten piece of toast. There's a pile of papers in a stack before him. The light from the windows filters in, illuminating his hair, his face. This moment has played out in my memories so many times: Rafferty young, smiling mischievously; and in my dreams: Rafferty older, his smile slow and wicked and—

"Morning," Raff says, his fingers stilling as they flick through the papers. He looks up at me. "How are you feeling?"

"I'm okay," I say softly, then I narrow my eyes at him. "I don't want you tiptoeing around me. I'm okay. I'm fine."

"Tiptoe around the most fierce Lia Peartree? Never." He smiles up at me, and it's neither mischievous or slow or wicked but something else altogether, a smile my imagination could never conjure up, then pats the space next to him. "Come here. Look at what I've found in these drawers."

I settle down next to him. The side of my leg presses up against his, and my body is a thousand tiny wires all lit up. A small part of my brain yells that this can never last, because once I leave here again I won't be coming back, but—still. Can't I be happy for a while with Rafferty Pierce too?

"What is it?"

His long fingers shuffle the papers. "Old letters. Documents. Books."

"About what?"

"The house. This place." He hands me a small stack of photographs and I riffle through them. Dark eyes of Briers past stare out at me. Briers on the headland where my sisters and I stood. Briers in the orchard where we swung from the gnarled boughs. Briers standing in front of the house, ivy crawling up the exterior behind them, the windows blank like extra pairs of eyes.

The final picture is of a man sitting in the sand in the cove, *our* cove. My mouth tightens as I look at his dark hair—so unlike mine and my sisters', which we obviously got from the Peartree side of the family. He's not smiling, just staring directly at the camera. My father, the final Brier to live and die here.

I shuffle the photos and pass them back to Raff. I don't want to touch these photos of my erstwhile extended family that I don't know, that I will never know.

"And there's this." He exchanges the photos for a newspaper clipping. I wonder who has so carefully cut it out. It's from a 1994 issue of the *Eastwind Gazette*, and the headline is in thick black letters: **IN THE HALL, WITH THE KNIFE?** And then in smaller letters beneath it: **POLICE CALLED TO BRIER HALL**. I skim the article: It's all about a death that occurred at the house. Unusual circumstances. Police stumped. No suspects.

I hand it back to Raff, who glances down at the scrap of newspaper, then looks back at me seriously. "There's an entire folder of clippings like that one."

My stomach drops.

Raff rustles through the pile of stationery detritus around him and then hands over a book, already flipped open. "Have a look at this. How much did you know about Brier Hall before you came here, Lia?"

I reach for the book, trying to keep my hands from shaking. "Nothing. My father left it to us when he died. It's been in his family for—well, I don't know. My mom might. A long time, at least."

I look down at the book and check the title. *Gone Home: Lingering Spirits in America's Most Haunted Dwelling,* by Dr. Anderson Carlisle, PhD. Raff has already opened it: There's a big picture of Brier Hall, full color, from an angle somewhere down by the gates. It looks imposing, frightening. To me, it's like one of those pictures that change as your eyes go blurry: It's both accurate and not, true and false all at the same time.

> *Brier Hall is, by all accounts, a sad and lonely place. A place that sinks under the weight of hiraeth. Hiraeth is a Welsh word, commonly described in English as "the feeling of missing home"—not just mere homesickness, but the deep longing that takes root in your bones. It's grief for the people whose eye color you can no longer remember. Grief for the lost places in your past, the places you can never return to, maybe even the places you've never been.*
>
> *Hiraeth is beautiful and sad, as so many things are. As Brier Hall was—and still is. Hiraeth is longing, lingering.*
>
> *Hiraeth is ghosts.*
>
> *And ghosts are something that Brier Hall knows well.*

I look up from the page to find Rafferty watching me. "Who is this guy, this author?" I ask. My voice sounds upset, even though I try to keep it even. "He talks about Brier like he knows it. Has he been here?"

"Apparently he's local," Rafferty replies. "He works at the local college up in Redlake, just past Fort Bragg."

"He *does*?"

Rafferty nods. "I looked him up. You know, Redlake's less than an hour away."

I flip to the author biography on the back flap of the book and examine the black-and-white photo there. Anderson Carlisle is a serious-looking man with dark skin and black curly hair, and he stares out intently from his picture. I'm pretty sure he never visited the house when we lived here—at least, I don't recognize him—but then again, I was just a kid who spent most of her time gallivanting around Brier's estate like she was its queen and not paying attention to much else.

I close the book with a thud. It's heavy on my lap. Maybe it's just the sun from behind the curtains, or the way the air is hazy with dust and memories, but I can't stand the thought of reading a stranger's view of Brier Hall, full of drama and gloom and melancholy.

Because I was happy for a while.

"And what's he say about it?"

"He basically says the same things I told you when you first moved in—do you remember?"

How could I forget? Meeting Rafferty Pierce on the beach, the sand under my toes and the strong breeze and a freckled, tanned, young Rafferty telling me the stories of the haunted house on the bluff.

"I remember."

"He talks about the history of this place. And honestly, no wonder everyone thinks it's haunted. There've been accidents. Suicides. Just . . . death. A lot of death." Rafferty pauses, and I know we're both thinking of Avery. "He talks about all the stories, really. But I know it's before you lived here because . . ."

"Because he doesn't write about us," I finish. And he would've. Everyone did.

I let the book fall open once more and scan the end of the chapter. No mention of the Peartrees. The final paragraphs catch my eye:

> *Some people think that the house itself chose every single one of its inhabitants. Why? No one can say—no one except Brier Hall.*
>
> *And for those who think it's strange to consider the house as if it's a living thing, I ask you this: What is a haunted house but something that has slowly grown sentient?*

I close the book hard and let it slip out of my hands. It falls with a thump to the floor, and I suddenly imagine that the windows are watching us here, and the closed front doors are keeping us inside. We are in the belly of the whale. We have been devoured.

"I want to talk to him," I say. "Maybe he can help us figure this place out."

Rafferty nods slowly. "I'll call the college and see if we can arrange a meeting with him. But Lia, you know he might say that it's all just a story. That bad things happened here, just like bad things can happen anywhere, and it doesn't mean that the house has become—*haunted*, or whatever."

I shrug, then gesture around at all the loose papers and books surrounding us. "These drawers used to be locked," I say. "They were locked when we left the house five years ago. And now they're open."

Rafferty sets down the sheaf of papers he's holding gingerly, like it might explode.

"Well, your mom probably locked them," he says. "Maybe she didn't want you as a kid to read about all the bad things that happened here."

"And now they're unlocked how . . . ?"

"Maybe your mom unlocked them too. And you just didn't know."

"Maybe," I mumble, but somehow I doubt it.

"We used to play hide-and-seek in here, do you remember?"
We were happy for a while.

I let myself smile, let myself remember. Force my thoughts away from locked drawers and locked doors. "I remember. It was one of our favorite places to hide—no, the second favorite after the briar patch."

Raff is smiling too. "Yeah, and Avery would always be the seeker."

"She said the oldest person got to be the seeker."

"She always would count to, like, two hundred."

"She just wanted some time away from us three annoying kids."

I close my eyes, remembering how the sound of Avery's loud counting would carry through the house, echoing up the stairs as we raced through the hallways, searching for hiding spots.

"I can almost hear her," I whisper. My chest is tight with longing, and I don't know if it's for the childlike nostalgia of Saturday hide-and-seek sessions or for my lost sister. Maybe both.

"Lia," I hear Rafferty whisper, and I open my eyes. I can still hear the echo of Avery counting—no, not the echo. It's getting louder.

Five, four, three, two, one.

The door to the library creaks open slowly. Small fingers curl around the edge of the door. "Ready or not, here I come!" says a voice, a loud, real voice, and then Avery—my Avery, my sister, the one I saw in the hallway, a bell jar Avery not a day older than she was when she disappeared—steps into the library.

My entire body goes cold. Avery is standing just a few feet away. My sister, but wrong. She should be older. *Think of the opposite of not growing up.*

Just stuck.

"Raff," I whisper. I don't move a muscle. I try to speak without moving my mouth. I don't blink in case she disappears when I do. "Do you see her?"

"It's not real," I hear from beside me. I don't know if Raff is saying it to me or himself. "This isn't real."

"It's not real," I echo.

Avery turns toward my voice. *She can hear me.*

Her eyes widen. *She can see me.*

Avery screams, and everything collapses around us.

That's the only way I can describe it: The room folds in on itself and Avery's screaming fills my ears, my head. I close my eyes and the screaming continues. It fills me up completely until I am not Lia anymore, I am just a scream made sentient.

What is a haunted house but something that has slowly grown sentient?

What is a haunted girl but a body overflowing with memories?

Everything is too loud, my senses are exploding around me, and when it suddenly all drops away—completely, the silence leaving a ringing behind—I open my eyes and find I'm alone.

No Rafferty.

No Avery.

The room is spotless; the mess of papers and books on the floor is gone. I carefully get up, my legs shaky and weak beneath me, and grab onto the desk to steady myself. I try the drawers: locked.

I close my eyes again, the panic rising within me, hot and fast. I sink to the floor and bend over, tucking myself into a tiny ball. I saw Avery—and Avery saw me. I'll think about what it means later because Avery's not here now—no one is. I'm alone in a quiet, locked library. A very different library from the one I left behind.

I grip the leg of the carved mahogany desk and squeeze. It's strong. Real.

"This is not real," I whisper. "Get a grip."

It didn't work when I panicked at school. It doesn't work now.

I wonder what my mom would think of me, her perfect, poised, straight-A's daughter, as I run to the door of the library and hammer on the wood. Hang on the doorknob; it doesn't turn and I'm not surprised. I'm not supposed to be in this place. This isn't the same Brier I was in before—or maybe it's exactly the same Brier and I'm just a fly caught in a different strand of its web.

Either way. "Let me out!" I scream until my throat is raw. How hard would I have to hit until the door disintegrated under my hands?

And then—

The door opens. I fall forward, a tumble of tears and torn nails.

"It's okay," Rafferty mumbles against my hair as I sink against him. I feel featherlight touches on my arms, the sound of Ali whispering frantically, "It's okay, Lia. You're safe now."

"What happened?" I try to whisper. The words come out cracked and broken.

"You were gone," Rafferty said. "I don't know. You were there, and then I think I saw Avery. And then suddenly I was alone. You just were . . . gone. Lost."

Once upon a time I would've told him that I could never get lost in Brier Hall, but now I know that's not true, not true at all.

SEVENTEEN

The three of us head to the car in a silent parade, but the air around us crackles with everything unsaid and raging beneath. Raff leads the way, my keys jangling too loudly from his fingers, and Ali follows, her eyes stormy. I trail behind them both, just feeling . . . empty. I don't want to close my eyes in case when I open them I'm all alone once more, a lost little girl trapped in an abandoned estate full of deserted rooms.

I know I should be tired, but I'm not.

I know I should be scared, but I'm not.

I'm just hollow. Not hungry, not tired, not cold, not scared. It's like I'm slowly ceasing to be a real person. Like I'm slowly ceasing to exist.

Raff is the one to start driving, steering carefully along the winding gravel path. The curlicued gate appears through the mist before us, locked tight.

"Will you get the gate?" Raff asks, the first words he's said since our frantic reunion in the entrance hall.

I get out of the car and head toward the gate. *You were just gone. Lost.* Raff had looked so scared when he'd said it, and that had hardened something within me. Raff was supposed to be the one who didn't believe. Who had an explanation. Who wasn't frightened of the house on the bluff. And so I'd tamped down my racing heart and brushed away my tears and stepped into Raff's role with a brisk, "It's okay, I'm fine. Let's go to Redlake and find this Anderson Carlisle guy—I have some questions for him."

I reach the gate and pull on the lock, suddenly wondering if the house knows we're trying to figure it out, and if it likes being unfathomable too much to allow us to speculate. For a moment nothing happens, and then the chain comes free and I push the gates wide open, allowing the car to pass through. My hand tingles, and I look down at it, at the scar that bisects my palm. This is the place where I received this scar, falling upon the gravel in a frantic bid to open the gate and get us out of here.

My scar is bleeding. It's open, the skin jagged, just like the night when I got it, when Avery disappeared. Red covers my palm, dripping down my wrist. Falls to the gravel below.

No. I clench my palm shut. It's just a memory, that's all. The scar has been healed for years, the bumpy white line nothing but scar tissue now, nerveless and numb.

"Lia?" Ali's voice comes from the cracked window. "What's wrong?"

I open my palm and breathe a quick sigh of relief. The scar is there, old and healed. It's not bleeding. *It hasn't bled in five years, Lia.* But as I hurry to the car, I pretend I can't see the drops of blood on the gravel where I stood.

"Is everything okay?"

I nod at my sister as I slide into the passenger's seat, unable to reply. Unable to lie.

I can tell she sees right through me. But she just says, "Then let's go," and kicks the back of the driver's seat.

Raff drives through the gates, and the gates let us go. We wind our way down from Brier Hall, and when we turn onto the main street of Eastwind everything seems so *normal* that I want to laugh. While we've been getting lost among the many twisting rooms of Brier Hall, Eastwind has gone on around us, utterly ordinary. Even though mist hangs heavy, teens in swimsuits, shorts, and flip-flops pace along the cracked sidewalk toward the beach, uncaring of the chill in the air. One of them catches my eye as I stare at them out the window, but there's no recognition there. Eastwind has forgotten its most infamous family. I know I should feel relieved, but I mostly just feel sad. Once upon a time this place loved me. *Knew* me. And now I'm just a memory.

The disconnect of Brier Hall versus the real world continues as we turn onto the highway and drive up the coast: Glimpses of the dark ocean flash through heavy groves of cypress trees and collections of coastal communities pop in and out of existence as we race straight through them. After being in Brier everything feels too vast. I'd almost forgotten the outside world exists.

It takes us just over an hour to get to Redlake, a small beachy town bordering the Pacific on one side and the sandy banks of a large lake on the other. The lake, despite the name, is a mix of murky indigo and sky-reflected cerulean without even a hint of red.

We follow small wooden signs to the local college campus, nestled on one side of the lake. It's a small assortment of bungalow buildings with students milling about, sitting in groups on the lakeshore or chatting happily away at the picnic tables nearby. Everyone looks so normal, so happy.

"It's like a different world," Rafferty murmurs as he parks, and I nod slowly.

The air feels lighter here, away from Brier, but my body desperately aches to return. Maybe I'm not meant to be in light places. Maybe I'm made to be in darkness. In silent locked libraries. Underwater, down, down, down . . .

"Lia?" I look up to see both Raff and Ali out of the car, staring in at me as I sit in the front seat, gripping my seat belt tightly with both hands. I loosen my hold and give a shaky laugh. *You're fine. Everything's fine.*

"Sorry," I say, and follow them out into the hazy sunlight that pushes weakly through the mist.

Rafferty leads the way, following directions on his phone. He talks too loudly, narrating everything as if he's trying to desperately push away the real reason we're here. Ali and I trudge along in his wake, letting his history lesson on Redlake wash over us like a wave.

We turn down a dead-end road, set back from the rest of the buildings and half hidden behind a cypress tree. It's a coastal bungalow painted the same dark blue-gray as the mist: It almost disappears. It's a building that wants to remain unobtrusive. A building that doesn't want to be seen. A small section of the lake is visible, but there're no students here, and the noise from the main campus is muffled in the fog.

We file inside. It's a long hallway, painted white. The first door leading off has a nameplate, and etched into the shiny silver is DR. ANDERSON CARLISLE.

"He wrote a book about our house and he's never even lived there," Ali's voice cuts through the silence. She leans forward to peer at the nameplate, eyes narrowed.

"He knows things we don't," I reply. "He can help." I try to infuse my voice with surety, hoping it will convince her and me both. "He knows the history, Ali. He knows things that happened there years and years ago. Maybe he even knew our dad."

Ali's lip curls. "Well then, poor him," she says.

I raise my hand to the door and for a moment I think Ali might try to stop me, but when I knock she just crosses her arms and takes a step back.

There's a pause, and then a deep voice says, "Come in, please."

The room inside is every inch a professor's office. Wall-to-wall shelves are packed with books, and papers overflow in great tottering piles. A man is sitting behind a desk covered with documents, a mug of steaming coffee in his hand. He's older than the photo from the book and his curls are now salt-and-pepper streaked, but he's obviously Anderson Carlisle, the author of the book Rafferty found in Brier Hall's library. He looks perfectly professor-ish, with a wrinkled beige shirt and contrasting tie and round tortoiseshell glasses. He surveys the three of us, his eyes drifting from Rafferty to Ali before resting on me.

"Hello, Dr. Carlisle," I say.

"Hello, Lia," he says, his voice serious and quiet. "Call me Anderson." He gestures to three spindly chairs packed in among the detritus of years of academia. "Please, sit."

We do, and there's a strange silence for a moment before I clear my throat. "Thank you for meeting with us on such short notice."

"It's my pleasure," he replies. "I must confess, I have long wanted to meet the Peartree family."

"You knew who I was, then," I say. "When we called. You already knew." I already know the answer; I can tell by the way he's looking at me with his piercing dark eyes. I get the feeling that not only does he know I'm Lia Peartree, but he's also been waiting for me to show up on his doorstep.

"I did."

"Then you probably know why I'm here."

He scrutinizes me. "I have my suspicions, yes." Everything Anderson does seems measured and controlled. Nothing is rushed. He takes a sip of his coffee and stares out the window of his office. Dimly, we hear shouts of laughter filter through the air, and Anderson gives a small smile. "Students celebrating the end of another year," he says. "Of course the shores of Redlake didn't used to have such celebratory tones by its water." He takes another tiny sip of coffee. "Redlake has seen much death."

"Oh, *great*," pipes up Ali, voice dripping with sarcasm. Her foot is jiggling incessantly, drawing on all our nervous energy. "That's just what we need." Her gaze slides to Raff. "You couldn't have warned us, huh?"

"I *did*," Rafferty snaps back. "If you'd have bothered to listen to me on the way over here. A town was flooded to fill the lake. The townspeople weren't warned—they should've been, of course, but through whatever bureaucracy and miscommunications they *weren't*. And the dam was broken, and the valley was flooded, and the lake was filled." He glances at Anderson, who nods encouragingly. Rafferty continues simply, "They drowned. And their homes are still down there. An entire drowned town, just below the surface."

"Excellent summary," Anderson says, as though this is a class and we're his students.

"Oh my god," I say, my stomach churning. "That's . . . horrible."

Anderson nods. "Yes. And even with so much light around Redlake now, some of the darkness remains." He seems to savor the macabre words. "Maybe that's why I was drawn here. I always find myself drawn to dark places." His eyes meet mine. "I'm sure you understand."

We stare at each other. I don't want to admit I know exactly what he means. "We found your book," I blurt out, because I can't let myself think of dark places and drowned towns. "*Gone Home.* You call Brier Hall America's most haunted dwelling."

"I do, yes."

"Do you really believe that?"

Anderson purses his lips, then speaks slowly, eyes still fixed on the cypress tree brushing its branches up against the window, like fingers emerging from the mist. "I'm a doctor of philosophy—I'm not, in fact, a ghost hunter or any kind of expert on haunted places."

Ali pipes in, obviously frustrated by this. "You literally wrote a book about it." She turns to me. "Why'd we even come here if this guy isn't going to answer our questions?"

My face flames at Ali's rude tone, but Anderson cuts in before I can answer. "Oh, on the contrary! I mean to answer your questions the best I can."

"Why?" Ali says, folding her arms across her chest like armor. "Why even take the time?"

Anderson peers at her. "My dear, I'm a professor. My job is to help wondering students. That's why I'm here." He pauses, then continues, "To answer your first question—do I believe Brier Hall is haunted? I study the fundamental nature of the world around us; this includes things we do not fully understand. I've researched many supposedly haunted places around the world. I would say Brier Hall is one of the more . . . *unusual* places I've visited."

"You've actually been in the house?" I try to picture anyone besides us walking its halls and find I cannot.

"I have, yes. I went there when it was still occupied by the Briers themselves." He clears his throat and meets my eyes again. "It's beautiful." I don't know why he says it—does he think to flatter me? Or maybe he can see Brier inside me, peeking out, and is attempting to mollify *it*.

"So you really believe that it's haunted?" The words come out desperately: I want him to *say* it. I want to know it's not all in my head. I'm not even sure how much I trust him—he seems to enjoy discussing morbid stories a bit too much—but I need someone outside Brier Hall to validate what I believe.

"I think," he begins, and he speaks ponderously, like he's weighing each and every word. "I think that Brier Hall is old. And old things have long memories. Old things remember. Brier Hall has stood on that bluff for hundreds of years; it's been in the Brier family for generations. It's had many iterations of families, but none have affected it so much as the final owners. The Peartree girls. You."

Ali leans forward, fixing Anderson with a serious gaze, and she drops the sarcastic tone. "We weren't supposed to own it. It was in our father's family—the Briers—not ours, not really. We didn't even know them. We barely knew *him* at all. It wasn't supposed to come to us."

"Or maybe it was," Anderson replies. "Maybe you were exactly who it wanted."

"How can it want things?" I whisper. I want to trust Anderson. But I can't help seeing the way his eyes glint behind his glasses, and I get the distinct impression that he's enjoying this. For a moment I wonder if this conversation will appear on some podcast, or in the news. Some five-year anniversary special of the Flight from Brier Hall, and we've just given Anderson one-on-one time with his biggest story yet. *Don't be cynical, Lia.* "It's just a house." Even as I speak the words, they don't feel true.

Anderson takes another sip of coffee. "Just a house? Is anything really *just* anything? Brier Hall is full of centuries of residual memories—some good, most bad, and all extremely strong—and those kinds of memories stick. And that's why I wouldn't call the house haunted, not exactly. It's not haunted *by* anything. The entire estate is just one huge tenacious tangle of memories and energy and history, all wrapped up in something *house-shaped.* It's something much more than *just* a house."

I think of Brier Hall, hidden from view in the mist and fog, its windows watching the waves break below in the cove. I think of it as a wild thing, an awake thing, a thing with a beating heart in its tower and veins stretching throughout its walls. A thing made alive by feeding off the Briers who came before. And then us. *Avery.*

Rafferty has pursed his lips, and I can't tell how much of this is sinking in for him, how much he's believing. Ali is stone-faced, her eyes also on the cypress tree reaching out of the mist, so I can't read her, either.

"What happened there?" It's what I'm thinking, so when the words come from next to me, I'm a little surprised, as if my voice has

ISABEL STRYCHACZ

come out of another body. Ali is leaning forward toward Anderson. "You said Brier Hall had a lot of bad memories. And it's apparently belonged to the Briers for years. So what happened there?"

Anderson considers for a moment, then taps his lip and says, "At the start, I think it wasn't so much the house but the family. They came from Redlake—did you know that? I suppose that's important. Yes, the Briers relocated before the valley was flooded. It's almost as if they knew."

"So the Briers moved to Eastwind? And the rest of the town—"

"As your friend told you," Anderson cuts in, nodding at Raff, then gesturing out at the slice of lake we can see through the window. "They are down there still."

I shiver, the sick feeling returning. I can taste salt in my mouth, just like the shot of vodka that turned to salt water. *Down, down, down . . .*

"But there have been stories about Brier Hall ever since they moved in. I mean, look at it."

All of us turn, almost unconsciously, to face the window, where somewhere miles away through the mist sits the house on the hill. I know exactly what Anderson means. Brier Hall, with its ivy-covered front and twisting briar patches, invites the stories in.

"Eastwind seemed to think the Brier family was bad luck," he says. "After all, the whole family avoided death very mysteriously."

"Wouldn't that mean they were good luck, then?" Rafferty asks.

"You've been in Brier Hall," Anderson says. "Does it feel like it has good luck there to you?"

Rafferty doesn't even need to reply. We all know the answer.

190

"And the bad things that happened there . . ." I prompt, trying not to sound desperate. I need to *know.*

"Yes—the bad things. I'll tell you what I know, but I can't prove anything—you understand. They were just stories."

"Is anything really *just* anything?" I echo, and for a moment there's silence.

"There were strange deaths," Anderson says softly. "And disappearances too. One by one the town of Eastwind would see less and less of the Briers, and the story was that they were just . . . gone. Swallowed up by the house. Swallowed up by the sea, the water finally reclaiming them, when they had avoided its clutches the first time. Who knows? And then others started going missing too. The Briers would hold parties and some people were just . . . never seen again. The Briers, of course, had reasons: they moved away, they left town."

"No one was suspicious?" Rafferty sounds dumbstruck, and I wonder if his ironclad logic-fueled certainty about Brier Hall and its grip on the town is finally breaking down.

"No one could prove anything," Anderson says. "And I think everyone was varying degrees of frightened by them. The Brier family swept into town like a storm, and destruction seemed to follow them."

My family. The Brier name doesn't feel like mine, but destruction has followed me too, so maybe the Briers and the Peartrees are closer than I ever realized. Still, I am suddenly intensely, overwhelmingly relieved our last name is Peartree, and that my mother never changed hers to become a Brier. I imagine briar thorns, prickly and cutting, wrapping themselves around a stalwart pear tree, around *us,* tighter and tighter. My childhood hideout in the briar patch always made me feel safe and secure, but now the mere thought of curling myself up below the thorny vines makes me shiver.

I tune back in to find that Anderson is still speaking. "It wasn't just disappearances, though. Soon after, the deaths began. People would go up to the estate and be found the next morning, dead with not a scratch on them. Just lying there in the grass in the orchard, or on the cliff's edge, peaceful as anything, as if they'd just fallen asleep."

"Murdered?" Rafferty asks, and Anderson shrugs.

"Perhaps. Or perhaps some sort of heart issue, something undiagnosed. That is the most obvious reason—and Occam's razor, of course, says that the simplest explanation is probably the likeliest."

I think of it: statue-still people lying quietly in view of the house's windows. Not asleep under the crab apple trees, though, as I'd often done when we lived there. Just gone. It didn't sound like the most likely explanation to me, but I couldn't think of what else it could be. Is *haunted* ever the simplest explanation?

"But you don't think it was any of those reasons," I blurt out. "Like I said: You wrote a whole book on Brier Hall, calling it haunted."

"I could've written what I thought would sell," Anderson replies smoothly.

"But you didn't, did you? You wrote it because you *do* believe it. I can *tell* you believe it." I meet his gaze and I know that I'm right. "You don't think those people were murdered. You don't think they had heart problems."

"Tell me, Lia, what do I think happened, then?"

Anderson's eyes are very bright, locked on mine. There's a challenge there. He wants me to admit to something, but I'm not sure what.

"Something's wrong with the house," I say, not as a question. Anderson sips his coffee.

"Please, answer yes or no—is the house haunted?"

Anderson surveys me, his eyes still bright. "Yes," he says.

I ignore Rafferty's tiny sigh from next to me: I'm not sure he'll ever truly believe, even with all the strange things that have happened in the past couple days.

"Are the Briers haunting the house?"

"In a way," Anderson repeats. "I don't think you'll find poltergeists in the halls of your house, but you might find other things that have gotten trapped there. Brier Hall has stood for centuries—it's had many, many owners. Many people who have come and gone, who Brier has claimed. Brier is haunted by memories and grief and stories."

For the first time I try to imagine the Briers who lived there before us: the mysterious family who arrived from a drowned town and settled in their new house on a hill. The Briers who disappeared, just like Avery. The ones who died, just like my father.

"My father died in the house of unknown causes," I tell Anderson. He nods. "I know."

"Do you think that's true?"

"Your father was the last Brier to live in the house," Anderson says slowly. "I think the house wanted you . . . but a place can't be full of Briers for that long without keeping some of the thorns."

This doesn't quite sink in fully, as I try to imagine my faceless father, son of a crooked legacy, heir to a crooked throne, bequeathed a crooked house. All alone up in the house, aimlessly wandering the same hallways I wandered.

"This all sounds . . . hard to believe," says Rafferty.

"Some things don't care if you believe in them or not," Anderson says, and I remember Ali saying almost the same thing to me when I first arrived. And maybe she's right: Brier Hall stands alone, and it will haunt us whether we believe in it or not. I know exactly what Anderson means when he talks about the memories and stories haunting the house. Even when I'm not physically at the house, it haunts me still, in memories and dreams. I can't forget it, no matter how hard I try. And I am the ghost of my past self, and Ali is of hers. And Avery . . . the memory of Avery haunts us every minute. And our father, his family. All the Briers who we don't know, who are still a part of us. If Anderson's right, they are lost—but not gone.

Lost but not gone. The thought scares me and intrigues me at the same time. If the spirits of Briers are tied to the hall—does that mean Avery is too? And if so, how do we find her?

Anderson sets down his empty coffee mug and stands up from the desk with a small cough, a polite yet clear dismissal. He continues, "Of course, this is all hypothetical. There's no scientific evidence to suggest a haunting. All we know is that odd things happen in that house. Take this old professor's words with a grain of salt."

"I will," Ali says, her voice hard. She stands up and picks her way through the stacks of books, arms crossed tightly across her chest. "First you say the house is haunted, but then you say there're no ghosts lurking around in the walls."

Anderson smiles. "I never said there aren't ghosts in Brier Hall. I can only tell you my suspicions. You came to find out more about the house's history, and I've provided that. Any conclusions you come to based on that and your experiences . . . well, that is completely up to you."

Ali huffs. "Helpful." She turns and heads into the hallway, the white clinical paint making her seem insubstantial. For a moment I am gripped with the fear that she'll disappear into the wall, and I'll be the only Peartree sister left. Rafferty shoots me a look and, with a swift apology to Anderson, follows her.

"I'm sorry for my sister," I say to Anderson awkwardly.

"There's no need," he says. "She's scared. And she should be."

I go cold at his words, but colder at his next ones.

"You be careful up there, Lia Peartree."

"I'm being careful," I whisper, gripping the doorframe, wishing I'd left with Ali and Raff. I feel pinned in place by Anderson's gaze, and once again, I get the feeling the old professor is enjoying the ghoulish tales and our fear just a bit.

"Good," Anderson says, sitting back down at his desk and flipping nonchalantly through a thick tome. The branch of the cypress tree scrapes across the windowpane, making me jump. "Because like I said, Brier remembers. I think it wanted something it never got from the Briers. You gave it love, affection. You called it home, in a way I don't think any of its inhabitants did before. And now that it has got you back, I don't think it will want to let you go again."

HOMECOMING

What did you want to know? That I called and called and the Briers came? That they left their houses and lives and came to start anew in the safety of the hall?

That the lake ran red?

I would have told you how the Briers uprooted. How they knew I'd entangled them, how they could feel the pull, how they despised it. How it didn't matter, because by then they were caught—*saved, I'd saved them*—and there was nowhere to go back to.

What did you want to know? That the more I tried to make them love me, the more they hated me? I would've told you how I clung to them, how they found my heart and tried to destroy it.

What did you want to know? There were parties held, and sometimes a Brier would try to leave, try to run. Giggling and gasping and running barefoot down the drive.

I wouldn't let them go.

I *saved* them.

They'd be found, later: George in the apple orchard, Sarah by the cliff. Molly-May in the library, Joshua and Oliver together in the cove. Stern people from Eastwind took the bodies away, and I let it happen, because I had the best parts of them anyways, and they couldn't leave me now.

And I suppose you would want to know about the final Brier, Montgomery, the last of them all. He left for a while, but I called him home. He didn't want to come. He tried to leave again, he tried to burn everything to the ground.

And so I saved him too.

Come home, Montgomery, come home! Off the cliff, into the waves. *Down, down, down.* And then I was alone, but it wasn't long before I felt Montgomery's Brier blood stir in someone new.

Come home, Lia, come home!

Yes, there were so many others, before you.

But you loved me most. You loved me best.

t's dark outside the library's windows, the pitch-darkness that comes when the lights of Eastwind turn off and the fog rolls in and covers the stars. Somehow the day has fled, but Rafferty's watch still says only a few hours have passed. My mind has been whirling ever since our visit with Anderson Carlisle, spinning as it tries to piece together what's happening at Brier Hall. Fragments of memories and dreams and the cold water of the cove and my sister's laughs and being lost in a maze and things that might not have even really happened cloud my head until I can't parse out one thought from the next.

We drove home in near silence, each of us lost in our own little world, mulling over the professor's words.

Rafferty breaks the quiet first. "What do you think about all staying in here tonight?" he asks, gesturing to the stacks of books surrounding us.

I've moved closer to him and I tentatively reach out, waiting to see how he'll respond. He lets me lean against his side, but his muscles are tensed. I know things are weird between us, and being here makes him nervous, regardless of what he does or doesn't believe about the house. I focus on the way we breathe in and out at the same time—*I'm still here, still alive.*

I nod in answer. "Safety in numbers," I say, although it sounds hollow even to my ears. It hasn't helped us much so far.

"Ali and I will get things ready down here," Raff says, and I don't see the look he shoots her over my head, but she doesn't say a word. She just stares out the window at the inky blackness outside and crosses her arms. "Lia, are you sure you're okay after this morning, and after that visit with Professor Carlisle?"

"I'm fine," I say. I haven't looked in a mirror since yesterday, and I'm sure I look a mess after this morning's terrifying drop into unreality and our ensuing meeting with Anderson, but it's ingrained in me to say *I'm fine* to everything.

"You just look pale, that's all," Raff says finally.

"I'm fine," I echo, but the words sound brittle. Everything Anderson said is whipping through my head, and I can't quite make sense of any of it.

When I turn to look at Raff, he's staring back at me like I'm made of glass. My eyes flick to my sister. Ali isn't looking at me at all.

"Why don't you go and just . . . take a minute?"

I suddenly want out of this room so badly it's painful. I hate how everyone is looking at me, like I'm about to break. I hurry away from Rafferty's side and leave the room.

When I close the bathroom door behind me, I wait silently for a moment, palms pressed against the door, in case Rafferty has followed me up. Armed with soft words and apologies. Maybe a gentle touch. I want it desperately, just for a second: I could collapse with the need to be held.

He doesn't come.

I guess I don't really know why I expected him to. Everything— all the past and present colliding in just a few moments—is still so weird between us. Our bodies are heavy with past memories, but not much else. I remind myself again I don't know this Raff, not really, and I can't expect him to be the Raff of my memories, who would run after me without a moment's thought.

He doesn't care, I tell myself. Fingers curl against themselves. *He doesn't have to care.*

When I finally move away from the door, I see that the bathroom is dusty, unused. As it should be. It's a dark, gothic room with mahogany wainscoting and malbec-painted walls covered in a wild assortment of gold-framed paintings, yellowed illustrations of anatomy, and glass boxes of pinned moths. The edge of a clawfoot tub peeks out from behind the mirrored dressing screen. I cross the room to the sink and run the water for a while until it's cold and clear and the basin is clean once more.

My eyes flick up to the mirror, at the me in the reflection. The *many* mes: the grimy ornate mirror over the sink reflects the mirrored screen as well, and I'm multiplied into millions. In these facing mirrors, I am infinite, and the infinite Lias watch and echo as I grip the edge of the sink and peer more closely at myself.

God, no wonder both Raff and Ali have been tiptoeing around me ever since we got back from Redlake. I look like death: My skin is too pale, stretched across my cheekbones. My pupils are fully blown out, swallowing the irises around them, and my hair has almost completely fallen out of the messy bun I tied it up in this morning. I barely recognize myself at all.

All I can see in my gaunt face and shaking hands is Ali.

Don't think about her.

Ali, and how her voice cracked even through a whisper when she told me I was safe, after I escaped the silent library and burst back into reality. The first real thing I heard after the thick silence of the empty, locked library and my own panicked screams that echoed through it.

Ali, and how she asked me if I was okay in the car, seeing right through me even when I lied.

Don't think about it.

I fill the sink basin with water and splash my face, the cold a welcome shock to my system, and then wipe my face on my sleeve and turn toward the door.

Movement in my peripherals: definite enough that I pause, gaze locked on the far wall where a huge downy moth is trapped in its glass cage, but swift enough that I immediately tell myself I imagined it. Still, I can't turn toward the mirror. I'm pinned in place just as the moth is. My vision turns watery; I refuse to blink.

The moth flaps its wings.

No, that can't be right. *You didn't see that, Lia.* The moth is still.

I shift my eyes to the side, where I can see just a sliver of the mirror. The infinite Lias are all lined up and also turned, held in time. Frozen, just as I am frozen.

I crook my pinkie, and the infinite Lias echo my barest hint of movement in a sinuous line.

I take a breath, my rib cage expanding painfully with thirty seconds of held air. So do they.

I'm about to turn away, and I watch as the other Lias turn too.

Except . . . except one Lia doesn't. Even seeing it in my peripherals, my mind can't comprehend what's happening. Can't comprehend how my reflection stays facing forward and watches me go with black-hole eyes.

The first flash of movement I saw in the mirror made me freeze up and flee—*stay still with all your arms and legs inside the bed so the monsters don't know you're awake.* Now my body surges with adrenaline as somewhere ancestral inside it recognizes a threat and prepares for a fight.

I turn and face my reflection fully. She stares back at me, almost identical but . . . something is different, and when I walk unsteadily toward the mirror she does too, but her movements are sure and calm.

I wonder if my head and heart will believe me if I try to tell them this isn't really happening. If I try to forget, to block it out, like I've been doing for the past five years.

And maybe that's what I've been doing wrong all this time. I can't fight something I can't see. I can't fix something I don't believe is real.

It's like at the Safeway, back in sun-drenched, ghostless Daley. I blink and the scene changes. *Blink*—the Lia in the mirror blinks back at me, off tempo. *Blink*—the Lia in the mirror has something in her hand. Lipstick. She uncaps it as I stand before the sink, as if I too am molded from ceramic. *Blink*—she places the tip of the lipstick on the mirror and writes slowly, her eyes never leaving mine. She must be writing backward, because the words look right side up to me. We have the same handwriting. The four words are written in stark ruby red.

Turn around
Bright eyes

I blink, and when I open my eyes again, a part of me expects to see a clean mirror. But the words are still there. It's just that the face behind them is different now.

I stare at my thirteen-year-old self. She stares back at me through the mirror, her eyes wide and scared. Little me. She's both familiar and not: just someone I used to know.

The tube of lipstick is heavy in my hands. I can't quite remember how it got there as I let it fall and stretch my fingers toward the mirror. My little reflection reaches out too, echoing my every movement. As if we're one, as if we're the same.

But we are not the same.

My fingers touch glass. The lipstick words smudge under my fingers and I stare at my bright red fingertips. The lipstick is on my side of the mirror now. The little Lia's tiny fingers are pressed against mine, but I can't feel them.

There's nothing but a sheet of glass and infinite worlds between us.

I can see the little Lia trembling through the mirror. She's more afraid than I am. Can it be possible she's real somewhere? My mind bypasses all thoughts of this impossibility.

Am I truly looking at myself?

Little me's mouth opens just as mine does, at exactly the same time.

As if we're the same.

When we speak, I see her mouth shape words and I realize we're whispering the same thing to each other.

"Who are you?"

US AND OUR SHADOWS

You remember now, don't you?

You remember waking up. No moon, nothing. You remember the darkness, and the confusion of not realizing why your eyes are open.

Until you hear the footsteps. The running.

At first you think it's Avery, or your mom. Because who else would it be? Who else would be careening down the hallways in the dead of night? You can tell the thing outside is screaming but the words are muffled, as if all your senses are underwater.

Are you underwater?

This doesn't feel like a dream but what else could it be?

Ali has woken up from the other bed, her eyes wide as they lock onto the door, where the handle is being turned this way and that. Violently. Whatever is out there is desperate to come in.

"What do we do?" Ali whispers to you, even though you're littler and it's supposed to be her who knows what do. It usually is her, but not now, not in the darkness.

You remember now, don't you? How just before you are about to respond, the banging on the door stops, ceasing immediately as if it had never been there at all. The screaming too is gone. The room seems larger when it's heavy with silence. Ali's panicked breathing is louder than usual. You can hear it in every corner of the bedroom.

You creep to the door, and you tell yourself that you're not

afraid but it's a lie. You're terrified and yet you move closer anyways, drawn onward. You're unable to help yourself.

You throw the door open, the soundtrack of Ali sobbing from
under the covers a strange comfort. There's no one there. Of course
there is no one there. Looking out at the empty hallway, a part of
you realizes that's exactly what you expected.

How did you know you would find an empty hallway?

Because you understand the inner clockwork of Brier Hall?
Because a part of you has realized something that your brain hasn't
yet? Because you're special?

Because you're special.

Down the hallway, the bathroom door is ajar, and light seeps
out into the corridor, casting shadowy figures on the walls that
jump and leer. Ah—it all makes sense now. It's Avery in the bathroom. Your mind is relieved at the easy solution, the answer that
makes sense. Avery in the bathroom—yes.

Of course it is.

"Avery?" you whisper down the hallway, waiting for your sister's blond braid to appear in the slightly open doorway. There's no
answer, so you tiptoe down the hall toward the light.

You are the moth.

"Avery?"

The door creaks under your touch, inching open to reveal a
bathroom containing everything a bathroom might have except,
of course, your sister. You walk over to the mirror above the sink
and stare, watching the reflection and refraction of millions of
nightgown-clad Lias.

For a second you think you do see Avery somewhere behind

you. The person in the mirror—behind you in the mirror?—isn't you. You whirl around to face—nobody.

"Avery?" Your voice quavers now. The fear sets in, the kind that settles deep within you. You begin to wish you hadn't left your room, hadn't left your bed, hadn't left your family's old, crowded apartment. You begin to wish you had never come here at all, but like all wishes of this sort, it's most certainly too late.

You turn back to the mirror and the wrongness settles over you like a cape.

You're not there. That's what hits you first: You can feel your body, the way your bare feet are cold on the black-and-white tiles, the dryness of your mouth. But in the mirror there's no one there at all.

You look behind you again, quickly, sure that you can feel someone else's breath on your neck, someone standing—looming— behind you. No. There's no one. You turn back to the mirror.

There's red writing there, words that you've been hearing for months now, echoing throughout the house.

A memory—weeks ago, sitting in the kitchen, seeing something through the open kitchen doorway that made you scream, something impossible that you pushed out of your mind right after, when your mom was frantically trying to calm you down . . .

You remember now, don't you?

You remember how you blink and you're back in the mirror and—it's okay, it was all a dream—the relief only lasts for a split second because it's not you in the mirror at all. It's an adult, someone older. Someone you've never seen before. Blond hair. Hollow eyes. A mouth like Avery's. A mouth like—yours.

You remember now, don't you?

How the fear becomes fear with a capital *F*.

How you step forward and put a finger to the glass, almost expecting it to shatter.

How you lean close and whisper, "Who are you?"

NINETEEN

Memories come fragmented, hurtling toward me before turning left at the last minute, right before I fully catch them. But I remember some things. I remember enough.

My mind is a maelstrom. It's trying to make sense of what it's seen, what it's realized.

I try to put the whirling thoughts in order. Here is one thing I know to be true: five years ago, I went into the bathroom and stared at a different face in the mirror. I didn't know who it was then, but now I am on the other side of the mirror and I know exactly who I saw that night.

Myself.

I stare into the mirror, gripping the edges of the sink, those four innocuous words burning themselves into my head. In the kitchen, five years ago: Now I know exactly what we saw back then that made us all scream. Not ghosts. Not intruders.

Us. I saw *us*.

So what does that mean? Think, Lia. You're smart, you're an A+ student. *Think*. The porcelain of the sink is cold beneath my fingers; it might be the only real thing in the world right now.

All that I learned during our time at Redlake is joining with what I just experienced, what I remember. Anderson telling us that he thought the house was a maze full of memories. *The entire estate*

is just one huge tenacious tangle of memories and energy and history,
all wrapped up in something house-shaped.

Layers of memories and spirits gobbled up by this place, all stacked on top of one another. I'm in one now . . . my fingers drift to the words written on the mirror once more, to touch the lipstick and assure myself it's really there. I remember feeling when I walked up the front drive just a day ago that the years collapsed in on themselves.

What if they did?

All the footsteps, all the banging, all the shifting rooms and disembodied voices that scared us so badly as children . . . all those things *did* happen in the house, just in a different part of its maze. And we heard the echoes. That's all I am: an echo.

I leave the bathroom, walking slowly down the hall as I try to consolidate my thoughts into something normal enough to present to Raff and Ali. *We're trapped in a layer cake of memories* won't quite do the trick.

As I walk by the door to the tower, it suddenly swings open. Just a crack, like someone's pushed it from the other side.

It takes all my effort to keep walking. To pretend I don't see it, feel the pull of *come here, come here.* I swear I hear a little voice say it.

I come back into the library so silently that it takes both Rafferty and Ali a second to notice I've returned. They're arguing—what's new. I can't bring myself to care.

I have to tell them.

I can't tell them.

How the hell do I tell them?

Finally they both look up, and Raff immediately looks concerned when he sees me just *standing*, staring out the window at the fog. I know I should pretend everything's normal, but normality is too far gone now. Normality is just another layer in this place, and I've slipped past it.

"Are you feeling better?" Rafferty asks.

Ali steps forward, eyes narrowed as she stares at me. "What happened?" she asks brusquely. "What happened up there?"

I open my mouth, ready for the *nothing* to spill out, but it doesn't come. "I . . . don't know."

"Something weird?" Raff asks, and all I can manage is a nod. I don't know why I don't feel more frightened. I don't even feel full of adrenaline anymore. I just feel a strange sense of numbness. Of unreality.

"Something weird, yeah."

"What was it?" Ali asks.

I take a deep breath. "I think . . . we need to calm down. Think of this rationally."

Ali raises an eyebrow. "Rationally?"

She's right—there's nothing rational about what goes on in the walls of Brier Hall.

"I think—I think I know what's happening."

Raff's fingers tighten around my arm, and for the first time I realize he's holding me up. I don't even remember when he came over to me. My thoughts have skidded past everything except the little me in the mirror and the red lipstick smudged on my fingertips. I let Raff direct me to one of the velvet wingback reading chairs and I sink gratefully into it.

"What are you talking about?" Ali asks, her voice rising aggressively.

No matter how I start this sentence, it will seem unbelievable. "I think," I begin hesitantly, "that it's just like Anderson said. There're *layers* to this place."

"Layers," Ali says flatly.

"A labyrinth?" says Rafferty.

"Maybe labyrinth isn't the right word," I say, locking eyes with Rafferty, trying to block everything else out. Trying to make him believe it, to make him understand. "Maybe a *maze* is better. It's just like Anderson said. So much happened here . . . and I think that somehow it all sunk into the walls, and all those lives are tied to this house, still able to affect us. This place is wild. This place is *alive*."

"You sound just like that professor," Ali says.

I ignore her. "It all makes sense—the things I've been seeing. The flowers dead, and then alive, and then dead—I'm just seeing a different layer of Brier somewhere in its maze."

"What, like a different time?" Rafferty sounds like he's trying to be supportive while still being inwardly incredulous.

"No, not a time, not exactly. Another reality, almost. All these Brier Halls pressed up against one another so tightly that sometimes we catch a glimpse of another one. A door closes here, but it might just be a door closing in a different layer." A door to a locked tower creaking open here, and in another layer, the two best friends unlocking it. Hearing ghostly echoes in the library, and in another layer, an older sister plays hide-and-seek. Looking in a mirror here, and in a different layer, the same-but-different girl looks back. I don't quite know how to bring up *that* particular experience.

"If that's true, what does it mean?"

I take a deep breath. "I think it means that some of the things we're experiencing here—and experienced back then—were caused by two layers pressing against each other. A layer of reality from right now, and one from five years ago. I'm saying that . . ." I pause. "I'm saying that some of the things that happened here, some of what we remember . . . was caused by ourselves in another layer of Brier."

Two sets of eyes stare at me uncomprehendingly.

And then: "You're saying we imagined it," Ali says flatly, then rounds on Raff. "Well, doesn't that just sound like exactly what our dear ol' bestie Rafferty has been saying this whole time. That we made all this up inside our heads. That none of it was real."

"What the hell, Ali?" Raff retorts. "I had nothing to do with any of this. I never said you made it up in your head."

"You did," Ali continues, interrupting him. "You act all innocent but you just want to be part of something, part of the drama, just like back then." She slides her eyes back to me. "Bringing him here was such a stupid mistake, Lia. I had everything handled and—"

"Stop it!" I snap. None of this big reveal is going the way I imagined—although, I suppose I shouldn't have expected that both Ali and Raff would nod in awe and understanding. "First of all, Ali, you had nothing handled. How could you? You don't know what's going on here. But I do, okay? I really think I do." I take a deep breath. "When I was in the bathroom, I looked in the mirror, and I saw myself as a kid."

"If you say Lia imagined this too . . ." Ali snarls, trailing off warningly.

Rafferty spreads his hands. "Ali, I literally said *nothing*."

"Stop it," I snap. "I saw myself. I didn't *imagine* myself as I was back then. I mean she was there, and we . . . we weren't in sync."

Quiet follows this.

"You weren't in sync?" Ali says.

"Are you trying to say that she wasn't a reflection?" Raff interjects.

"Yes," I whisper. "I'm saying she wasn't a reflection."

"Lia . . ."

"No, listen. I also remembered things—things I'd forgotten. Moments from when we lived here. Just last night, when I ran through the halls, when I thought I saw Avery? Ali . . ." I turn to her beseechingly. "Don't you remember when we *heard* someone running at night, screaming? Don't you remember the person trying to get in?" I continue on without waiting for Ali's reaction. "And five years ago when we lived here, I saw something in the mirror. A person who wasn't me. Well—" I break off with a short laugh. "A person I didn't *know* was me at the time. After leaving Brier I forgot, or blocked it out, but now . . . now I think I might've seen myself from tonight."

"That's impossible," Rafferty says, and although he says it gently, kindly, Ali turns a look of barely leashed fury on him.

"How can you say that?" she demands. "After all the shit we've seen, how can you *still* cling to your impossibles?"

For once I agree with my sister. "Time not working correctly is impossible," I say. "Me disappearing and reappearing from the library is impossible. And yet here we are. How is it possible? I don't know. How is any of this possible? I don't think Brier Hall cares much about impossibilities, if I'm being honest. So will you both *listen* to me?"

"I'm sorry," Raff says, nodding. "I'll listen."

Ali rolls her eyes but doesn't retort, so I take that for a *yes*.

"Just like Anderson said: I don't think we've been experiencing ghosts. I think that we've been experiencing ourselves, just in a different layer of reality. And the house has been pulling us back all this time, trying to bring us home."

"So what you're saying is," Ali starts, then breaks off and shakes her head, looking down at her tightly clenched fingers.

"I'm saying," I continue, "that Brier Hall *is* haunted. I think we've been haunting ourselves."

Ali is shaking her head more, eyes firmly locked on the ground. "No."

"I think . . . I think we have."

"*No.*"

"Ali—"

"It wasn't us!" her voice erupts as a scream and I push myself back into the chair. "This place is haunted, Lia! This place ruined our lives! And I'm going to get revenge on it—I'm going to burn it to the ground, I'm going to knock down every wall until it doesn't call me back anymore! I'm going to destroy it so that no one else will ever have to go through what we did!"

I launch out of the chair now, grabbing her arms. "We can't," I say, surprised at how calm my voice sounds. "We can't, Ali."

Ali's eyes are black holes, just like my wavering reflection in the lineup of infinite mes in the bathroom. Her fingernails grip my upper arms tightly, digging into my skin.

When she next speaks, every word is carefully controlled. "Why not, Lia?"

I try to figure out how to form the words I need, how to make my final point. "Ali, you were right. I don't think Avery's dead."

Ali shakes her head, turning her face away, but not before I see her expression crumble. "Don't."

I know she doesn't want to hear it. The girl who believed so much can't quite believe this.

I press on, desperate to make her understand. "You were right. She's not dead. I don't even think she's gone."

"Lia, stop!"

"She's here, Ali!"

"Lia—" Her voice breaks, but I speak over her, speak so loudly that my words seem to hover in the air, taking up all the oxygen.

"She's here! Right here! Just not here right *now*."

Still holding on to Ali with one arm, I reach out my other, waving it around in the air.

I swear I feel the touch of fingers on mine.

Raff is quiet and so is Ali, but they're both listening, and Ali's eyes are wet. Each word lands where it should, like Brier Hall is guiding my tongue. "This house is a tangle of many versions of our realities."

"And now they're colliding," Rafferty rasps.

"Yes," I whisper back, thinking of all the collisions I've had with myself, with Raff, with my sisters, with the ghosts of ourselves. "Yes, exactly. And if Avery's not gone, if she's still *here*, somewhere, then that means we can rescue her." I look between them, Rafferty's face unreadable, Ali's broken. "That means we can get her back."

THE COVE

Time is a game played beautifully by children.
—Heraclitus, *The Fragments*

TWENTY

The bathroom feels oppressive with all three of us crowded near the sink. We reflect again in the mirrors—all of us—so that it looks like there're thousands of us jostling for space.

"So how do I see myself?" Ali asks. She's acting pricklier than ever but she hasn't questioned a single word I've said. Almost like the impossibility of reality bending and weaving in this house was something obvious, something to be expected. I find I don't mind prickly Ali because it's better than the Ali who is both dull-eyed and paranoid. The Ali I last saw in the parking lot.

At least now my sister has some fire back in her eyes.

"Look in the mirror, I guess," I begin. The mirror is still covered in the red words and a capped lipstick is on the tiled floor. I don't remember dropping it. I don't remember *using* it.

"Helpful."

"It just *happened*," I snap. "I didn't do anything. I just looked up, and she was there."

Ali faces the mirror. "Come on, me. You need to appear and lead me to Avery." She leans in; her breath fogs the surface. "Come *on*."

"I don't know if this will work," I say.

Rafferty cuts in, saying the words I knew I would hear from him at some point. "Is this even a good idea?"

Ali pushes up away from the mirror with cold hands. She grips the sink and stares into the mirror before her, then flicks a glance over her shoulder. "No," she says. "Not at all."

"Because what happens," Raff continues, "if it *does* work? What, you think the younger version of yourself is going to come popping out of her layer of this house and just lead you through the maze to Avery?"

Ali's eyes are defiant. "That's exactly what I think is going to happen. It *will* happen. I'll stand here forever if I have to."

A prickle of unease tickles the back of my neck. Somehow I think that's exactly what the house would want, but I don't want to contradict her so I just watch her carefully, keeping my breathing quiet. "What do you see?"

"Myself," Ali replies.

"A normal reflection?"

"Yes."

I try to quell my frustration and turn away from Ali, meeting Raff's eyes instead. "It really happened," I say, more to myself than anyone. "I know what I saw." But the surety that was there when I told the two of them about my ideas, the collapse of realities within these walls, that we could use mirrors to see ourselves in the other layer and maybe find our missing sister this way . . . that surety is gone. Because even if it's true, and we could crawl between all the layers of Brier that are pressed up against each other, *how* do we even do it? It's always happened either abruptly or completely unknowingly before.

I tilt forward, resting my forehead against Rafferty's chest. His shirt is soft and I count his heartbeats, ticking them off in my head. *One, two, three, four, five . . .*

It reminds me of us, our little selves, playing hide-and-seek. The patch of heather and briar. The library. The cove.

Five, four, three, two, one . . .

Ready or not.

I haven't been ready for anything, and yet here I am, still going.

Ali makes a noise—a tiny noise, just a tiny, breathy "oh" of surprise. There's no swearing, no shrieking, no sobbing. Just an exhale, enough to let me know she's experiencing something too.

I stay pressed against Rafferty for a minute because I can't bear to turn around and see little Ali. *My* Ali. In Brier, there are ghosts everywhere, but not the kind I thought. There're so many versions of ourselves in this house that we're spilling over: ghosts in the mirrors, ghosts in the walls. Ghosts playing down in the cove. Little ghosts hiding under their beds.

If I turn and see little Ali, it will be like seeing a ghost staring out at me.

Except every fiber of my being *knows* that somewhere in this house, little Ali and little Lia still run free down the hallways, being followed—as always—by their diligent older sister. Maybe just in my memory. Maybe just in the depths of my grief. Maybe just in the corner of my mind that wants my sisters back so desperately, it's cracking under the pressure.

Maybe in Brier Hall, memories and grief and desperation and ghosts are just different names for the same thing.

"Oh," Ali says again. I hear her take a deep breath; I don't hear the release. Rafferty does a sharp intake, and I wonder what he can see over my head. Here, at least, is proof for Rafferty. Proof that I was right. We might not ever agree on *what* happened all those years ago when we were children, or what exactly has happened the past few days—but here is proof that *something* did. Proof he can't explain away. And right now, standing in his arms, that's enough.

"Oh," says Ali, and this time the "oh" is just a stand-in word from someone who's heart is breaking. I can hear the pieces falling around my sister like stones.

And then there's a giggle from outside the bathroom door, and I know that sharp-toothed giggle. I look up just in time to see Ali whip her head from the mirror—the mirror with no reflection, just a sea of inky black—toward the door. She hears it too. She knows it's hers.

And then she takes off running.

"Ali, wait!" I yell as she pushes past me, desperate to catch the little her, to dive through every part of this house together until they find Avery. Ali's desperation feeds mine, and panic roils inside me as I chase her—chase *both* of her—down the hallway. I can't let her out of my sight. I'm terrified I'll never see her again if I do. But she had a head start, and the hallways start careening out of control as I run.

The house doesn't want me to follow her. The house tries to stop me.

The floorboards scream as I race over them, and the carpet hallway undulates under my feet. I collapse against the wall, breathing heavily as the hallway stretches out, until it goes on and on, and Ali is just a tiny speck in the distance.

"Stop it!" I scream at the house. "Don't you want me too?" And I mean it, and I'm angry and scared, but I'm also a little hurt. What I really want to ask is *Don't you love me best?*

The hallway rubber-bands back in on itself and there's Ali, just ahead. She's scrabbling at a door—at the tower door. And for the first time, it opens and lets her through.

"Ali, wait!" I scream at her, and she tries to stop the heavy door from shutting behind her—all I can see is her white and terrified face—but then it slams shut with a horrible, final-sounding *thunk*.

I run up to it, and a second later Rafferty comes to hover behind me, leaning against the balustrade and eyeing the door warily.

I turn the key and then the handle and wait for it to open, like it's always done before.

Nothing happens. The door stays shut, locked. I try again and again until I'm fumbling with the key, my fingers slipping off of it as my dread and anxiety surges, threatening to drag me down with it. *Down, down, down* . . .

But the door doesn't open. The house has let Ali into its heart, but it has shut me out.

I'm not screaming now, just panting hard. My mind races, thoughts colliding with one another, piling up in teetering towers and then freefalling down, too fast for me to catch them.

Ali.

Where did you go?

How do I follow?

Her name jumbles into one thought that supersedes every other: *Alialialialialialiali*—until it doesn't even sound real anymore, and I don't know if I'm thinking her name or my own.

Like this.

"I have to get through there too," I say. "Raff, I *have* to get through."

225

"Lia, you have no idea where she went! I can't let you walk through a door to fucking Nowhereland! Do you understand—do you even—" His words jumble as well, and he lets them drop. I can see the whites of his eyes.

"Do you remember our hideout in the briar patch?" I say abruptly.

Raff just looks at me like I'm not making any sense.

"We would have picnics," I say. "You would tell me my house was haunted. When we heard footsteps and voices we would lie there in the heather and you would tell me it would be okay."

"Yes." His voice is hoarse.

"Will things be okay now?"

He doesn't want to answer. He just swallows and stares at his fingers.

"Raff," I say. "Please. I need you to just—lie. Will things be okay?"

It's as Rafferty woodenly tells me of course everything will be just fine that I realize it's raining, the kind of California coastal downpour where the clouds store up all their rain for the entire year and then release it all at once in a wash-the-house-away flood.

I go to the bathroom window and pull the curtains apart, peering out. Far down below, I see little lights bobbing in the sudden storm. Lights? I peer closer, and then it hits me all at once. *Flashlights*, held in the hands of three little girls, running inside mid-game to escape the weather.

From somewhere down below, I hear a door slam.

"Oh," I say, just as Ali did, and now I realize why: When it truly clicks, when all the neural pathways light up and illuminate the truth, it's not a gasping-out-loud sort of thing. It's quiet. Some-times the life-changing truths are the ones that sidle softly in the door, the unassuming and uninvited guests. I don't need a calendar or a clock when I say with certainty, "It's five years since we left."

"I know," says Raff, confused.

"No," I say, the echo of a little giggle drifting up from down-stairs. "It mean it's *exactly* five years ago, tonight, that my family ran away from Brier Hall. Five years, *tonight*, that Avery went missing."

When I was telling Ali and Raff my big ideas about reality, there was more than I imagined. More than I could fathom. The connections were there, floating loosely around, waiting for some-one to line them up.

Clarity brings Brier Hall into sharp focus.

I understand now, and I know what I have to do.

COLLISIONS

~~~

It starts raining while you're playing out on the bluff, too near to the edge, but you've all sworn each other to secrecy.

What are sisters for, after all?

The rain starts as a sprinkle, but before you can look at the sky and say, "Hey, I think I just felt a drop of rain!" the skies open up and everything turns to shades of gray: the roiling sky overhead, the silver-glass sheen of the grass as you run toward the shape of your house that looms through the mist.

You don't want to go inside.

This is supposed to be your fairy-tale princess castle, but you can't stop seeing and hearing things that shouldn't be there. Things that scare you. You can't get the face of the woman in the mirror out of your head, the one who stood where your reflection was supposed to stand, who stared at you as if she were looking right at you.

Who whispered, "Who are you?" just as you did.

You wish you could stay outside, where the blustery air rips any scary thoughts from you and flings them to the wind.

You wish you could stay at the cove, splashing in the water, but the weather is turning colder now, and the sea monster who swims below seems more of a threat when the days are dark and windswept.

Ali and Avery push their way in the door, giggling together.

You hover uncertainly, rain pouring over you, until Avery appears back in the doorway and gestures toward you. "Come on! What are you doing?" She's smiling and illuminated by the light in the hall. She looks like an angel.

You don't know why, but you feel . . . sad.

You follow her in because she's your big sister and she told you to.

"Shoes off," Avery says.

You take them off.

Because she's your big sister, and she told you to.

The storm is safely shut outside now, but the booming thunder gets louder by the minute. You're shaking uncontrollably, but you can't tell if that's because of the water soaking through your clothes or if it's the face in the mirror that haunts you, or the fact that you feel a sudden need to take hold of Avery's hand and not let it go.

Do you remember how you spot it first?

How you start crying, because you are just a kid, after all. How all you can do is point at the wall, where huge, waist-high writing spells out *Bright eyes*. A Sharpie lies on the ground at the baseboard, lonely, capless.

"Get upstairs," Avery says, and her voice is more scared than you've ever heard it.

You go, because your big sister told you to.

And as you go, things *happen* before you, as if something is running ahead, causing discord in their wake. As you get to the top of the stairs, the ornate vase tumbles to the ground, smashing with the crash, the thick ceramic shards scattering onto the carpet.

Ali screams, and on the end of her scream comes music, bursting into life from some unknowable place. Bonnie Tyler's voice is singing mournfully, so loudly you can't hear yourself think. You're crying again, and Avery pulls you forward down the hallway, deeper into the house. Toward safety.

But houses aren't always safe.

This is when you learn.

All the doors in the hallway burst open, one by one clattering forcefully against the wall. Paintings fall from their places, canvases and frames crashing to the floor. The entire hallway is in chaos, and the screams of the three of you are echoed by the screams of your mom as she comes flying down the hallway stairs.

"Get out, get out!" She's panicked as she catches Ali's hand and pulls her back the way we came. You grab hold of Ali's other hand.

You remember now that Avery was behind you. You remember looking back at her, and seeing her running, and seeing someone else there too, running alongside her. Someone that faded in and out. Not there. Not *all* there.

And then they are gone, and the doors are slamming shut, and the flower vase shatters against the wall opposite you as if someone threw it, hard. You duck just in time.

The chandeliers overhead flick on and off, on and off, spotlighting your frantic retreat in staccato illumination.

The front door is already open, the storm outside spraying salty wind and rain into the entrance hall, slicking the wooden floor. You almost slip, but between Ali's hand pulling you forward and Avery catching you from behind, you right yourself. Avery slides in her sock feet too, and then is jerked sideways in a strange, unnatural motion.

Like she's being held.

"Run!" screams Avery, pushing you toward the front door among the clamor, even as something pulls her backward. "Run!"

You run. Because your big sister said to.

And then you're all running, your hand slipping in Ali's, your legs cramping. You fall. You remember falling, how the gravel cuts into your palm and slices deep, but the pain is dulled, like it's already happened a thousand times before in some other life and this is just an old wound now, scabbed over, a red, raw scar.

You mom is just ahead, her nails breaking as she fumbles to get the gate open so you can all run through to safety. It's still raining when you're through the gate, but just barely. The storm has abruptly turned to a drizzle, like someone turning off a tap.

Ali's crying, her feet cut from the gravel, and your mom is bending over her, her arms shaking.

You're the one who notices first.

You were always the one who noticed things first, don't you remember?

You look around and ask, "Where's Avery?"

TWENTY-ONE

The storm breaks against the bathroom window with a brilliant bloom of lightning. I rush to the cabinet by the side of the claw-foot tub, scrabbling to open the top drawer—I already know what I'll find there. My mind is catapulting forward while a tiny part of it tries to remember the past.

But it doesn't matter because the past has already happened.

In another layer of Brier Hall, this night and all its events have already occurred. The tangled maze of timelines within this house are fragmenting tonight.

In the drawer is a tube of red lipstick.

I take it and turn toward the mirror, peering into the reflectionless space. I'm there somewhere, though, separated by reality and grains of sand.

I step up to the mirror and uncap the lipstick, pressing it into the glass. I know what to write because I've already written it, and in another moment the infamous refrain from "Total Eclipse of the Heart" runs red in lipstick letters.

"Wait . . ." Rafferty says from behind me, but I can't wait for him to put the pieces together. Because as another crash of thunder comes, shaking the walls of Brier Hall, I'm more sure than ever: Somehow my *now,* my reality, is colliding with the night we left five years ago.

The memories of that night whirl into my head, snippets of

a night I've tried for five years to block out. The storm is washing them back in.

"You wrote it," Raff says as I let the tube of lipstick fall to my feet.

"Yeah," I say, walking quickly to the bathroom door. "I'm beginning to think I did a lot of things. So far it's been accidental, unknowing." I pause with my hand on the door. "Well, not anymore."

I run out into the hallway, letting the door slam open. This is the first act: All doors will be slammed open and shut tonight; I might as well get started. The light in the hallway is strange, a hazy half-light that makes everything look blurry. Unreal. The floors warp away from me, stretching out before rubber-banding back like some sick imitation of a fun house.

This house is *not* a labyrinth: one way in, one way out. This house is a maze: full of branching pathways that shift and spiral, keeping you trapped inside.

I end up crawling to the far end where a thin staircase cocooned by the walls rises to the third floor. This is where my mom's office was; it looks out over the sheer drop down to the waves below, with a clear view of the cove where we would spend most of our days shrieking in the water. I give Rafferty a *look* and he returns it, wide-eyed, as if he knows this is the start of something. Or maybe the ending.

I push on the door; with a creak, it opens. And even though I know what to expect when I poke my head in, my heart still jumps into a painful double time.

My mom sits at her desk, her back to me, her hair up in the messy bun she always used to sport.

My mom is in Daley.

My mom turns toward the open door, her brows coming together in confusion as she sees—well, apparently not me. She looks young. Her eyes are clear: they don't hold the terror of this final night, or the media scrutiny, or the disappearance of her daughter.

But they're about to.

All I remember about that night was my mom coming running down the stairs, panicked. And now I know why.

As her eyes rove over the empty space where I stand, I slam the door as hard as I can. So hard the hinges shake. She jumps, a strangled half cry getting tangled in her throat.

"Kids?" she calls out. "Is that you?"

Yes, Mom, I think. *It's me.* And then I cross to stand beside her by the desk, and very deliberately sweep my arm across the top. Papers go flying; her keyboard cracks to the floor. The paperweight rolls off with a loud, jarring bang. Pens and pencil litter the rug.

My mom pushes herself away from her desk, a single scream growing as one by one her books are thrown around the room. As I chuck a book at the glass window, I wonder now if she has ever thought in the next five years about the fact that all of her books seemed to miraculously miss her.

The paintings come next. They thud to the floor, frames splintering.

My mom is screaming now in earnest, and she ducks a final flying book to scrabble at the door. I follow her out, sprinting past her down the steps, down the hallway, Rafferty flying in my wake. "Lia!" he yells, but I can barely hear over my mom's panicked cries.

Far below, from somewhere in the house, I can hear the sound of giggling, the *thwack* of muddy shoes being taken off and thrown to the ground. Three little girls, blissfully unaware that this is the night where everything changes.

But maybe it doesn't have to—not this time.

Not tonight.

I can't hear my mom anymore; time has looped, swirled. The girls will run into her when they go upstairs—it's already happened.

"Jesus, Lia!" Rafferty cries as we stampede down the grand staircase. He pulls me to a breathless stop at the bottom, where I can't help my eyes from zeroing in on the three girls crouched at the front door, taking off their shoes. "What the hell are you doing?"

Memories hit like steel-tipped arrows.

Little me, frenzied at the sight of the song lyrics that started our stampede from the house. And all along, it was *me*. A message for myself.

The Sharpie I took from the floor of my mom's office is burning a hole in my pocket, and I step toward the wall. I'm laughing now, laughing so hard that when it turns to sobs I barely notice. I write a huge *B* on the wall, drawing over paint and wallpaper.

"Lia, stop! What are you—"

"I'm being bad, Raff," I say, hiccupping, my nose running as I continue writing the words. "I'm haunting us. I'm getting us out of here. Don't you get it? It was me. That whole night was *me*. I'm the one who made us leave."

Raff doesn't answer, but when I step back from the writing on the wall he slips his hand into mine and squeezes it.

BRIGHT EYES

The two words adorn the wall now, the words *I've* written, and I turn to face the little girl who's staring at the words, slack-jawed. I let the Sharpie drop numbly from my fingers. The past and present collide before me.

"I'm sorry," I tell her, but she doesn't hear.

Instead, she runs.

Now it's time for my second act.

"Stay here," I tell Raff before taking the stairs two at a time ahead of little me and my big-little-sisters, sending the vase at the stop of the staircase smashing to the floor. Everything is still hazy as I crash open doors and slam the ornate oil paintings lining the hallway to the floor. Oh—here's my phone, in my pocket, as if it never left. As if I didn't leave it in the bedroom charging over a day ago, filled with its phantom texts I don't remember sending. I know exactly what I'm supposed to do with it: I turn up "Total Eclipse of the Heart" and play it as loud as I can as I follow us through the hall. At one point, I think little me looks back and locks eyes with me.

Reality bends, and right on time, here comes my mom, sprinting down the thin staircase and herding the three girls downstairs again.

I follow, preparing for the third act. Because this is the part I don't remember, the part I don't know. Somehow, this was when Avery got left behind. This is when Avery disappeared.

Not this time.

Surely this is why the house has brought me here, all these years later: to make us leave, and make Avery leave too.

"Raff, get the lights!" I yell, and Raff sprints to the light switch. The chandelier swaying overhead flicks on and off, on and off.

I keep my eyes focused on Avery, not letting her out of my sight. This is when we lost her before.

Don't lose her, don't lose her, don't lose her . . .

There's a brief jam at the front door and I try to keep Avery in my sight—when her wet blond hair appears from behind Ali, who she's shepherding out the door, desperation overtakes all conscious thought and I reach out for my sister.

I grab her hand.

I am a ghost—I *thought* I was a ghost.

But Avery's hand is solid in my own, and she screams. I realize then, in one swift heart-stopping moment, all I've done wrong.

It was me.

I was haunting us.

And the final piece clicks into place: It was *all* me. Avery screams and pulls away from the invisible force grabbing at her, clear panic overwhelming all her senses. She rips her hand from my grasp.

She sprints back into the house, away from the force—away from me—as the rest of my family sprint out into the pouring rain, thinking she's right behind them.

"*No!*" I scream, so loud my words breaks in my throat. "Avery, *no!*"

And I'm chasing her, a ghost through the halls, following the ghost of my childhood that's been haunting me for years.

Avery runs for the first door she sees: the plain, rounded door set into the upstairs hall that leads to the tower. The tower I saw the first moment we arrived at Brier Hall, the one that looked like a fairy-tale tower that a lonely princess might sing from, hoping to be rescued.

Now all I can think of is the lightning-struck tower, the Tarot tower. A card of absolute change. A card of absolute chaos.

That's the tower door she's headed for now, chased by her ghost. The tower door that always opened for me but hardly ever for my sisters. But it opens for Avery now, the true princess, and she falls through, scrabbling up the first few steps. Her breathing is so loud I can hear it from the hallway.

"Avery, come back! Please, come back!"

Raff is coming up behind me, but I follow Avery into the dark stairwell. Of course I do.

She's my big sister.

The door slams shut. Avery is still running up the steps, her bare feet slapping on the stones. I turn to the door and try the knob: It turns but doesn't open.

"Raff!" I scream through the door. "Get help! Please, go and get help!"

There's no response from beyond the door. Raff might've disappeared entirely for all I know. It wouldn't be the first time.

All I can do is hope he hears.

I turn toward the stairs where the echoes of Avery's frenzied breathing float down the circular stairwell.

Avery.

I won't lose her again—I can't. Not now, just steps ahead of me. Not again.

I start running, her name a refrain that pulses with each heartbeat. *Avery, Avery, Avery, Avery . . .*

I climb. The steps to the tower room were about two flights, straight up, but these steps keep going up. I climb, chasing the last remnant of my sister. My breathing is loud in my ears. I climb, but the stairs keep going up and up and up, and around me layers of Brier flash by like a flipbook, rushing over me, layer after layer after layer after layer after—

TWENTY-TWO

The ground is soft beneath my cheek.

The ground is—a rug. My eyes open slowly, and even blinking doesn't dissipate the thick, heavy feeling that's settled over everything. My body is too heavy to get up. I am a rock, carved into the shape of a human.

I lie on the ground, curled up like I'm brand-new, just born, until the cottony feeling lifts slightly. I roll over, every part of my body aching, but even the ache doesn't seem to reach my senses. I hurt, but I can't cry and I don't seem to feel any pain. It's more like a part of my brain realizes I'm hurting but can't quite bring itself to care.

I'm lying in front of the door to the tower. It's closed, as if I never opened it and scrambled up its inner spine. The last thing I remember is going up, thighs burning, mouth dry, up and up and up. But the door is closed as if it's never been opened, ever.

It takes a moment for me to realize that the sound I can hear are my own breaths, slowly rattling in and out. I can hear my groan as I get up, knees quaking as if they can't believe they've ever held up the weight of the rest of me. The sound rebounds toward me. Everything else is silent, like the house is holding its breath.

I cough and, crawling to the thick wooden railing, peer down to the entrance hall. There are no words written on the wall. No muddy shoes left in the entrance hall by a fleeing family. Brier

Hall, it seems, has reset itself. Or perhaps I'm in another layer, running parallel to all our others. One that no Brier or Peartree has touched.

"Avery?" I call out. "Ali?" The house swallows the sound.

I stand at the top of the grand staircase. The vase stands solitary on its table instead of lying in shattered pieces on the ground. As I reach the entrance hall and walk across the hardwood floor, I suddenly realize that my footsteps don't make a sound. I stomp near the door. Nothing.

There's a mirror hanging in the entrance, and I peer in. The mirror reflects the hall behind me, but my reflection has completely vanished once again.

I'm still a ghost in my own house.

I'm still not here.

I can't bring myself to feel anything: not scared, not confused. All the chaos of the past few hours has narrowed down to right here, right now, and the heavy silence is the only real thing in this world.

I turn away from the mirror and head outside. I want to see if it's just Brier Hall that's soundless, I want to hear the wind whistling off the bluff, the crunch of heather underfoot, the roar of the sea. As soon as I throw open the door I know it's no use: This place I've found myself in is just . . . quiet. I cross the usually creaky old porch and pick my way through the overgrown front gardens, down to the crumbly bluff-side path cut into the side of the cliff.

My feet know where I'm going before my mind catches up: By the time I realize, I'm halfway down the path to the cove. It's unconscious, this need to be back by the waves. To sit on the sand where we used to play. Even if the sea is now soundless, if I'm caught in the web of this motionless landscape.

I can't let myself think past the cove.

Do I sit by the shore in this quiet place forever, alone and unmoored?

I keep walking, my feet slipping on the sandy path. *Don't think of it.* It's easier now, easier than it's ever been. The panic that usually sits and waits right around my collarbone is absent, tamped down. I think I've used up all my panic, all my anxiety, all my *everything*. Now I'm just hollow.

The cove comes into view as I skid down the final lengths of the cliff path and collapse onto the beach. I breathe in, my hands burrowed into the sand. Although this place is soundless, it still smells the same. The scent of salt and sand and seaweed is overpowering, and I shake the sand from my fingers to brush away the tears.

I ache with absence. I miss my sisters. I miss laughing, miss splashing each other in the waves. I miss the Lia who saw Brier Hall as a princess's castle. I miss the Lia who wore glasses rosy enough to think that. The Lia who had a family, and sisters to fight with and cuddle with, sisters who only whispered "I hate you" under their breaths when you'd used their nail polish, but then rolled their eyes and painted the rest of your nails.

Sisters who never, ever meant it.

I kneel in the sand for a while. It could be seconds or hours or anything in between. Then I get up and walk toward the waves. It's only when I get closer that I notice the figure on the beach, kneeling just as I did in the sand, just close enough to the water that the waves lap over her knees.

It's Ali.

Ali, my sister. My sister who shakes and spits and loves everything and anything that removes her from reality. Loves everything and anything more than me. Who's glassy-eyed and angry and who screams at me *I hate you* and means it.

The sister I can't bear to be around any longer.

The sister whose mere presence usually makes my teeth involuntarily clench, my eyes stare at anything else, my heart race, and my mind chant, *It's okay, it's okay, it's okay.*

The sister who, when I see her on the beach, makes me break into a run, makes every inch of my body feel weak with relief.

"Ali!" I scream, and for a second I'm terrified that no sound will come out, and I'm a ghost to everyone. I thought I was invisible to my family in the aftermath of Avery's disappearance, but I've never realized what being truly alone is. But then the words rip free, so loud and sudden in this quiet place that even I jump.

And Ali hears.

She scrambles to her feet and runs toward me, not slow motion and graceful like in the movies but frantically, her face contorted. I think she's about to hug me, but when she gets close enough, she stops. Waits. She's wary, paranoid. But this seems different. It seems *real*, in a place where not much else is.

"Which Lia are you?" she asks.

I stare at her, unsure how to answer. What's happened to her since she fell through the mirror? Did she arrive right in this silent landscape or did she have to fight her way to it?

"I'm—me," I say. "I was with you before."

"All the Lias were with me before," she rasps.

"I was with you in the bathroom," I amend. "You ran to the door of the tower, and when I tried to come through after you, the way was shut. The door was locked. I couldn't get through and—"

She slams into me, arms tangling against my back.

"Oh, thank god," she says, the words breaking as she draws me in close. I can feel her thin body shaking with sobs. I haven't heard Ali cry in years. The sobs don't even sound like they're coming from her. "Oh, thank god you're mine," she says, the words muffled against my hair.

And her words sound like *you're me*. And I hug her back, my life raft of a sister, who my hate burns through the silence and my love drowns, the one who says *you're mine* and means *you're me*, and in that moment, I am.

"Where are we?" I whisper to her. We stay coiled around each other like we're one person.

Ali shakes her head. "I don't know. But . . . I'm glad you're here."

"It's quiet here."

Ali nods, her hair tickling my cheek. "If we're in some *layer* of Brier, I don't think this layer gets much use."

I remember running up the stairs in the princess tower, how I was running up but felt like I was falling, glimpses of other lives within lives flashing by.

"Hey!" the voice cuts through the stillness like a knife through butter. Warm and loud and real. Ali and I break apart as if we've just come up for air after being underwater for far too long.

"Was that you?" I ask, even though I know that it wasn't.

She shakes her head, her eyes latched on something at the far end of the beach.

I turn, then stumble back a step. Stumble away from Avery, Avery as she should've been, grown up and not gone.

Walking right toward us.

'm running before I realize I'm running. My feet are moving, carrying me forward, and my mind has to hurry to catch up from its place of shock. I can feel Ali next to me, her fingers gripping my fingers, the back of my shirt.

We won't lose each other again.

"A—Ave—?" I'm panting, the word coming out too quiet for her to hear. But Ali hears, and she lets out a strangled sob from behind me. Because it *is* Avery. As we get closer, I slow down, causing Ali to chafe against my side.

How can my missing sister be just . . . there?

She's backlit against the gray and silent sky, watching as Ali and I stumble closer. I recognize her immediately because even though she's aged, she was always the older sister. Her eyes are the same. Her frown. *Her.*

But will she recognize us? Her little sisters, all grown up?

We all stare at each other. Ali and I creep close enough to see Avery's pupils, wide and shocked.

"Oh," she breathes. A glittering of water shifts in her eyes. "Oh," she says again, then adds simply, "You're here. I was wondering if you'd show up."

The Avery from five years ago would have expected Ali to speak first; after all, Ali was the fiery, stubborn one. But Ali is silent behind me, and I step forward. We're not the same girls as we were back then. I can't stop staring at Avery, this grown-up before me. *None* of us are the same.

"Are you . . ." My voice is scratchy. I clear my throat, and then try again. "Are you really Avery?" Now I think I understand what Ali meant when the first thing she asked me was *Which Lia are you?* As I stare at Avery, missing for five years, I can't help thinking of all the other Averys and Alis that I've seen in the past hours—and the past years. The older and younger versions who switched without a breath. The reflections that stared back, before turning away in the mirror. The little girls who ran up and down the hallways.

Which Avery is this?

"I am," Avery replies, and her voice sounds different but familiar. It's like watching a home video and knowing the little girl running rampant is you. Somewhere deep inside, you know. And looking at Avery now, I *know*.

"Do you know who we are?" I whisper, taking a step forward. I dreamed for years about reuniting with Avery, mapped out everything I would do. How I would cry, scream, run toward her. Hysterical, joyful. But now it's happening, and I'm just . . . still. Like an off-center world has suddenly been shifted back in balance and one bat of my eyelid might be enough to shatter it.

"You're my sisters," Avery says, her voice breaking. A single tear rolls down her face. I step closer; she does the same. I reach out a hand—so does she. I'm half convinced that there's a mirror between us and I'm just seeing myself. Another of Brier Hall's tricks.

But Avery's shaking fingers touch mine, and they're cold and calloused and blissfully, gratefully real.

We still don't hug, just stay there with our fingers linked.

It feels like enough. It feels like everything.

"Are you okay?" Avery whispers. "Have you been okay?"

"Yes, we're fine," I say, speaking around the lump in my throat because Ali is still crying behind me, and I don't know how to sum up the disastrous downward spiral of the last five years other than *yes, we're fine.*

Avery pulls on my fingers and I trip forward, Ali stumbling along after me, until suddenly her arms are enfolding us both tightly. I can feel her breath on my neck, her nails digging into my shoulder blades.

Real.

"You're a liar," she breathes, but it sounds more like *I love you.*

"That's what little sisters are for," I whisper back against her neck, and I mean it like *I missed you.*

"Come on," she murmurs, pushing me back. Her eyes rove over me, then flick to Ali. "Before you tell me how you got here, let's go sit down." She takes one of our hands in each of hers and leads us farther down the beach. If I strain, I almost think I can hear the echo of waves in this silent place. Like this frozen dimension is being gently sucked beneath the current.

We sit in the sand, on either side of Avery. I squeeze her hand tighter and I can see Ali doing the same on her other side.

Before Avery can speak, I interrupt. As little sisters should. "How are you here? *Where* is this? Where did you go?"

Avery lets out a little sigh. "I can't answer all your questions. How could I? To me, this is what happened: We were leaving the house—we were scared. And then something pulled me back."

I pulled you back.

"I ran. I was in the tower, going up . . . that's all I remember. I must've blacked out, or something, but when I woke up, I was lying back in my bed. But I was *here,* in this other Brier, in this quiet place."

"So it's true? Brier's a maze of different timelines, different layers?"

"A maze," says Avery. "If that's true, I think this place is Brier's heart, the center of the maze. The last layer. It's just . . . nothing. It's just the house. That's it."

"So you're the only one here?" Ali asks.

"As far as I know," Avery says.

I feel cold all over, sick. "You mean that all this time you've been stuck here alone?"

"Yes," Avery whispers. "But I don't remember all of it. I just walked through the house, walked on the beach, swam in the cove. Time went by as if in a dream."

Life is but a dream.

On the other side of Avery, Ali looks like a statue. "You've been here five years."

"Is that how long it's been?" Avery says, and she sounds surprised.

Ali stares at us for a second, and I can see some emotion bubbling up in her eyes right before she snaps. She shoots to her feet, entire body shaking, and screams, "What the *fuck*!" The words sound painful, like they're being ripped from her.

Avery gets to her feet too, reaching out a placating hand. "Ali, it's okay—"

"It's not okay!" Ali screams, her face turning a blotchy red. "It's *not* okay!" She crouches suddenly, as if her legs have given out, and her hands go into her hair, digging into her scalp.

"Ali—"

Ali makes a noise that doesn't even sound human anymore.

Avery is standing there, arms still outstretched, but she looks at a loss. It's then I remember: Avery may be our older sister, but she's the older sister of two little girls who don't exist anymore. Two girls who hadn't known much loss. Two girls who still giggled and played and loved each other with a love that felt like love. Who loved each other simply, easily, and didn't have to *try*.

I remember now that Avery doesn't know the girls on the beach. She doesn't know the new Ali and Lia, forged in fire. Forged in grief from loss—the loss of *her*. She doesn't know how to handle this Ali, but I do.

Right now, in this world, in this reality, I'm the only one who does.

I fall to my knees by Ali, the sand sinking beneath me.

I don't think about what I want to say or need to say. I just look at my sister before me, heaving with uncontrollable grief, and the words just come out, rising above her sobs.

"I thought I hated you," I say.

She takes a deep breath before continuing to cry. But I can tell she's listening, that my words make her pause.

"I hated you so much I couldn't stand to be around you. I hated the choices you made, I hated that you drowned yourself in drinking and lost yourself to drugs and got to escape while I didn't." I grip her shoulders and slowly, slowly, she raises her head to look at me. "I hated that you could be bad, and that I had to hold it together. I hated that I couldn't lash out like you lashed out. I hated that when you *did* lash out it made things worse. The things you said made me hate myself. And I hated myself for hating you, and then I hated you even more for that."

Ali stares at me through glittering eyes. But she's not crying anymore. She's listening to every word. As I knew she would. Because maybe we're more alike than I ever understood: *like this.*

"You said that you wished I was dead. That you wished I wasn't your sister. That it had been me instead of Avery." Ali's shaking her head, tears dripping down her nose. "And I'll never be able to get those words out of my head. But the reason I hated you for saying it was because I loved you—so—much."

I think about what Rafferty said back in the bedroom at Brier. I know it wasn't all that long ago, but it feels like forever. *You do care, Lia. You've cared about her so much for so long that it's ripping you apart.* I couldn't face it then. I couldn't have him be right.

But I look at Ali now and I know.

"But you know what?"

Her mouth moves, forms an unuttered "*What?*"

"You're also the one who knew we had to come back here. You're the one who was determined that Avery wasn't gone, that she was alive. Whatever happened between us before, you're the reason we're back here now. Whatever happened before, it all led to here. It led to now. So it can't be all bad, right?" I shake her shoulders. She's gazing at me, eyes glazed, but when she blinks her eyes look clearer.

"I'm sorry," she whispers. "Lia, I . . ."

"I know," I say. I suddenly don't want to hear it. Because it can't change anything, can it?

"But I—I'm *so*—"

"I said I *know*." I look at her and I'm not sure what I feel. Is this forgiveness? It feels too raw, too unbalanced. I don't feel warm and peaceful. I feel like my skin's too tight, like my eyes are prickling, unsure whether or not to cry.

Ali's eyes slide to Avery. "I'm sorry you've been stuck here for so long," she rasps.

"It wasn't so long," Avery says simply. "It was just . . . a dream. But I'm sorry that you're here now. Stuck. Trapped." She sits down on the sand again, staring out at the water. Ali and I share a glance over her head—*stuck, trapped?*—and then sink down on either side of our older sister once again. "But we're all together now."

"Avery," I begin. "Are you trying to say that there's no way out of here?"

Her eyes don't leave the water. "Don't you think I've tried?"

"Five years' worth of trying," Ali mumbles.

Yes, I think. *Five years' worth of trying: what we've all been doing.* I try to find the place within me that's panicking, like I rationally know I should be. But I reach out and link my fingers through Avery's, and it's hard to feel scared when my lost sister is found once more.

It's hard to feel scared when we're together. We're not lost things anymore. We're not things left behind. We're not lost at all: We have each other.

"Do you remember when we were happy together?" I say.

"Yeah, I do."

"I do too."

My next question is on the tip of my tongue: *Do you think*

we can ever be that way again? But the words stay spooled in my mouth, unsaid.

Maybe there's too much hurt for us to ever be back to the way we were. We might never be able to put things right or truly forgive. My heart aches, because the thing is, I'm still mad that all this happened. I just don't know who I'm mad at anymore.

Maybe I will be wondering for the rest of my life *what if.* What if we'd never come here. What if this entire twisted maze of a house had never occurred. What if Avery's disappearance had brought Ali and me closer rather than driving us apart.

But nothing happened in the way I wanted, in the way it should've.

And now everyone is hurt, and everyone is haunted, and I'm so nostalgic for the past I feel physically sick with longing.

Maybe I'll forever miss who we were before Brier, before everything fell apart—and who we might have been.

And maybe that's okay, I think as I watch Ali's head drop onto Avery's shoulder as they stare out at the waves. I dig my hand into the sand and then let a handful of it swirl away in the wind, settling back to where it came from. Maybe I can move forward in this unmoving place while still mourning for everything I lost.

Because the truth is, I will never not miss her.

I will never not miss the fifteen-year-old that Ali was, wicked but wonderful in the way all fifteen-year-olds are.

I will never not miss the naive little girl who was her little sister, the Little Lia, who trusted that there were monsters in the lake and monsters down the hall solely because her wicked and wonderful sister told her there were and made her close her eyes.

I will never not miss the Avery I knew, who wasn't perfect but was held as a saint in my mind, enshrined in her vanishing as quickly as if it were death. Who should've been allowed to grow up, to grow old, to be bad, to be something—anything—besides the sister that I miss; the sister fated to drift down the stream that is Brier's heart, *merrily, merrily*, for five years. The sister whose disappearance broke us all.

I will never not miss the me I might've been.

The me I should've been.

The me that maybe—somewhere, in another life, in another layer—I *am*, the me who is unbroken and unmoved by storms; the me with no secrets, no memories, no past; the me who is still, happy, whole; the me who sits by the shore and watches the waves with her sisters.

HOME

Let everything happen to you: beauty and terror.
Just keep going. No feeling is final.
Don't let yourself lose me.

Nearby is the country they call life.

You will know it by its seriousness.
Give me your hand.
—Rainer Maria Rilke, "Go to the Limits of Your Longing"

ALL THE THINGS THAT CAN'T GET LOST

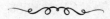

You decide you will live forever.

Your sisters are huddled together, muttering, but they do that sometimes. They're older. They put their heads close and link arms, a wall against you, and they keep secrets and you try not to care, because you're looking up at the true-blue sky and it's warm and for once there's no breeze. And you will always live here, and everything else can leave but you will be here.

Always.

Safe.

You know it in your bones.

As long as you don't leave Brier, you'll be safe. The thought is overwhelming. You're not quite sure where it came from.

Sand flies up as your sisters approach.

"Hey," Ali snaps. She's gotten more snappy as of late. You know it's because of the nights, when you both lie awake and unseen things run up and down the hallways, banging to please, please be let in. The nights have sunken into her. You're able to brush them off as soon as daylight hits.

A bad dream.

"I saw something last night," Ali says.

The sun is hot today. You close your eyes, sleepy.

Maybe you should just sleep.

"Hey!" Ali says again, irritable now.

"Lia, listen," Avery adds, and you finally sit up. For the first time, you notice that Avery looks upset too. Her face is pinched. She worries at her lip. "Ali saw something weird. In the mirror."

You've seen lots of strange things in mirrors.

"Tell Mom, then."

"I did. She didn't believe me."

Of course she didn't. Things that waltz around and try to crawl through mirrors aren't really there. Things that crash down hallways aren't real.

You're imagining it.

You're all imagining it.

You feel the worry, then, don't you? The ice-cold slick of fear the slides between your ribs, like your sisters have carried something diseased over and infected you and your perfect, live-forever day.

You can't quite remember why you want to stay here forever.

In fact, the more you think about it, the ice pick of fear grows. You can't quite remember why you want to stay alive forever. It doesn't sound like the perfect idea it did just moments ago. You squeeze your eyes shut, trying to keep the thoughts that aren't yours from finding you.

But they find you anyways, don't they?

They always do.

"What if we leave?" You say it first. It's unimaginable. "What if we run away?"

"What about Mom?" Avery has bit her lip so consistently that it's started to bleed. You notice that while she's being rational, she hasn't said no to your running away idea.

"Do you think we can?" Ali whispers. She sits down next to you on the beach. "Do you think the gates would let us go?"

You stare at each other. You don't feel little anymore. You feel too old for your body, like another Lia has taken over and is realizing things that you, as a thirteen-year-old, shouldn't be having to think about. Shouldn't realize are real.

Real, as it turns out, is a very tenuous thing.

"We could swim," Avery says finally.

"Yes!" You alight on the idea; you grip it with both hands. "We could just keep swimming out of the cove, around the headland, out to the big beach, and—"

"No."

"We'd get away!"

"No, we wouldn't," murmurs Ali. "The monster would get us first."

A part of you always thought the monster was a story. Knew it was a story told by wicked older sisters. But now you tilt your head to look up at the bluff rising above you, where Brier Hall perches on its edge like an overgrown bird of prey. Watching you.

Maybe not all monsters live in the sea.

Maybe some monsters are closer to home.

"The monster wouldn't get us," I say, turning away from the windows of Brier.

"It would."

"Not if we swam really hard."

"Even then."

"I could get away." You are resolute.

Ali isn't looking at the waves either. She's also focused on the house on the cliff above you. "Well," she says slowly. "Maybe you would. But someday it would get you. It waits forever. It always waits."

You try not to let yourself be scared. You've heard this before. Many, many times. It's Ali's favorite story: the monster who waits. And there's always only one ending: that no matter where you go or what you do, the monster will get you.

Ali looks your way and smiles, slyly, like she knows. "Are you scared now?"

"No," you say, but the tremor in your voice gives it away.

Ali stares at you, and then chews on her bottom lip. She narrows her eyes, and there's a different look there suddenly, something softer, something you haven't see in Ali's eyes in a while. Something the late nights hiding under the bed have carved out.

Or maybe not, because her gaze softens, and for the first time ever she clears her throat and tells you a different ending to the story.

"You don't have to be scared, Lia," Ali says. "The monster wouldn't get you anyways."

You stare back at her, wordless, because this isn't how the story goes.

"Me and Avery. We're the ones you can hide behind. It would see us, get us, and let you go free."

You don't know what to make of this new story.

Somehow this feels worse than the original, when some nameless sea creature gobbles you up and your older sister giggles and grabs your foot underwater.

"But I don't want it to get you," you whisper.

Ali glances up at the house, then looks out at the waves. The day is turning chilly. The sky is turning a slate gray, clouds pushing in against the blue. "Better us than you," she says, and she's serious. "After all, that's what big sisters are for."

TWENTY-FOUR

Sitting on the soundless beach under a washed-out sky, we tell each other a story. Just like our mom used to.

Avery begins it. She's the oldest and the one who's been missing, so Ali and I let her. It feels right to hear her say the words: "Once upon a time." She clears her throat and doesn't look at us. "Once upon a time there were three little girls. And they were the best three girls in the world."

She's quiet for a while, and when I glance over, tears are dripping down her face.

I take a deep breath and continue. "And they lived in a house on a cliff. And they ran wild and caused their mom a lot of grief. But they were happy in their house."

"Until things started changing," Ali breaks in. "Until the hallways started to change and move. Until they'd get locked in rooms during hide-and-seek and stay there for hours until the door would open suddenly."

"Until they'd see other reflections in mirrors."

"Until things would go bump in the night."

"They'd hear music where there shouldn't be music."

"They saw ghosts," I say, when what I mean to say is, *they saw themselves.*

When Avery speaks next, it's a whisper. "They got scared."

We're quiet for a moment. Speaking about it like this, it almost *feels* like a story. Everything is muted like it happened to somebody else and not us.

"The three little girls were scared, but they had each other," I whisper. "Until one night they didn't."

"One night everything changed," Ali takes over. "They left the house on the cliff, but there were only two little girls by the time they got out."

"The third sister got lost in a maze," Avery begins slowly. "And no matter which way she turned, the doors never led out. And everything was gray and quiet and she was alone."

"And the remaining two sisters weren't very good without the third," Ali cuts in. "And one of those little girls tried to grow up, because she wasn't anyone's little sister anymore, and she just couldn't bear it. And when she couldn't grow up, she tried to forget she used to be a little sister. She tried to forget she was *anyone's* sister. She tried to forget she was anyone at all, because it was easier to be nobody than to remember what she'd had and lost."

Ali finds my hand in the sand. She doesn't squeeze it or hold it but she touches the tips of fingers hesitantly to my skin, and it feels like an apology.

We're all silent for a long time, but of course people are never really silent, and even in this silent, breathless world I can hear our breaths, and the sound of the sand as we shift, and Avery's shaking shoulders, and Ali's sniffles.

It's my turn to tell the story, my story. I try to speak around the tightening in my throat. "And the other little girl tried to stay little, but both her sisters were gone in different ways, and it's hard to stay little when there's no one to be little for. So instead she tried to be

265

good. No, not good; she tried to be *perfect*. But underneath she was crumbling, and she waited for someone to notice. She was a liar, an actress. But no one ever noticed, so no one helped, and she was falling to pieces. To keep herself together she got angry and used that fire inside to keep her going." I tilt my head toward Ali. She's not crying anymore, but her eyes glitter with tears. Her fingertips shake on top of my hand once again, the memory of being close enough to touch.

"One of the lost little girls went back to the house," whispered Ali. "Back to where everything fell apart."

"The other little girl followed," I add. "She was angry, but she couldn't help but follow her sister."

"Even though her sister told her not to come," Ali says.

"The little girl was never good at listening," I say, and Ali snorts with a rare burst of quiet laughter. "So she followed her sister back to the house on the cliff. Back to the maze of rooms. And they looked for the third sister."

"They missed her," Ali says.

"Everything went wrong when she wasn't there anymore," I say.

"They were determined to find her," Ali adds.

"They wouldn't leave without her," I agree. "And because of that, they found themselves somewhere they never thought they'd be." I gaze out at the sea, the waves that keep breaking silently on the sandy shore. It doesn't feel real, any of it, but definitely not the fact that this is final. This is the ending place, the end.

Avery clears her throat. She's been quiet while Ali and I have told our tangled vine of a story. "It wasn't supposed to be the end of the story," she says, her voice choked. "But at least the sisters were together at last."

This is the end, I think to myself over and over until the words run together. We'll stay here until our days begin to run together, until everything feels like a dream. But as Avery said: We're together. At least we're together.

Then Ali asks, "And?"

Avery's forehead creases. "Hm?"

"And what?" I say. *This is the end.*

"And?" Ali says again, forcefully, and I finally get what she wants—no, *needs*—to hear.

"And the three little girls lived happily ever after," I finish quietly, and for a single moment it doesn't feel like a lie.

But then all of a sudden I think of our mom. The stories we're telling, they're hers. All of us are hers. My heart clenches, painful and too big for my chest. I'm glad I'm here with my sisters and I'm glad we are together, but all I can think about now is my mom, the Peartree left behind. The only one of us left.

I don't want her here with us—here in this shadow world. She's escaped; she's the lucky one of us. But she won't know it. She won't feel it.

Losing one of us broke her. What will losing three do?

I want to cry. My head is aching, wetness welling up in the corners of my eyes. Why was I so content to just sit here in the center of this maze forever? Why was I okay with letting Brier Hall wrap its thorny arms around me and drag me away? I try to push the thought of my mother, alone and worried and heartbroken, out of my mind. Instead, I get angry.

And it works. My throat is choked and my cheeks are hot but I don't cry. Sometimes it helps to be angry. Sometimes it keeps you lit. Keeps you alive.

And then suddenly, as if it's been summoned by the fury at being stuck here, at the unimaginable unfairness of it all, a tiny pinprick of light flickers through the grayness at the edge of the horizon. Out beyond the waves—it bobs and dips on the ocean.

A light.

I stand up, sand cascading down my legs.

"Look!" My voice comes out too loud, amplified by the stillness.

"What?" Avery says. Her voice is drowsy. Is this how she's had to live the past five years, wandering this empty place, trying to sleep away the pain?

"Look!" I say again, pointing out across the waves. "It's a light! There's a light in the distance!"

"No, there's not," Avery says, dismissively.

"Ave, *look.*"

"You don't know how many things I've imagined," Avery replies. Her voice is dull.

"This could be the way out!"

"There is no way out." Her voice is flat, and she stays sitting down, her eyes locked on the sea, on the light flickering valiantly against the expanse of gray.

I lock eyes with Ali for a moment, but I can't read her anymore, and I don't know if she's thinking of backing me up or Avery. In the past, it was always Avery, and I was the third wheel, the little sister tagging along. How easily we fall back into our same dynamic.

"I'll swim to it," I say.

"You can't swim to it," Avery says immediately. "You'll drown."

"I won't drown."

"No," Avery replies, and finally she stands too, folding her arms tightly. "I mean you'll *really drown*, Lia. You don't know how many times I've tried." She swallows hard. "You think I haven't tried? You think I've just been sitting here dead-eyed and weak for five years?"

"I don't think you're weak—" I begin, but Avery cuts me off.

"I tried, Lia. When I first found myself here I tried to leave over and over and *over* and I couldn't get out, okay? Every time I end up back where I started. Sometimes by the briar patch on the headland. Sometimes in the house. I'm not here, not really. I'm like a ghost, drowning over and over again." Her voice breaks. "There's no way out."

Ali steps up besides Avery, tucking her fingers into the crook of her arm. Avery looks away from me, shaking her head slightly.

"But you've never had us," I whisper. "Avery, we have to try."

Avery just sighs. "You don't get it, Lia. You just don't."

I bite my tongue, hard enough that copper fills my mouth. The thing is—she's right. I don't get it. But a part of me is sure she still sees me as little Lia, her baby sister. Someone to be sighed at.

But five years is a lot of time to change, and we're sitting here together but we're all wishing for something else. Ali longs for the bonds of the past. Avery misses the sister I was and even Rafferty misses the girl I used to be, and all I can think of is how I am none of these people anymore and all of them, all at once.

"Avery, please," I say, taking her hands in mine. "For me. I have to get home. *We* have to get home. You've never tried with us before."

Her eyes lock on mine. They're the same as they were five years ago.

"Please," I whisper. There's a light in the distance, and I know we have to go toward it. I'm not sure of much, but I'm sure of this.

"We should try," Ali suddenly says. "Yeah. We should try."

Avery chews on her lip, looking between us. "I—I can't do it again."

I look up at the house rising above us, the spider at the center of the web. The monster who watches. *It would get us and let you go free.* Ali said that to me, long ago. Now we're back in the cove, and the words have more meaning than ever.

"You both swim," I say, and the words are freeing. They feel right. "I'll stay here. The house wants someone to stay behind, doesn't it? It wants one of us at its heart. It would let you go if I stay. I know it."

"No," Avery says. "That's not happening."

"Absolutely not," Ali says, her words running over Avery's, mingling together into one chaotic protest. "What are you even thinking? What are you—?"

"I'm staying," I say, sitting back in the sand. I'm adamant. This is how my sisters will get out. This is how Ali will have a chance to get better. This is how Avery will have a chance to actually *live.*

Ali fingers are a vise on my upper arm. "Get up, Lia."

"No."

Ali's eyes are fire, and then suddenly she snaps, "Okay, fine."

And she sits down in the sand next to me with a thump. "If you don't go, neither do I."

"Ali—"

"We all go, or none of us go," Ali says. Her leg presses against mine, and she turns to face me. She holds up her hand.

Two fingers, crossed.

"Together or not at all," she says. "Like this."

TWENTY-FIVE

We hold hands as we wade into the water.

It's colder than I thought, colder than I remember, and the water rises slowly as the sandbank sinks away under our bare feet. We rise up on tiptoes. We left our shoes on the beach, three sets lined up in a neat and orderly row.

A reminder that this happened, that we were really here together.

"Don't let me drown," Avery whispers. Her eyes are set ahead, fixed on the light.

"I won't," I say, and Ali echoes the words. Her grip is tight in mine, and I can feel her watching me. She's suspicious, worried.

Like she can see right through me.

The sandbank takes another steep drop and is completely gone, heading off toward the ocean floor. *To where the monster lives,* I think, and I have a sudden urge to laugh.

We pull our hands apart to swim but stay close, our legs kicking out against each other, our arms tangling. All of us are unwilling to drift too far apart, and we swim hard against the current. A wave comes, washing over us, the sound still muted as we break through it, sputtering and coughing.

"Everyone okay?" I yell.

"Fine," Avery calls back.

"Yes," Ali says, out of breath. I feel her fingers keep grabbing the back of my shirt.

The light is getting closer and closer.

"Keep going!" I call out. No one answers, but I can hear my sisters panting and spitting out salt water on either side of me.

"I'm—tired—" I hear Avery say, and then—there—the light gets bigger, and out of the thick gray fog a form emerges. The light is attached to the form.

The light is attached to a *boat,* and inside the boat is Rafferty.

His mouth is opening and closing, but we can't hear a thing. He looks wet, like he's being rained on. Rafferty's right in front of us, and yet he's *not.* We're still in the quiet place; we're still stuck.

My heart is breaking open at the sight of Rafferty Pierce.

Please, go and get help: the last thing I yelled to him, when the door had shut between us and the labyrinth of Brier Hall had separated us. But he heard. He heard through locked doors. He heard across realities, across infinities.

Or maybe he didn't.

Maybe he just knew what I would do—knew what little Lia, who was his friend so many years ago, would do. I think I've changed so much but maybe I haven't.

Maybe everything can change about a person except when they're sad they cry for their mommy and when they're trapped they head for sea.

Trapped. The word worms its way inside, and I drag my eyes away from Rafferty, desperately searching an empty sea for the three people who are right in front of him.

We're still trapped. The realities are bumping up against one another, but whatever separates the different layers is holding firm.

My eyes drift up to the house, presiding over the three little girls frantically treading water. The house wants someone to stay.

You know what to do.

I don't know if the voice in my head is my own but I don't care, because as the idea forms I feel the certainty of rightness flood through me. The house always liked me best anyways, and it knows what I'm going to do before I do it. Maybe in some other reality I already *have* done it, and it's just waiting for me to remember.

I could wait forever for you.

As soon as the thought solidifies in my mind, as soon as Brier realizes that one of us will stay caught in its web, it happens instantaneously. One moment we're treading water desperately on a silent, fog-covered sea, and the next the sound crashes in on us like a wave itself and we're drowning in an explosion of noise. It's raining, a downpour, and the rain on the ocean is so *loud*. Rafferty is yelling our names to the sea, the words carrying over the howling wind.

The gray veil has ripped open and we're buffeted by the storm, gasping for air as the waves suck us down. For a moment, we've broken through the layers.

"Lia!" Rafferty screams against the gale.

"Here!" I gasp, pedaling my feet, trying to keep my head from going under. Rafferty is shouting in surprise as we all appear in the water, broken free from Brier's grasp at last. Hot, living panic rises within me as the sudden noise crashes over me. I wasn't scared before, but now I can't breathe, now I can't swim . . .

Get a grip, get a grip! I scream the words in my head as I always have before as I try to find purchase on the edge of the boat. *You're okay, it's okay* . . . All the things I've been told to tell myself in times of panic aren't working because I'm *not* okay and it's not okay and I can't get a grip on the edge of this boat.

I try to breathe. To keep breathing. That seems like a good start.

My fingers find the slick edge and as I cling to the boat with one hand I push Avery toward it with the other. "Get her!" I yell at Rafferty. "*Please*, get her!"

Rafferty starts dragging Avery up over the side of the boat. His hair is stuck down against his forehead in the downpour. He might be crying—I can't tell. The rain washes everything away.

I'm crying too, and the ocean doesn't care. What is more salt to the sea?

Avery is in. Avery is safe. *It's okay, it's okay* . . . I breathe, trying to push out the panic. Avery is not lost anymore. She's not trapped. And I have to keep it that way.

The thought helps. *I have to keep it that way.* Even while my body is furiously keeping itself alive in the water, my mind is suddenly calm where my body's not.

Keep them safe.

I said on the beach we'd all go together, but I didn't say I would stay. *It's all of us or none of us,* Ali said, and I agreed. But I lied. Because someone needs to be the one they can hide behind. Someone needs to stay behind and appease the monster.

Will Rafferty be able to get us all out of here?

Just one more unknown, and I can't risk it.

I need to make sure the layers of Brier Hall stay ripped open long enough for my sisters and Rafferty to get away, far enough that the house can't call them back. Brier Hall wants someone to stay—a sister for a sister—and so I'll stay.

My body is flooded with adrenaline, rebelling against what it's already decided to do.

I wait until I see Ali clutch the side of the boat with both hands, her dark blond hair lank and wet around her face. Rafferty goes to her, grabs her hands. Avery huddles in the boat, head bowed against the rain.

We're still trapped, but a trap is only a trap if you're caught. A maze is only a maze if you're lost.

And I am not lost.

I am exactly where I need to be—where I've *always* needed to be. For so long I've been the moth dragged toward Brier Hall, its beating heart calling to me. Now I'll face it head-on. I'll be the one to stride up its driveway, banging on the doors, demanding to be let in.

Now I will be the light, the kind that can't go out, even when broken, doused, drowned.

The kind of light that draws all attention to me. Me, and not my sisters.

Better us than you.

Before I can think about it, I push myself over the edge of the boat and let my body go limp. I open my mouth to the sea. I hear a scream, but it already sounds far away, lost to the wind and rain. I make my choice and Brier accepts the trade.

Yes, says Brier. I can hear it calling me through the waves. *Yes.*

The salt water rushes in.

THE MONSTER WHO WAITS

You were the one who loved me the most. I was yours. I was home.

You always knew that it would be you. That you were the one. Didn't you?

I knew it too.

TWENTY-SIX

The monster drags me down, down, down . . .

Everything is dark, and in the darkness I see things that can't be real, but nothing that's happened can be real, *and yet*. I must be dreaming, drifting, dead, because at the bottom of the ocean there are houses.

An entire drowned town, just below the surface.

Down, down, down . . .

And there, in its center, is another Brier Hall, sodden and half-collapsed, a ruin of itself. Instead of a sandbank here is the cliff, crumbling away into the depths. Here is the tower, pointed, regal. The windows are all broken.

Where are its people? Maybe *I'm* its person. That's what it's been waiting for all along. Someone to swim among its rooms, wade through its maze.

I'm pulled closer to the underwater house. In the darkness, a light shines in the cracked window of the tower. A shadow crosses in front of it—someone is there, someone is home.

They were swallowed up by the house, swallowed up by the sea.

I thought the gray place was the innermost layer, but I was wrong. This waterlogged house, broken and alone at the bottom of the sea, is the heart of Brier. This is where the monster lives.

The front door opens, a gaping dark hole beyond. The light in the broken window flickers—

It's been waiting for me forever—just like Ali always said.

And then a tentacle wraps itself around my middle and I'm being dragged away. I don't know which direction I'm heading but the light in the window gets smaller and smaller and then suddenly I'm breathing air instead of water. Ali is holding me, pushing me toward the boat. Not a tentacle—an arm.

I'm coughing, coughing up water and coughing up salt and then as Ali helps Rafferty drag me into the boat, I'm coughing up everything that's broken between me and my sister.

The water washes it away.

"Lia?!" My name is said by three people at once, and then hands are touching me, helping me sit, helping me cough. Brushing back the wet hair from out of my eyes, tucking a damp blanket around my shaking shoulders.

Avery kneels over me, and I close my eyes against the flood of tears.

"Are we out?" I whisper, voice craggy. I'm scared to hear the answer. Scared that any minute the boat will dissolve around me and we'll drop back into the water; the gray fog will descend and blanket us in silence.

Scared that a part of me is still down in the underwater house, breathing in salt and living in sand.

Scared that this is all a dream.

"Look," Ali says. Her voice is scratchy too, and I peek at her. Her eyes are red-rimmed. She dove down into the water. Hauled me out. "Look. We're out."

I turn my gaze to the sea around us. Raff is steering the boat out of the cove, rounding the bluffs. The storm that made his entrance so difficult has dropped away, as if its sole purpose was to hinder him. To keep us apart. Everything is wet but calm now, and the three of us sit huddled in the boat.

"Is this real?" Avery whispers, and none of us reply.

I don't know anymore.

I'm not sure if I will ever know again.

I can't answer, so instead I move to where Rafferty stands, his hands clamped white-knuckled on the wheel of the boat. The edge of the blanket around my shoulders flies up in the breeze like a superhero's cape.

I think of the first time I ever saw him, standing on the beach in his cutoff shorts, dark curls tangled. How I felt like I already knew him. And then just days ago, when we met for the first time in years, and every single bit of me remembered him. I slip my hand into the crook of his arm and tilt my head to his shoulder.

"Thank you," I whisper.

"Lia . . ." he says, and then trails off, and there's something so raw in his voice I want to cry again.

"I didn't know if you heard me." I see the door to the tower slam shut, the handle turning but not opening, the surety that Raff and I were no longer separated by just a plank of wood . . .

He gaze lands heavily on me. "I didn't hear a thing."

"Then how? How did you know to come here?"

For the first time, I see the hint of a smile form. "How? Because I know you, Lia Peartree."

"But . . ."

"I just knew, Lia. I just felt a—I don't know. A *pull*. And where else would you be besides the cove?"

I know you. Things will never be how they were five years ago, but as Rafferty smiles at me, I settle into the idea that maybe we can walk some new path together, one that I didn't manage to imagine. One better than I even could've.

Raff jerks his head toward the back of the boat, at the forms huddled together. "It's her, isn't it? She looks older, but that's . . . that's Avery."

One breath, two. Talking about Avery like she's here, like she's alive. Because now she is.

"Yes."

He doesn't say it's impossible because it's not, doesn't say it can't be real because it is. He just lets out a heavy breath. "You really did it. You found her."

Saying the words sounds unreal. "I found her."

"Where was she?"

Gray. Silence. A trap. "She got stuck in the house," I say slowly. "In its maze, in its heart. The whole time she was *stuck*. It was like . . . a different world, Raff."

"What was it like?" His voice is a whisper.

"Cold," I say. "And silent." I shake my head, trying to clear it of the memories that cling like cobwebs. We're nearing the Eastwind beach now. It's empty and dark, the moon shining a streak of silver in the water.

"It sounds horrible," Raff says. "It sounds . . . sad."

"Yes," I agree, because that's exactly what I felt in that silent realm, and when I looked at its waterlogged heart. "It was sad."

"Then why did you try to stay, Lia?" His voice is quiet and he doesn't look at me, and I know that if I don't reply, or if I change the subject, he won't push it.

But I don't. It feels good to talk. I don't want to keep any secrets inside me anymore. There's no room. "Someone had to stay," I whisper. "It was the only way out."

"Lia, you threw yourself out of the boat."

"It was the only way you three would be able to get out," I insist.

"By *drowning?*"

I shrug. I don't want to think of the other Brier, the underwater light, the monster pulling me down, back to the house, the front door swinging open, welcoming me home . . . "It wanted one of us," I say. "It wanted *me*."

"It didn't get you," Raff says firmly. "Never will."

I look up at the house on the headland, at the tower rising above the mist, and don't reply.

The boat bumps up on the sand. Rafferty helps us out one by one, and then we walk, barefoot and bedraggled, up to where Raff's car is parked. *We're out.* This, too, feels like a dream. Gravel under the soles of my feet, wind whistling off the coast, waves lapping on the shore. I want this to be real.

"Look," Avery says, almost dreamily, and she stops by the open car door, staring up at the bluff, at the house on the hill. "Look, all the lights are off."

Ali squeezes her from behind. "Yeah."

"I want to see it," Avery adds suddenly. "I want to see it from the outside."

She sits in the passenger seat as Raff drives slowly up the narrow gravel path, peering out the front window. Her expression is rapt. For so long she was stuck inside this estate, and now she's on the outside looking in.

"Look," Ali whispers as we get closer. "The gates are shut." She's right. A heavy chain and padlock hang around them, keeping them closed. "And it's dark," she continues. "It's . . . it's like it never even happened."

Avery turns to us in the back seat, face screwed up against tears. "Is this a dream?"

"No, this is real," Ali replies immediately.

"Look at it," Avery continues, sobs choking each word. "The gates are locked and the house is dark. I wandered around for so many years and now looking at it—it's just a house! It's just a *house*."

Nothing is just *anything*, I think, but I don't speak.

Next to me, Ali is crying too. Tears drip down her chin, disappearing into her already soaked shirt.

"Are you okay?" I whisper to her.

"I can't feel anything," Ali whispers back. But she smiles. "I can't feel it anymore, Lia. There's no pull. It's not calling to me anymore. You too?"

She turns around to look at the house.

"Me too," I murmur to the back of her head, and Ali is staring up at Brier Hall and she doesn't see that I'm lying, and I don't tell her, because that's what sisters are for.

TWENTY-SEVEN

We sit in the parking lot of the Eastwind Hotel as dawn breaks over the sandy streets and peeling paint of the town. Streaks of buttery yellow line the sky, peeking out from behind the thick headland fog rolling in off the ocean.

My sisters are sleeping in the back of Raff's car, folded over each other like some creature with many arms and legs. I sit on the edge of the curb and Raff stands in front of me, leaning against the hood of the car with his arms crossed against the chill. Our clothes have mostly dried, but they're salt-soaked and stiff.

My phone sits on my lap. Rafferty found both it and my car keys at the bottom of the boat, even though I left them both in my bedroom at Brier Hall. The phone is waterlogged now and won't turn on, but I fiddle with it anyways just to give my hands something to do.

"So, Avery," Raff says. I hear the question in her name. He crosses his arms and looks away, down toward the beach where Eastwind is just waking up. Eastwind is unaware of everything. "She's been missing for five years. What will you do—what will *she* do—now?"

I shake my head. "I know." I sigh. "I mean, I *don't* know. I have no idea what to do next."

Rafferty nods slowly, eyes flickering back to me. I push myself off the curb and cross to him, wrapping my arms around his waist. He hesitates for just a second, and then I feel his arms echo mine, snugly surrounding me.

"Raff."

"Hmm." I can feel the vibration against my cheek.

"Thank you for making sure I had a *next*." I tilt my head up. "The night in the hotel, when I first saw you again. You were going to kiss me, all spiteful. You asked if I wanted it to happen."

Raff groans. "Lia, I . . ."

I bring my lips closer until they're hovering right over his. "I never answered you."

"What would your answer have been?" Raff asks, his voice low, slow. He's softened since I reunited with him; the anger has drained away. But his eyes still light up as they roam across me. I remember how I would dream of reuniting with Rafferty: the grand gestures, the long speeches.

I don't need any of that anymore.

I stand on my tiptoes and press my lips against his softly. His hand comes up to cradle my cheek, and I relax against him. I remember back in the hotel room when we were this close, he seemed dangerous and mysterious, and my entire body was electric. Now, there's none of the crackling electricity in my veins from the aftermath of our fight in the hotel. *Everything's changed.* We're no longer just kids, the best of friends, *like this.* And he's not the Rafferty I invented in my head over the five years apart, the perfect Rafferty, perfectly in love with me. But when I look at him I still feel that I know him, that some part of me recognizes him.

We're exhausted and drained and our lips touch so lightly it's nothing more than a featherlight breath of a kiss, but somehow all our infinite branches still narrow back down just now, right here, and for that split second things make sense.

I just feel warm.

I think of the house, and all the other Lias wandering lost in its maze of hallways, and I hope that they feel this warmth too.

I break away first. Raff's cheeks are red, and I bite the inside of my lip so I don't smile. "I would've said yes," I whisper, and it feels like a promise.

We're in a parking lot filled with weeds, and our clothes are itchy with salt, but it's better than anything I imagined. It's just me and Rafferty, and I know exactly who he is and vice versa, and neither is wishing we were anything else.

We stand for a moment, arms around each other, and I listen to his heartbeat. Strong, reassuring. Real. One thing, at least, I know that's real.

"I don't want you to go," he murmurs against my cheek when he pulls away. His eyes are dark. "Honestly, Lia, I'm worried I won't see you again."

"You will." I go up on my tiptoes to kiss him. I want to fall into him, but standing in this circle of his arms will have to do for now. "You're my next thing, Rafferty."

He doesn't smile, just chews on his lip. "It'll be hard, when you go back."

"I know." I sigh and press my face into his chest as if I can block out the rest of the world. "The media will have a field day. 'Missing girl returns from haunted house on the anniversary of her disappearance! She didn't run away after all!' You know, that sort of thing."

"Yeah."

"We'll have to get the police involved. They'll want to question us."

"Yes."

"We'll have to tell some lies. We'll have to tell *a lot* of lies."

"I know we will."

"You might be the infamous weird haunted house guy at Dartmouth."

Raff's mouth twists into a half smile at that. "I'm okay with it."

I peek up at him. "Even with Avery back, everything might not be better, Raff."

"But it might be," he murmurs. "That's the thing with living— you just never know."

In the car, Ali begins to stir, pushing herself off of Avery and wiping blearily at her eyes. I turn back to Raff.

He opens his mouth to speak, but I shake my head and silence him with another swift kiss. "Don't. Don't say anymore. It'll make it too hard to leave."

"Lia—"

"Don't," I say.

"Okay, I won't," Raff says. He catches my chin again and meets my eyes. "I won't say a thing. But you know, don't you? You know what I want to say."

"Yes," I whisper. "I know. And Raff—another thing I know? I'll always come back here. Back to you. Back home."

Raff just nods, his jaw tight. "You better get going."

It's a short and simple goodbye. But it's better than nothing. Better than fleeing in the dead of night. We got our goodbye, our kiss, our promise. It just took time.

And time is one thing that Brier Hall gave us.

I open my car and I slide into the driver's seat, Ali getting in next to me. Avery gets into the back—she's been silent ever since Raff parked back at the Eastwind Hotel. I inch out of the parking lot, Raff walking beside the car, following it out to the main street. It's too early for the beachgoing tourists to be up yet, and the street is foggy and quiet. For a moment my heart clenches with sudden fear, and I throw the car into park and roll down the window, listening to the wind, for birds, for *sound*.

Before, Avery kept asking if this was real. She couldn't believe she was out of the quiet place; that this must all be a dream.

For a moment I wonder if I'm dreaming too. If I'll wake up back in my bed at Brier. Back on the sandy beach in the cove, watching the still waters with my sisters beside me. Back under the water, salt water in my eyes and ears and mouth, the monster who lives in the water and the walls dragging me down, keeping me forever.

"Lia?" Raff says through the open window. Beyond him, a seagull screeches loudly and flaps its wings, eating a crumb off the pavement.

My hands are shaking on the gear stick.

"Lia?" Ali whispers, putting her hand over mine. "Are you okay?"

"Fine," I say. I am fine, I'm here and safe and alive, but there's a part of me that wonders if I'll ever feel truly fine again. I can't stop my body from trembling. *Down, down, down . . .*

"You're here," Ali says.

Down, down to the light in the underwater house . . .

"Come back," Ali whispers. "You're not lost."

I close my eyes, feeling the salt water filling my mouth. "I might be lost."

"You can't be," Ali says, squeezing my hand until it hurts. "Not with us here. Some things can't get lost." Her fingers, for once, don't shake at all. Not even a little bit.

"Come on," she says again. "Come on, Lia. It's time to go home." I take a deep breath and open my eyes. My mouth still tastes like salt. I think a part of me is still underwater. Raff reaches in through the open window and touches my cheek, just briefly. He smiles, encouragingly.

"Home," he says.

I glance in the rearview mirror at Avery, who's staring out the window at Brier Hall. She slowly turns away and meets my gaze, then smiles. "Home," she echoes.

Just for a moment, I let my eyes rise to land on Raff, who raises his hand in goodbye, and behind him, the house alone on the bluff.

Home.

Then I start the car and pull away.

I realize I will never, ever tell my sisters that every part of my body aches to return. That I see a shadow moving behind the curtains in the princess tower, and the gates stand open, and the front door hangs wide, and the house's windows are all blazing with warm golden light, as if someone has turned on every single lamp in the house to welcome me home.

MOTHS

You leave. I let you go.

You said a trap is only a trap if you're caught, but is a trap a trap if you're simply let out?

Is a maze a maze if you don't know you're still running through it?

You've left, but I know you'll return.

I loved you best, all along.

I could wait forever for you, probably.

ACKNOWLEDGMENTS

All I've ever wanted to do is write books, so I feel extremely lucky to get to write these acknowledgments for my second novel. Some iteration of this book has been around since 2016, and I am so thankful to everyone who helped shepherd it into readers' hands.

First and foremost, thanks to my brilliant agent, Taylor Martindale Kean, whose smarts, know-how, and excellent advice never fail to astound. I couldn't ask for a better partner on this journey. And thank you to everyone at Full Circle Literary, which is truly the best agency around.

To Nicole Ellul, for your ever-insightful guidance and editorial magic, and for seeing this story through years of iterations and loving the heart of it throughout—thank you times a million!

To everyone at Simon & Schuster Books for Young Readers who had a hand in this book—THANK YOU! You are all brilliant. Huge thanks especially to Managing Editor Kimberly Capriola, my copyeditor, Kayley Hoffman, and my proofreader, Sophia Lee, and to everyone who has worked so hard at getting this book on shelves.

Thank you to Lizzy Bromley, who designed the perfectly eerie cover, and Sarah Jarrett for the most stunning artwork. Together you created the atmospheric gothic cover of my dreams!

To Allison, for our long-distance read-alouds that gave me the confidence to continue, and for our brainstorming sessions that made this book what it is. My plot would be just a vague gathering of vibes and Pinterest boards if it wasn't for you.

ACKNOWLEDGMENTS

Thank you to my writing group The Lunch Mob—Sarah, George, Kayla, Catriona, Mel, Christine, Eva, and Pia—for feedback and cheerleading and group chats and the best GIFs and writing retreats and not ever being able to keep a straight face on Zoom. And a special shout-out to Sarah and George for beta reading! #HoldMeBack #8kFriends #LimbManualMince

Huge thanks to my families on both sides of the pond for your unwavering support. Thank you to my husband, Henry, for your constant love and encouragement—I love you so much. And to my daughter, Imogen Grace, who made finding time for writing trickier but made everything else in my life infinitely better.

And finally, thank you to my readers. You're the best, and you're making this author's dreams come true. THANK YOU!